MURDER FOR TWO

MURDER FOR TWO

NIYLA FAROOK

First published in the UK in 2025 by
PICCADILLY PRESS
an imprint of Bonnier Books UK
5th Floor, HYLO, 103–105 Bunhill Row, London EC1Y 8LZ
Owned by Bonnier Books, Sveavägen 56, Stockholm, Sweden

A CIP catalogue record for this book is available from the British Library.

ISBN: 978-1-80078-937-1
Also available as an ebook and in audio

1

This book is typeset using Atomik ePublisher
Printed and bound in Great Britain by Clays Ltd, Elcograf S.p.A.

bonnierbooks.co.uk/PiccadillyPress

For Mum, for everything.

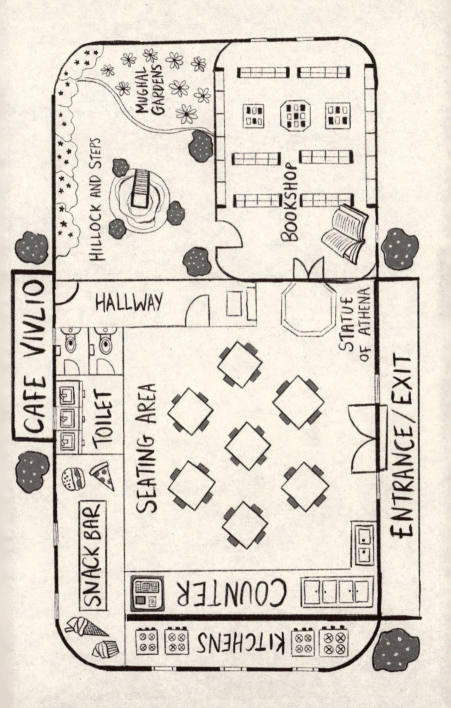

1

ANI

Today has been murder.

Everyone else in my year has been taking photos, signing T-shirts and leavers' hoodies. There's been no time for sniffing out a mystery. My classmates are fine but they're not my friends. They don't share my keen interest for sleuthing. Every second I've been waiting for the bell and in seven minutes we're going to break up for summer. Finally. It'll be just me and all my summer sleuthing plans.

Well, I'll invite my best friends, Helin and LaShawn, to sleuth with me. So no time to think about starting secondary school in September, with intimidating teenagers.

But the only problem with summer is that it ends. Just like life. Meaning autumn is summer's successor as funeral rites are life's successor. How grim.

Mx Henderson, form teacher extraordinaire, insists we talk about our futures. 'Ani, you're up.' They beckon me to the front. I walk with my head held high. Mrs Kostas

1

always says to 'fake it till you make it' and that's what I've been doing since I started here two years ago. 'You're the last one to tell us your career aspirations.'

My answer is never-changing, even when Dad asks me over and over again.

'I want to start my own private supersleuth agency called the Tariq Ultrasecret Supersleuth Centre. Shortened to the TUSC. Just like the CIA and the FBI.' You'll understand the name in a minute. I look at my classmates, who stare at me, unsurprised by my answer. 'Some of you wanna be superheroes. Some superstars or supermodels. But I'm going to be a professional, *paid* supersleuth.' Even though Dad would love for me to be an IT consultant like him.

Disclaimer: I already *am* a supersleuth, by my standards. Only I don't get paid. Yet.

Right now, *you* don't have clearance to view my portfolio. You will soon. Patience.

Mx Henderson wants more information, so I add, 'The TUSC will solve everything from mysteries to murders. It's going to be an international agency but will most definitely *not* be associated with law enforcement. I mean, how appalling is the rate of stop-and-searches for people from ethnic-minority backgrounds here in the UK?!'

Half of my classmates appear to be listening to me. Others either daydream while gazing at the clock behind me or scrolling on their desk-hidden phones. Maybe Mx Henderson hasn't noticed the phone-using rulebreakers because they're not a supersleuth.

I continue, 'So, yes, I will change the entire world's laws

2

to cater to the TUSC's ways. Obviously I do believe in justice for the innocent and consequences for the guilty. Just not how it's handled in today's society. There's not a chance in he—'

'Ani Tariq, do you want to be the first person in our school's history to get detention in the last hour of the last day of Year 6?' Mx Henderson's face reddens. Why are adults so grumpy? I was only going to say the four-letter word for the afterlife of sinners in some religions. How is that detention-worthy? It's in the curriculum!

'Yo, Mx, cut us all some slack,' Frankie Chase says from the back of the class, not looking up from his phone. He isn't defending me – he doesn't even know me. He's simply defending himself. Then looks up. 'Can we leave early?'

See what I mean? I don't need to see their expression to know the answer; Frankie frowns and returns to his phone.

Mx Henderson stands in front of me. 'Well?' they say, expectantly.

I should respond. But instead I'm processing Mx Henderson's official TUSC profile. All profiles include a person's full name, gender, pronouns, age, three physical characteristics, their occupation and one observation.

TUSC PROFILE

Name:	Mx Alex Henderson
Gender:	Non-binary
Pronouns:	They/them/theirs
Age:	30 years old

```
Occupation:   Year 6 schoolteacher

Physical characteristics:
    1. Normally pink-faced
    2. Wears round thick spectacles
    3. Bright red hair with a fringe


Observation:   Always wears same three shirts on
    rotation
```

The green shirt, AKA the least appealing, is now getting crinkled as they fold their arms at me.

Despite my strong defence, I press my lips together. Head back to my seat. 'Watch your tongue' is always Dad's advice to me when I find myself in conflicting situations. Whenever I get detention, he gives me the same boring old lecture in Pakistani English (yes, calling it *Pinglish* is offensive). While I love him, I'd prefer lecture-less summer holidays.

The bell rings. My class works as a team to exit in record time. Backpack on, I skip out of school.

The weather has also realised it's summer – sunrays dazzle me. I shove my sunglasses on. I'm glistening with sweat already, uniform sticky, but still pick up my pace.

As I do, I unlock my phone. Press 'record'. Then speak into it, 'Supersleuth's log. I'm finally free from attending *that* educational institution forever. Summer is the best and mine will be jam-packed! Major TUSC case workload. First stop: Cafe Vivlio.' I stop recording and look around.

Castlewick, the West Yorkshire town where I live, is always busy and beautiful. Population: 80,000. Always people around. I like that but it often makes mysteries too easy to solve because there's always a witness or two. Wobbly cobblestones serve as stepping stones for me. My arms are aeroplanes so I can balance. Walls with brightly coloured graffiti are in sight. In Castlewick, graffiti is a celebrated art.

A bus hisses nearby and I hear much more as I walk on. Bike handlebars rattle. People chat. These are the background sounds that make Castlewick and I love them. My ADHD means that my brain works better with background sounds.

I decide to take a shortcut through the town centre. Tourists admire the courthouse's stonework. The tour guide is talking so loudly that I feel like I'm part of the group.

'Most buildings are Victorian, including the landmarks and statuary. You can see our finest example here.' Without meaning to, I glance at the clock tower at the same time as everyone else. It's a fancy tower on top of a museum I visited with school once. Nice place. Ancient.

'The brochure reads: *Spires fill Castlewick's skyline while trees fill its landscape so let's take a look.* How beautiful are they?'

Very. They look like they could be used as the swords of giants. Rich-green trees are in the background. Sometimes, me and Dad go for countryside walks. I love exploring Castlewick. The town, between Bradford and Leeds, is multicultural. Many South Asian, Afro-Caribbean, Arab and Eastern European people live here.

5

'The central statue is of our famous Mr Dexter Walterson,' the guide continues.

Dexter was a big deal, like, a million years ago. Had to do a school project all about him once. Forgotten a lot now except that Castlewick used to be a mill town and he owned the biggest one. Dexter's legacy and his statue are overrated but it's expected that he is immortalised in the town centre. What about the masses of immigrants who worked in his mills and were treated unfairly because of their skin colour and religion?! I shake my head, exasperated. If I squint past Walter's statue, I can see Cafe Vivlio. Nearly there.

OK, after getting personal, political and historical with you, let's get introduced.

The name's Imani Tariq, but you can call me 'Ani'. Like a posh version of 'Annie'. Or even better, say 'ahh' then 'nee', and you'll have it. If not, I won't hold it against you – my dad is from Pakistan's snowy mountains so we are used to people being unable to say our names. Try saying Dad's name – Abderrazzak. Can't? Well, I'll teach you.

Ready? It's Ab·der·raz·zak. Yes, all in one breath. No, unlike me, he doesn't answer to nicknames (nope, not even Zak) but does to titles including The World's Best Hugger, Un-Funniest Dad and Most Talented Nail Painter.

I'm eleven years old. I haven't lived in Castlewick forever but I don't remember much about where we were before because I was too young. When me and Dad first moved to Castlewick we lived in a council house until he got a fancy job two years ago. Fun fact: LaShawn now lives in our old house. Dad and me moved into a posh flat in a block called

The Skyscape. It's paid for by Ellextrus Tech, the company Dad works for remotely. As you can see, there've been lots of changes in my life so far.

But one thing that'll never change is Cafe Vivlio, the best place on earth.

Its owner, Mrs Kostas, told me that 'vivlio' means 'books' in Greek, her native language. For all my fellow code-crackers, that means it translates to 'cafe books'.

Cafe Vivlio is a cafe *and* a bookshop all-in-one.

Now, here's what would go on my gravestone if Muslims were encouraged to have such things: I would die for manga! And Cafe Vivlio stocks manga. Manga and mango juice. Mrs Kostas keeps mango juice especially for me, refrigerated, by the snack bar. Pretty sure I'm the only one who buys it.

I like to think of Cafe Vivlio as a vintage spaceship. 'Vintage' is the cafe – exposed-brick walls and high, wide windows. Neon lights and plants hang from the walls, along with old mirrors and framed Greek proverbs. Seats are either wooden or armchairs, all unmatching. To make it cosy, Mrs Kostas added pillows and rugs on the hardwood floor. Mimi (one of the many cafe regulars) told me that Cafe Vivlio's 'aesthetic' is 'on point'. Whatever that means. During busy hours, queues tend to go outside because people like to overstay their welcome. Especially with a good book.

That's where 'spaceship' comes into the mix – the bookshop, behind the statue of Athena, Greek goddess of knowledge, is all white. No corners there either. Mrs Kostas got inspiration from the Tianjin Binhai Library in China. She lived there for a few years. Books are shelved with their covers front-facing. Different genres are stocked – not just manga – and they have new books and second-hand ones. Customers pay for books at the cafe's till.

TUSC PROFILE

Name: Mrs Polina Anastasia Kostas,
               'Mrs Kostas' to most people
               and 'Polly' to some adults.

Gender: Female

Pronouns: She/her/hers

Age: 57 years old (age confirmed
               unethically)

Occupation: Cafe-bookshop owner

Physical characteristics:
   1. Glasses with a hexagon-shaped frame
   2. Bright blue eyes and greying straight hair
   3. Always wears dresses (she doesn't feel
      the British weather's bitter coldness)

Observation: Her signature scent is the
   cinnamon, walnuts and cloves with lemon zest
   of karidopita (AKA Greek walnut cake, which
   is also her signature dessert)

```
Bonus fact:    She gives me advice in the form
       of Greek proverbs (in Greek, which she then
       translates)

Bonus bonus fact: In return, I watch Bollywood
       movies with her and translate them.
```

'School's out for summer already, Ani?' Mrs Kostas asks, as I sit at my usual table in the corner below an alcove. I like to think of the spot as my public sleuth office.

'I've been waiting forever for this summer, Mrs Kostas.'

What's funny is that even though I refer to her like I do to schoolteachers, she's my mother/grandmother figure. We're super close. She's my unofficial guardian when Dad works late and needs quiet time. It works out because she lives on the floor beneath us. Her flat is smaller than ours but homier.

'Let me guess . . .' She quickly wipes the counter before limping (she has arthritis) over to me. Now that she's near, I can smell karidopita on her. Cafe Vivlio has a chef but only Mrs Kostas can make karidopita the best so he doesn't even try. She puts a slice in front of me. 'Ready to solve new mysteries this summer?'

'Of course.' I take a few mouthfuls. Somehow, Mrs Kostas's karidopita always tastes better than the last time I ate it. 'I trust you've made some up for me.' Mrs Kostas is partly (if not mostly) responsible for my mystery-solving obsession – she's made me treasure maps that led to actual treasure (new manga, collectibles, bright socks) and writes riddles for me.

She chuckles, confirming that I'm right. '"Wisdom begins in wonder." Socrates said that. I can't wait to be the first-ever sponsor of the TUSC when you've set it up . . . *after* completing school.'

Because I know her all too well, I know exactly what she's going to say next. We say it simultaneously: '"The roots of education are bitter but the fruit is sweet."' Aristotle.

Mrs Kostas laughs. 'Now, tell me what your classmates are doing this summer.'

I know it's rude to roll your eyes at an adult but I can't help it – Mrs Kostas is always pestering me about befriending my classmates. But I'm not interested. LaShawn and Helin both go to my old school. Besides, having two best friends is a lot, so I don't have any vacancies, which is what I always tell Mrs Kostas.

'One's going to Mallorca and one to Mumbai. Two to Santorini and three to San Diego. Someone's going to the Lake District. Someone else is going to Cornwall. Scotland and Wales, the usual,' I drone on in a bored tone. I only know this meaningless information because of Mx Henderson's silly last-day-before-summer activities. Of course, I won't tell Mrs Kostas that – let's let her think I found all that out on my own.

'Good.' Then we talk about wonderful nonsense. Time flies by.

She glances at her watch. It's now 4.30 p.m. 'Rodolfo!'

she shouts down the hall to the cafe's kitchen. 'I'm going out back for a bit. Can you cover?'

He nods, walking towards us. Rodolfo's been the chef since Cafe Vivlio opened two years ago, when Mrs Kostas moved to Castlewick. He has yet to warm up to me. He's a grouch but his culinary skills are spectacular.

TUSC PROFILE

Name:	Mr Rodolfo Espinoza
Gender:	Male
Pronouns:	He/him/his
Age:	57 years old
Occupation:	Chef at Cafe Vivlio

Physical characteristics:

1. Jet-black hair with even darker eyes and tan skin
2. Full-sleeve tattoos on both arms
3. Approximately 160cm tall

Observation: Speaks in a strong Spanish accent

Rodolfo mutters something under his breath. Mrs Kostas rolls her eyes.

'I take it he's still grumpier than normal because you want to hire another chef,' I say.

She nods. 'I put the vacancy up today.' I don't say anything. 'Thanks a lot, Rodolfo.' Mrs Kostas sounds loud and pitchy as if she doesn't mean it. She wipes her hands then gets her handbag.

'Remember everything you've thanked me for, Polly,' he warns.

'An attitude like that and you wonder why I'd want to hire another chef!' she retorts. My eyes widen – I've never heard Mrs Kostas speak like this before. And in public too?! I know there's been some recent friction between them but I didn't realise it was this bad. What's going on?

It's an unusual day at Cafe Vivlio in more ways than one. Normally there are eight members of staff on rotation each day. The cafe is open from 7 a.m. until 7 p.m. and there are always three on a shift at one time, plus Mrs Kostas and Rodolfo.

Mrs Kostas goes on to no one in particular: 'I don't know where Clarissa and Linnet –' the two baristas covering this shift due to a mass staff sickness '– are. I tell you, they know not to take breaks that overlap. *I've* had to be the third barista today.'

'A bathroom emergency, they said,' Rodolfo grumbles. 'Food poisoning. Not my food. Because our facilities aren't working, they've gone to the supermarket opposite.'

'Deary me, it could be norovirus. That's what's got the

rest of my staff off sick. Maybe I should stay here then.'

'No, I can handle it.' Rodolfo goes behind the counter. Doesn't look at Mrs Kostas.

'I appreciate it, Rodolfo,' she says, softer.

'If it gets too much –' Rodolfo continues with a bitter tone – 'then I can always go outside and play guard.' His dark eyes meet Mrs Kostas. 'Right?'

I trail my eyes over to Mrs Kostas's face. She looks as if she's seen a ghost.

'Get your stuff, Ani.' She sounds suddenly hoarse. 'Let's go.'

'Where?'

She forces a smile. 'Why, to The Secret Garden of course.'

I squeal with glee. The Secret Garden is so much more than *just* a secret garden on a hillock behind Cafe Vivlio. It'll help me to forget this adult weirdness.

Me and Mrs Kostas built The Secret Garden a year ago. It started with Mrs Kostas making a Mughal Garden for me in a secret patch of land behind her cafe. Think, colourful flowers. A half-working fountain. Fruit trees. Bright grass. Eight garden steps leading to the hillock. Dad helped us add a cabana and deck chairs. Plus, a swing set because – as Mrs Kostas agrees – you're never too old to go on a swing.

I follow her down the cafe's long hallway in large strides. This will be the *best* start to summer.

We're at The Secret Garden now, and I stop short. *Oh no.* This is the *worst* start to summer.

2

ANI

How could this be happening?! Mrs Kostas and Dad have arranged a barbecue.

A barbecue, of all things!

Sure, summertime is great for barbecues, and I wouldn't say no to shish kebabs, corn on the cob and marshmallows (halal of course). But in the Tariq family, barbecues are bad omens. And true, it's unconventional to organise an *entire* barbecue for three people but it's become a thing of ours. A thing that I hate. Should I feel betrayed by Mrs Kostas for luring me here? No, she means well.

At our barbecues, there's always one piece of bad news with the savoury food.

And another with the sweet food.

That means it's twofold. Twofold bad news. I've survived four barbecues in my life:

THE BARBECUES OF BAD NEWS (BBQoBN)

Note: sweet potatoes and mango juice are served each time

BBQoBN 1:

Age: 6 months old

Note: Ani Tariq has zero recollection of the foods and events of this BBQoBN. This is based on Dad's account.

Savoury food: Hariyali chicken tikka skewers
Savoury bad news: Parents are getting divorced
Sweet food: Roasted pineapple
Sweet bad news: Mum and my evil twin are
                       moving to America

BBQoBN 2:

Age: 6 years old
Savoury food: Lamb chops with spicy mango salad
Savoury bad news: I have to go to the doctor to
                       officially be diagnosed with
                       ADHD (doctors are intense)
Sweet food: Gulab jamun
Sweet bad news: I'll be on medicine for life
                       (update: this ended up being
                       bittersweet because the
                       medicine helps me but in
                       the moment I felt bad).

BBQoBN 3:

Age:	7 years old
Savoury food:	Paneer skewers
Savoury bad news:	Chloe Li, the super-fun teaching assistant who was so helpful after my ADHD diagnosis, is enrolling in the College of Policing
Sweet food:	Rasmalai
Sweet bad news:	She's moving to Manchester

BBQoBN 4:

Age:	9 years old

AKA the year Dad tried — and failed — to become vegan.

Savoury food:	Plant-based 'chicken' kebab burgers with grilled avocados
Savoury bad news:	It's too hard for Dad to drop me off at my old school (the same as LaShawn and Helin)
Sweet food:	Vegan jalebi
Sweet bad news:	I have to move schools

As you can understand, barbecues and me don't have a good history. But I'm more alarmed that it's the *start* of summer and Dad has to deliver two pieces of bad news.

What could it be?

Oh, I know. His job with Ellextrus Tech is on the line. So, we'll probably have to move. No problem there – I can still walk over to Cafe Vivlio to see Mrs Kostas.

Because I'm a supersleuth, I'm confident I'm right. Also, congratulations – you have stuck with me this far so you now have clearance to view my sleuth profile and portfolio overview while I eat my barbecued masala fish.

TUSC PROFILE

Name:	Supersleuth Imani Tariq
Codename:	Asdfghjkl
Gender:	Female
Pronouns:	She/her/hers
Age:	11 years old
Occupation:	Director of the TUSC and school student (listed in order of priority)

Physical characteristics:

1. Chubby cheeks

2. Taller than the average 11-year-old

3. Has a few freckles on nose and cheeks

Observation: Never wears black socks

Successful cases:

- The Case of the Missing Tie
- The Case of the Ripped Trousers
- The Case of the Lost Cat
- The Case of the Runaway Squirrel
- The Case of the Spilled Milk

Unsuccessful cases:

- The Case of the ███████ ███
- The Case of the ██████ ████████

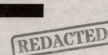

For the first time ever at a BBQoBN, I feel good – I've figured out what the bad news is so I'm ahead of the game. I'm eating yummy food with no dread. And I'm so ready to eat kheer (South Asian rice pudding) after this.

Dad rubs his hands together, clears his throat.

TUSC PROFILE

Name:	Abderrazzak Muhammad Tariq
Gender:	Male
Pronouns:	He/him/his
Age:	34 years old
Occupation:	Computer scientist

```
Physical characteristics:

    1. Dark hair is always in a bun and he has
    a short beard
    2. Hazel eyes (that I didn't inherit)
    3. Wears shirts and ties but with jeans

Observation:   In school, he used to be a bhaṅgrā
    dancer

Bonus observation: He never calls me by my
    nickname
```

'Imani, you enjoying the fish, yeah?' he asks. 'I added harissa this time. New recipe.'

'Nice.' I lick the sauce off each finger. *Pop*. That gets me a glare from Mrs Kostas.

'Uh . . . R-ready for kheer, no?'

I walk over to the bin. Throw away my empty paper plate. 'Yes, please.'

But before he gives it to me, he says, 'Imani, this summer is going to be different.'

Yes, because we're moving out of The Skyscape's poshness. 'That's fine, Dad.'

He blinks. 'Really? Because you'd take it quite bad, I thought.'

I almost tut at his shock. I'm such a good sleuth that I tend to forget that other people can be shocked that I know so much without being told. 'Well, it's only –'

'So, it's OK with your mum and sister visiting us from America?'

Everything goes silent. My mouth and eyes widen. 'What? No!' I don't want to see either of them. The only family I want is Dad, Mrs Kostas, LaShawn and Helin.

Dad's forehead wrinkles. 'But I thought you'd found out already. You said –'

'I got it wrong,' I snap. I'm normally so good at bridging gaps with conclusions and evidence – that's the job of a supersleuth. But this time, I'm off. Maybe it's the hot weather getting to me.

'Imani, it's only for the summer.'

'So? They'll ruin everything! I don't *ever* want them to visit!'

'Sweetheart –' Mrs Kostas smiles – 'you haven't seen them in three years.' She's right – my parents divorced when I was six months old but it wasn't until I was eight that things turned rocky. The visits stopped. We drifted apart. 'It'll be good to reconnect,' Mrs Kostas adds.

'No!' My eyes brim with tears. My body quakes with anger.

'Ani –' Mrs Kostas says in a firmer tone – 'take a few breaths. Remember what I always say – "the tongue has no bones but bones it crushes."' She gets lost in her own world for a moment, as if the words of that Greek proverb have triggered something.

I'm too overwhelmed to heed her words. 'I don't want to reconnect! I just want to solve mysteries and be with LaShawn, Helin and you.'

Dad pinches the bridge of his nose. 'Well, they're landing tomorrow.'

I see red. Not my proudest moment but I let out a loud grunt that turns into a roar. 'Argh! Why didn't you ask me about this?'

Dad gives me a look like *I've* crossed the line. 'Because the parent here is me.' He sighs. 'I didn't tell you because it was your last week of school, I didn't want to disrupt it.'

'Dad, I can disrupt my last week of school all by myself, thanks very much!'

'I realise that now. Mx Henderson rang me, you know. You nearly got detention on your last day for saying something bad?' He sounds so disappointed.

But I'm *more* disappointed. 'Don't change the subject! I don't want Mum and *her* here!'

'She, you know, is coming to Leeds to set up another UK office for her job. And it's good for you and Noori to see each other.'

I don't want to see my evil twin or Mum. My heartbeat is pounding at this new information. 'Is she going to stay in Leeds to run the office?' I don't want Mum and my evil twin living nearby whether it's a brief stay or forever. It'll be worse if it's forever, though.

Dad replies, 'Your mum, she doesn't know for definite yet.'

I wish he could say that Mum and my evil twin are definitely not ever coming here. I grit my teeth in anger and give him a sidelong glare. 'Do you want to make *Mum* your wife again?'

'No, Imani. We'll be mature about this, OK? Me, Mum, you, Noori.'

I shudder at the second mention of my evil twin. 'I won't visit them at the hotel.'

Dad clears his throat. 'That's another thing –'

Mrs Kostas's deck chair creaks as she stands up. She jumps at the sound, which isn't like her. Takes the bowl of kheer out of Dad's hands. Passes it to me with a small smile. 'Have a spoon or two first,' she encourages, softly.

I would decline it, but Mrs Kostas's soft tone always comes with hard eyes. I take one spoon. Then two. The second spoonful is flaked with almonds. As usual, the kheer is delicious – perfectly milky and sugary – but I don't change my expression. 'What else, Dad?' Here it comes, the sweet bad news. I brace myself.

He swallows. 'Noori won't be staying at the hotel.' I raise my eyebrows and my eyes widen as I wait for him to elaborate. 'She'll be staying with us, you know.'

I inhale a calm breath. Not what I wanted to hear but I don't think it can get any worse. 'So will I be sleeping on the sofa? Or will you, Dad?'

Dad exhales. 'Noori will be staying in your bedroom with you.'

I don't say anything, or scream, or cry.

Instead, I run out of The Secret Garden. Far away from Dad and Mrs Kostas.

3

RIRI

The only problem with airports is that there are so many people – therefore, so many germs. Like bathrooms and supermarket carts. And library books. But that's a risk I'll always take . . . with gloves, that is.

There are plenty of good things about airports. For example:

1) The shops
2) The food
3) Watching aerodynamics first-hand

I shift in my seat; my butt hurts. Oh, I just thought of another problem – airport seating. Me and Mom arrived at Leeds-Bradford Airport about ten minutes ago. The flight from LAX felt longer and more turbulent than it was because of crying babies.

'Riri, put that book away now,' Mom mutters to me in between her phone conversation. I don't know who she's talking to – she's always on phone calls so it's impossible to keep track. Her phone voice makes her Californian accent nearly blend into a Texan one. I'd laugh, but she'd give me one of her warning looks to shut me up.

Natasha, my mom, is a thirty-two-year-old workaholic. She's very pretty – brown, glowing skin usually made up, curly black hair and frequently wears pantsuits and always has on high heels. Whereas my skin is a darker shade of brown, I have hazel eyes and prefer comfy clothes. Besides, the hair beneath my hijab is pin-straight. I wear the hijab because it was my choice to, and Mom doesn't because that's her choice. Aunty Mona, Mom's sister who lives in New York City, wears it and I decided I wanted to start wearing it last year.

'Why? We're just –' I cringe at my lisp that makes me say the letter 's' as a 'th' even though Mom says I should own it – 'waiting for the Uber.' Mom's being cryptic about where we're staying during this trip. She told me all about how NovaStarr Labs – the pharmaceutical company she is on the Board of Directors for – has appointed her to spearhead the setup of another UK office. She said we'll be back home to the palm trees, sunshine and beaches of California soon. But I wasn't born yesterday – I remember that Castlewick, where my dad and sister live, is nearby. Maybe that's only a coincidence.

'Well, I need your undivided attention to talk to someone.'

'Who?'

'. . . Your dad.'

A lump forms at the back of my throat. Last time I saw my dad, I was eight years old. I remember enough about

24

him; Pakistan-born, he moved to England at ten years old. Mom, California-born with Pakistani parents, moved to England when she married Dad. She moved back when they divorced, with six-month-old me but not my twin. I remember Dad being nice, good at board games and bad at bowling. But in the last three years, me and Mom haven't spoken to Dad and my sister. Life happens, I guess.

'What does he want?' I sound panicked because, well, I am.

Mom keeps her eyes locked on her phone as she shrugs. I get a whiff of her strong perfume – lavender and musk. 'To check in and see if you need anything.'

'Why would I need anything?' No, I'm not the average eleven-year-old – I don't need the latest toys or games, even though Mom always offers them.

Mom types on her phone. 'Because you'll be staying with him and Ani all summer.'

I freeze. So, no hotel then. Is NovaStarr Labs poor now?! '. . . And you, right?'

Finally Mom locks her phone and looks at me, eyes heavily lined with kajal, as usual. 'No, sweetie, *I'll* be staying at a hotel . . . in Leeds.'

I gasp. 'Mom!' I'm not a loud person so when I shout, it isn't glass-shakingly loud.

'Calm down, Riri.'

'You're gonna make me live with strangers in a strange place all summer? That's so unfair!'

Mom gives me a pointed look and I shut up. 'First of all, they're your father and your twin sister, *not strangers*, so button it. Second of all, it's not unfair when it's a nice

25

opportunity for you all to bond. Your dad is kindly hosting you, and you and Ani are getting older. We want you both to get to know each other.'

I huff.

'No huffing,' Mom warns. 'No tantrums or sighs either. I'm dialling him now, OK?'

I hold back a sigh – I clearly have no choice. 'OK,' I mumble.

She puts the call on speakerphone. I find no problem ignoring the airport's background noises to hear Dad softly say, 'Assalaamualaikum, Natasha.'

'Walaikumassalaam, Abderrazzak. We're at the airport. The Uber's nearly here.'

'Good. How was the flight?'

Mom clears her throat, uncomfortable. 'Good.'

'. . . Is Noori there?'

'Yes, she's here. Riri, go ahead.'

I swallow. I don't know why I'm nervous. My palms are sweaty. I wipe them against my jeans as I squeak out a meek, 'Hello?'

'Assalaamualaikum, Noori,' Dad says and I feel queasy. How can he sound like both a stranger and a long-lost relative at the same time?

'Walaikumassalaam.' I pause, unable to say the word 'Dad' to him. It's been three years too long. 'Um . . . how are you?'

'I'm good, alhamdulillah. You?'

I look at Mom, who's fiddling with her sparkly watch. 'I'm . . . cold.'

Dad chuckles. 'Castlewick is much colder than California. All of England is.'

I smile, until I realize he can't see me. 'What's your house like?'

'It's a flat –'

'Apartment,' Mom whispers to me.

'– in Castlewick, like four-star hotel. Cool paintings inside and play area –'

'She's eleven years old, Abderrazzak,' Mom cuts in.

'Well . . . Imani still goes to the play area.' He sounds defensive.

Before anything, I hear a commotion on the other end of the call. A door slams open.

'Imani, why you do that?' Dad's voice is muffled like he's covering the mouthpiece.

'Because I'm still angry!' screams my twin sister.

I'm still as I realise that I've heard her voice for the first time in years. It's louder than mine, firmer. It sounds – and feels – familiar but her anger is off-putting. I would never speak like that to an adult.

'Well, your anger, it needs to disappear,' Dad commands. 'Now!'

'No! I don't want them here and I really don't wanna share my room with a *stupid* –'

'Enough!' Dad sounds like his voice isn't made to shout. 'First, you storm off at the barbecue yesterday. That was rude to Mrs Kostas. Now this? Apologise or you're grounded.'

There's a long stretch of silence, as if everything at the airport has stopped. I exchange a look with Mom, both of us feeling just as tense as if we were in the room with them.

'Abderrazzak –' Mom clears her throat – 'can I speak to Ani?'

Dad sighs, loud and exhausted. 'I don't think that's a good idea, you know. Don't worry, she'll be fine by the time you come here.'

Mom sharply inhales. 'I hope so. Hudafiz.'

'Hudafiz.'

Mom hangs up and we're stuck in an unspeakable spell. Until, 'Great, the Uber's finally here.' Mom stands and holds out her hand for me. Back in California, she lets me walk around independently, without holding her hand. But in this strange place I hold hers tightly.

Fighting gusts of cold daytime air, we leave the airport.

The Uber is somehow even colder than it is outside.

Mom's ringed fingers brush mine. After half an hour, she asks the driver if he minds her turning up the heating.

'So, Mom . . .' I say. 'Are we going to the hotel now?' I hope she's forgotten that she's arranged for me to stay with Dad and Imani.

'No, sweetheart. We've been through this and I'm happy to go through it again and again, but it won't change the plan.'

Despite myself, I have an argument with her. My cheeks burn and tears threaten to spill but I keep fighting my corner. How can she abandon me for a hotel?!

'Riri, I'm not abandoning you! I'll try to visit each weekend and call every day. I'm going with you to the apartment now and I won't leave until I know you're settled.'

'But –'

Mom sighs. 'Do you remember Mrs Dimas?' I nod, remembering the old woman fondly. I wonder where she is now. 'That nice lady who used to babysit you? She used to always tell you quotes, remember? One, I believe, was, "Always make the best of it."'

I shake my head. 'You've oversimplified Epictetus's words. "Make the best use of what is in your power, and take the rest as it happens."'

Mom feigns scolding herself. 'But can you? Do that for me?'

I bite the inside of my cheeks, hesitant. 'I – I can try.'

'Thank you.' Mom hands me a small container. 'I packed your favourite biscuits.'

I can't fight my automatic smile at the smell of cumin. We call them jeera biscuits. They're sweet and salty, crispy and crumbly. I thank Mom and eat them like there's no tomorrow.

I don't know how long later, but the city lights turn into a blurry array of colours and I fall asleep on Mom's lap.

I feel groggy as I wake up when the taxi comes to a stop.

I remind myself that:

1) I'm staying in Castlewick all summer long
2) With my dad
3) And my angry twin sister who hates me
4) And who I dislike

To further explain point number three: I'm a rational person.

My eating and sleeping patterns are the same every day without fail. If not, then they throw me off-kilter. My clothes must be ironed inside-out and folded in a specific way. Mom promised me that Dad knows all my schedules and routines.

Even my career aspirations are rational – I would like to become a lawyer or a judge or even the President of the United States. Jobs that don't have any blurred lines or grey areas.

To me, that is all rational. Rationality and rules help make the world go round.

My only irrational thing is my dislike of Imani.

I dislike her because of her over-the-top behaviour. Why can't she enjoy that me and Mom are visiting? Mom and Dad got divorced when we were six months old. They had a barbecue while they were planning their futures . . . apart. Mom got custody of me and Dad got custody of Imani. It wasn't an easy decision, according to Mom.

For the first few years, we tried to keep in touch. Our visits involved me and Mom flying to the UK. As toddlers, Imani and I were compatible. Mom and Dad were still friendly for our sake. As a pre-schooler, I would excitedly ask Mom every day when we were returning to Castlewick.

But when we were seven years old, we didn't know how to appreciate each other's differences. That led to The Great Twin War. It lasted all summer long. Imani wanted me to play spies with our new spy kits. All I wanted to do was use the invisible ink pen to write in my diary. When my invisible ink pen ran out, I borrowed Imani's spy pen because it also had invisible ink. She didn't take it well.

That summer, we had so many fights that we both lost our voices. Next summer, when we were eight, our parents thought that The Great Twin War would be over.

They were wrong. If anything, it was worse. The first week of that summer repeated each fight from the year before. Our parents tried to intervene but Imani wasn't so forgiving. I even spent my life savings on new spy pens! She didn't accept my peace offering. It got so bad that me and Mom flew back to California early.

Mom and Dad decided that they would not reunite us for our ninth summer. But at that time, their careers were taking off and keeping in touch got harder. Birthday cards and Eidi – Eid money – were sent. Mom and Dad tried to do video calls for big days. But whenever Imani heard something she didn't like, she'd hang up.

The strain of continuing at a distance took its toll and Mom and Dad's relationship soured too. Then commenced The War of Parental Independence. Contact has been scarce ever since.

Last summer, Mom and I went to Disneyland and stayed in a hotel in Anaheim. We also spent a day at Echo Park Lake. Another day was spent touring Hollywood.

In conclusion, last summer rocked.

And this summer will suck. But I know there's nothing I can do.

'We're here, sweetheart,' Mom says with a yawn.

I stretch, blinking blurry eyes open. Sleeping in jeans is horrid, my tingly legs tell me. 'What time is it?'

'It's nearly 5 p.m.'

'When did we land? Was it today?' I follow Mom outside as she gets the suitcases.

'We landed an hour ago. We're in Castlewick now.' There's a huge illuminated building in front of us with a sign that says THE SKYSCAPE. Mom inhales deeply as someone comes rushing out of the building to help us take the luggage. He's wearing a uniform so Mom and Dad probably made the arrangements for someone to help us before. Just like a hotel. Even though I now see another sign, this one saying that The Skyscape is an apartment complex.

Mom swings her arms, something I've never seen her do before. She's clearly nervous and I think I know why. 'Do you think you're ready to see your dad and sister now?'

I exhale. I don't have a choice but sure, is what I want to say, but that would be rude, so instead I go with the last word. 'Sure.' Three years later, how different can they be?

Mom looks at me a second too long as if trying to call my bluff. Even if she does, what good would it do? 'OK, follow me.'

I follow her through The Skyscape lobby and up to the apartment. I'm surprised when Mom opens the door and walks straight in. It's spacious and minimalistic, with impersonal framed pictures, as if Dad and Imani don't consider this their home. Based on what I know of my sister, I was expecting a messy, inside-out, colourful explosion. She must be good at tidying up. Or good at leaving while Dad tidies up.

In the living room, Dad stands, appearing nervous. I remember that we have the same eyes – a shade of hazel that stands out against our brown skin. He looks like he hasn't changed that much. The air feels weird – different. This is the first time we're all together in person in three years. Even thinking about it makes me feel like I've got a full belly and a warm blanket around me, which sounds nice but in summer, it just feels uncomfortable. I don't know what I want but I did know that this would be awkward. You know, in the *hours* I had to emotionally prepare for this reunion.

'Noori, beti.' Dad sounds affectionate and steps closer.

I look up at him, arching my neck because he's tall. 'Hi,' I say. I appreciate that he doesn't force me into a hug.

'Do you want a tour of your new summer home?' He smiles.

I nod.

'Riri, use your words, sweetheart,' Mom says. Even though she tries hiding it, I notice her discomfort.

'Yes, please,' I tell Dad.

He smiles and motions for me to lead the way even though I'd be instantly lost.

As I walk out, I see Imani in a staring competition with Mom, whose smile wavers.

The tour ended up being quite boring. In California, our house is 'Bohemian', as Mom describes it. It has lots of indoor plants and rugs – even some tacked to the walls – and lots of bright colours. It's interesting because Mom appears to be quite a serious person, but she's not really. She designed our house herself and guests always say they love it.

Dad has two TVs – with subscription services, thank

goodness – two tablets and lots of self-help books. The apartment has two bedrooms – one for Dad and one for Imani and, I guess, me now. Worse than abandoning me for a hotel, Mom prepped me about the '*non-negotiable*' arrangement about me sharing Imani's room. I tried volunteering to sleep on the sofa but it was no use. Still, I got my tantrum out of my system in the car and have since decided to be the bigger person. There's nothing I can do about it, anyway.

There's a big kitchen and bathroom, plus a bigger living room. The last room, which was locked during my tour, is Dad's home office. I bet Imani's the reason it's locked.

Dad takes me into Imani's messy room again. He was apologetic and insisted that he'd tidied it up this morning. Now, she's incoherently mumbling into a phone as she sits on her bed.

Side note: how unfair is it that she has her own phone and I don't?

'Supersleuth's log –' she keeps her unblinking gaze on me – 'there has been an invasion of my *private* TUSC office. Time: 5.09 p.m. I think I know exactly how to proceed.' In a flash, she jumps off her bed and lands on my airbed. Her intimidating gaze is still locked on me. I stare back then blink. She thinks she's a sleuth? Wow.

Dad stands between us. 'No, you don't. Imani, be nice to your sister.'

'She's not my –'

'Do you want to be grounded all summer long?'

Imani works her jaw. 'I suppose not.'

'Good. Now, welcome your sister and be nice to her for the next six weeks.' He looks at me and then at Imani again.

Mom comes in as soon as Dad finishes talking as if she was listening outside the door. She smiles at us. My heart warms then stings at the fact that we'll be separated all summer long. In my peripheral vision, Imani squirms.

'Imani –' Dad nods at her – 'say goodbye.'

'Goodbye.' Imani then woodenly walks out. At least she didn't stomp off.

Mom gives me a bright smile. I speed over to her and give her a tight hug. Her perfume tickles my nose and makes me feel lightheaded, but in a good way. 'I'll miss you.' I blink away my tears.

'I'll miss you more, Riri.' She pulls away, sniffs, then wipes her eyes. 'I love you so much. Be nice to your sister and good for your dad. Your dad said he'll let you call me whenever.'

I nod. Dad follows us as we walk out of Imani's room. He forces Imani to come along as well and she drags her feet over to us. Once Mom has left, I head to the window and look down. Dad's apartment is on the fourteenth floor and I can see Mom shuffle into the Uber. Before she shuts the door, her head sticks out and she waves up towards the apartment. I wave back, placing my hand on the window, then watch the black car drive off. I continue looking even after it's gone.

Imani turned away ages ago.

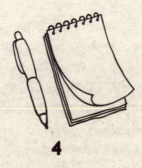

4

RIRI

Dad settles me and Imani back into her room. 'I'll let you two catch up.' Then he leaves.

I look around, fully taking it in now, noticing the similarities and differences between her room and mine back home.

Similarities:
- There's a bed, desk and window
- A copy of the Quran is on a high-up bookshelf
- A blue wardrobe with our initials on it

Differences:
- Her room is double the size of mine
- The theme of her room is mess — posters, newspaper clippings and *clutter* on her walls cover the wallpaper.
- My room has a reading nook, whereas Imani has . . . a sleuthing nook. Her window bench is littered with scrunched-up papers, a fingerprint testing kit, a map and a human skeleton diagram.

'Done staring?' Imani jumps onto her bed then taps my airbed with her foot. She wears checked capri pants and a neon vest. 'Take a seat.'

'I'd rather stand.' I'm grateful that Dad doesn't allow us to wear shoes inside the apartment – she seems like the kind of person to always have dirty shoes. But then, I bet she has dirty feet as well. Oh, dear.

'What's your name?'

'You already know, but it's Noori Tariq. I was born seven minutes after you.'

Imani looks at me dubiously. 'Chicken or fish?'

'Neither. I'm vegan.' Me and Mom have been vegan for three years now. Plants take some getting used to, but they are yummy.

Imani scrunches up her face in disgust. 'Books or movies?'

'Books.'

A sigh. 'Comics or movies?'

'Books.'

That makes Imani chuckle. 'Sunshine or rainstorms?'

That's easy. 'Rainstorms.' Why? Because the science behind rainstorms – warm air rising into cool air, causing water vapour to turn into raindrops – is much more exciting than the science behind sunshine. I mean, who cares about the sun's core turning hydrogen into helium during nuclear fusion, which creates the energy we feel in sunshine?

Plus, I suffer from hay fever. My hay fever is controlled in California, and Castlewick is cooler so hopefully I'm not affected.

'Puzzles or puddles?'

'Puzzles.'

Another sigh. 'Oh dear, that's a match. Deserts or desserts?'

'Uh . . . neither.' The Sonoran Desert's ragweed flared up my hay fever. And desserts are great but I prefer savoury foods – they're more nutritious.

She sighs yet again, this time super loud. 'Painting or feinting?'

My eyes widen. 'How is fainting enjoyable?'

Imani gives me a lopsided grin. 'Not *fainting* but *feinting*. F-e-i-n-t-i-n-g. Like a pretend blow when you're boxing to trick the other boxer?' Imani stands on her bed and fakes giving a blow and then taking one – with sound effects too.

'Oh. Then feinting.'

Imani raises her eyebrows. 'What?'

'I said "feinting".' Imani blankly looks at me, so I decide to explain. 'I box. I'm quite good, actually. I'm one of ten Junior Boxers in California.' I don't like gloating and whenever it feels like I am, it's awful. Just like now.

I patiently wait for Imani to respond while her face contorts. I'm looking into eyes that are the same shape and size as mine, only a different colour. Despite being non-identical twins, we do look alike. Her face is rounder and her nose is upturned whereas mine has a slight bump. I can imagine people doing double-takes during my stay here, even though I wear a hijab and she doesn't.

I continue to wait and wait; Imani is speechless. Funnily enough, she's biting the insides of her cheeks as if to *physically* stop herself from talking. What's her problem?

The silence between us is tense. She ties her curly hair up in a bun, reminding me of Mom.

'Well, I can shout superbly!' Imani blurts out.

I can now do one of two things. I can:

1) Talk in a civil tone

2) Try to match her volume

It's summer, the time of courage and change, so I decide to go with option number two.

'Well, I can play piano superbly!'

'So what? I can run brilliantly!'

'I can read dictionaries brilliantly!'

She thinks for a second. 'I can solve mysteries and riddles successfully!'

'I can solve crosswords and equations successfully!'

Dad barges into the room. 'What's happening here?'

I point at Imani. Simultaneously she points at me. 'She started it,' we say.

Jinx.

Dad gapes at us, then lets out a dry chuckle. 'Definitely twins. Imani, could you take Noori to Cafe Vivlio? I need to attend an important work call, you know, and I can't have any distractions. I might be a while. I'll pick you both up after and we can get ice-cream, yeah?'

'He's going to find out if he's lost his job or not,' Imani stage-whispers.

Dad says, 'Go now. Be good.' Imani opens her mouth to speak but Dad holds up a finger. 'Both of you together. On best behaviour. I should be done by 6.30 p.m.'

He hands Imani an oversized lightweight cardigan. I'm

still wearing my yellow pinafore.

'You might want to speed up,' Imani grumbles without looking at me. She opens the door and finally turns. 'Because I walk very fast.'

5

ANI

Sunrays shine on cracked cobblestones. Birds peck at pavement litter. Buses and their posters pass me by. Cars zoom down the streets. As good a time as any to resume my supersleuth's log.

Unfortunately I'm unintentionally walking in sync with my evil twin. We've rounded the corner from the flat and Cafe Vivlio's at the end of this straight pavement. Speaking of the cafe, I haven't seen Mrs Kostas since my outburst yesterday at the BBQoBN. I need to apologise to her.

I crouch, fake tying my shoe. My evil twin is so foolish, she hasn't noticed.

At least three steps behind her now, I get my phone. Press 'record'. I pretend to scratch my face as I murmur, 'Supersleuth's log.' I move my eyes around to search for any watchers. Never making any sudden head movements. 'I'm on the street. On foot. Keeping true. The weather is nice. Not too cold but not too warm either. The afternoon is over. It's 5.45 p.m. now but summertime means it still feels and looks like the afternoon. I'm walking in tow with my evil twin.

'Conclusion: I do not like her.'

My evil twin abruptly stops. Turning fast, her hijab tries to catch up with her. She chuckles at me like *I'm* pathetic. 'Seriously? You do your detective's log outside as well?'

I go closer to her in warning. She's drawing attention to me. If I were being followed, like all the best sleuths, then I'd have already been made by now. 'It's a supersleuth's log.'

'Sorry but is there a difference?'

My teeth grind as I glare at her. '*Yes!* Of course there's a difference! Sure, they both solve mysteries. But a detective works for the government, in law enforcement. And a sleuth can work for themselves and be super ultrasecret and cool.'

My evil twin frowns. 'But . . . a detective can also be that too. Ever heard of private detectives or PIs?'

'It's a *nuance!*' I exclaim. She stares at me, clearly not interested in the difference. 'I've solved *loads* of cases as a supersleuth.' I tell her about my most notable cases, including The Case of the Missing Tie and The Case of the Lost Cat.

'But those aren't *proper* cases.'

I gape at her. I officially hate her more than ever, and she only arrived today. 'It's – that's not the point. A case is a case. Besides, Mrs Kostas is going to set me some mysteries to solve this summer so you'll see.' She doesn't say anything. I glare at her. 'I'm a supersleuth. You wouldn't understand because you're just an evil twin.'

'Whatever you say. And "evil twin"? It's easier to call me

Riri. Everyone, including Mom, does. And . . . I've heard Mom call you "Ani." Can I call you Ani?'

I don't want to admit it but 'Ani and Riri' and 'Riri and Ani' sound good together.

However, at the moment, I have something pressing to address. I glare at Riri. 'It's not *air-nee!* It's *ahh-nee*.'

She tilts her head. 'So . . . like Arnie?'

'It's *Ani*!' I storm ahead to Cafe Vivlio.

'Whoa,' my evil twin says as I hold open the door for her. 'This place looks so cool,' she breathes. Wide-eyed with wonder. I'm not surprised at all – Cafe Vivlio is the best place ever. Let her fall in love with my town before returning to California forever. I hope she misses Castlewick a lot. No, I don't plan on welcoming her back here next summer.

'It is the coolest.'

Huh, first time I've agreed with her.

The smell of pastries greets my nostrils.

Riri sniffs the air. 'I can't wait until I'm allowed to drink coffee. Don't you love the smell?'

'Nope. Coffee smells of Monday mornings and schoolteachers. Come on, let's go to *my* table.' I march toward my spot. Three steps. I don't get far. She taps me. Keeps her hand on my shoulder. Warm. It . . . fits on my shoulder.

'Yes?' I ask suspiciously. Our eyes lock.

My evil twin quickly removes her hand from my shoulder. 'Sorry. Can I just say, it's so cool that you have your own table at this awesome cafe?' She points at the plaque on the wall that reads: ANI. Last year's birthday present from Mrs Kostas.

I nod. My hair curtains my face and tickles my cheeks. 'Noted.' I point to the statue. 'Behind Athena is a whole bookshop.' She gasps then squeals, looking delighted as she scurries off.

I head over to my table and settle into my chair. Comfy thanks to Mrs Kostas' hand-sewn cushion. I'm glad the AC is on.

I glance around Cafe Vivlio. Mrs Kostas isn't at the counter. In fact, no one is. There's a chalkboard near the menu with daily staff rotas.

Name	Role	Working today?
Mrs Kostas	Manager	Working
Rodolfo	Cook	Working
Clarissa	Barista	SICK
Linnet	Barista	SICK
Peter	Barista	SICK
Ava	Barista	SICK
Jack	Barista	SICK
Hassan	Barista	SICK
Heather	Barista	SICK
Rakim	Barista	SICK

Mrs Kostas is usually either in the cafe's bookstore or doing errands but she's never out for too long. I need to find her ASAP so I can apologise to her for running off yesterday. Dad has always told me to never leave things on a bad note.

But something doesn't feel right.

If everyone is off sick then Mrs Kostas should be here. Rodolfo grumbles something, lip curled, as he jogs between the counter and kitchens. Barely acknowledges me. But I know that he knows I'm here. Mrs Kostas must have left him in charge again like yesterday when she took me to The Secret Garden.

'Hi, Rodolfo!' I wave. His response is a sigh that further hunches his shoulders. Then he goes into the kitchens. 'He'll be back,' I tell myself.

One of the Cafe Vivlio regulars turns to me with a pleasant smile. 'Hi, Ani.'

TUSC PROFILE

Name:	Mr Fred Hunt
Gender:	Male
Pronouns:	He/him/his
Age:	34 years old
Occupation:	Aspiring screenwriter (technically unemployed)

```
Physical characteristics:

    1. Light brown moustache and goatee and
       balding head
    2. Wears frameless glasses
    3. Always wears bowties


Observation: He tells the worst jokes
```

'Fred! How's it going?'

'Probably not as good as you – how excited are you that, as of yesterday, school's out for summer?'

'So excited! I'm ready to solve so many cases. What about you? How's the fight scene going?'

He winces. Maybe I asked the wrong question. But if my memory serves then he's been stuck on that scene for so long. Weeks. Might even be a month now.

'It's keeping me up at night,' he admits. *Just like how my cases keep me up sometimes*. 'It's hard to get it right.' He pauses. I take it as my cue to say something helpful but instead, he adds, 'You see, Ani, what the illustrious Columbia University taught me was that you can never rush perfection. Even if it means sitting on a scene for weeks, even years. That's actually happened before. It took me two years to write an emotional scene once.'

'Oh. Well, I'm sure you'll get it perfect soon, Fred. You were a student and then a teacher at Columbia, right?'

He nods, overenthusiastically.

'Well, I'm sure you've got all the knowledge to do it right.'

Before he can tell me more about 'the illustrious Columbia University', I get up and stroll behind the counter (I'm allowed) to the kitchen. My aim: to find Mrs Kostas.

'Get out of my kitchen, Annie,' snarls Rodolfo. He has a butcher's knife in his hands.

'It's *Ani*. And I only came to see if Mrs Kostas is here.'

He sets the knife down and it clatters. 'She isn't. What does that sign say?'

'"Staff only". Fine, I'll go. If I have to listen to the sign then you have to follow the rules too. Pretty sure they state that a chef should be nice,' I quip.

He takes a step toward me. His bushy eyebrows almost conceal his eyes. 'Go now. I'm in charge until Polly comes back from wherever she is.'

I walk out. The counter is two steps away. One step later, I bump into someone.

There's hair in my face and it's not mine. It's long, blonde, straight and coconut-scented. My eyes are dazzled by a necklace with a fist-sized amethyst on it.

'Ani! Hey.' Mimi gives a high-pitched giggle and rubs her elbow. 'I feel like it's been, like, forever since I last saw you. Looking taller!' She twiddles her fingers on the chain of her necklace.

'Pretty sure it was four days ago.'

I get a perfect smile from Mimi. 'Sorry for bumping into you. I hope I didn't hurt you,' she squeaks. I locate her TUSC profile in my brain:

TUSC PROFILE

Name:	Miss Tammy 'Mimi' Jacqueline Bloodworth
Gender:	Female
Pronouns:	She/her/hers
Age:	36 years old
Occupation:	Technically unemployed but 'professionally figuring it out'

Physical characteristics:

1. Trademark blond hair is never tied back
2. Wears cycling shorts with vests no matter the weather
3. Always wears the same amethyst necklace

Observation: Her phone is *never* out of her hands

'No, Mimi, it's fine.' Even if I were injured, I wouldn't say anything. A supersleuth shouldn't make a scene unless it's a big reveal. 'I saw your newest TikTok. Looks fun.'

Dad doesn't let me go on TikTok. But from Helin showing me Mimi's profile, I know her social media is definitely where she's 'figuring it out.' She doesn't have many views or followers.

Helin's sister's gone viral loads of times. She's even quit her 9–5 job because she's earning money from social media. That's Mimi's aim, even though she doesn't have a 9–5 job to quit once she becomes an influencer. I hope she makes it.

'Really? Thanks so much. It took me so long to film!'

'Well, if you ever need help, I'm sure Helin's sister wouldn't mind.'

'Thanks. See you later.' She bins her empty coffee cup. 'Can you tell Mrs Kostas to put it on my tab?' I nod. 'Thanks. See you, Rodolfo! Maybe for the fourth time today!'

The grumpy chef replies, 'Yeah, whatever.'

As Mimi strolls out of Cafe Vivlio, someone else comes in. It's only Derek Chase, my big brother from another mother. He doesn't acknowledge me because his vlog camera is recording him talking. He posts live videos every day. His phone in his other hand. He's a busy guy but he's always nice to me. Always on my level. His video might be about coming to his favourite cafe – his viewers would watch him watch paint dry. They are loyal. A bit stupid.

'Right, I'm going to have some of Mrs Kostas's world-class coffee and sausage rolls,' he says to the camera. Smiles. 'I'll see you all in my Live tomorrow. Peace.'

Derek locks his phone and sets down his camera. He sits in his usual chair, right by the window looking down the street. He stretches and grunts. Rubs his face. 'Mrs Kostas?' he looks around. 'Wherever you are . . . I'll take my usual.'

TUSC PROFILE

Name:	Mr Derek Chase
Gender:	Male
Pronouns:	He/him/his
Age:	31 years old
Occupation:	Vlogger (owner of the DerekChasesTheGlobe YouTube channel, 1.83 million subscribers)

Physical characteristics:

1. Black skin, small afro, stubble, nose ring and lip ring
2. Wears sunglasses inside ~~(because he thinks he's a big deal)~~
3. Always has a leather jacket on.

Observation: Looks like he can play the guitar and sing but he cannot (unethically proven)

I glance at the hallway and wait for Rodolfo to come from the kitchens to take Derek's order. He doesn't. He's probably busy draining the sunshine from the skies.

'Yarr,' I tell Derek. 'Yarr' is a South Asian informal way of saying 'friend', that Derek understands. 'You seem tired,' I say, referencing how he's grunting and rubbing his face.

He looks up at me. Smiles, but it's small. 'It's the daily vlogging, yarr. Sometimes it's too much.'

'Well, you love the perks,' I half joke. He gets invitations to exclusive parties and events in London and LA. It doesn't take a genius to know that Derek loves freebies and designer clothes – things he only gets because of his popular channel. 'But do you have to vlog every day? Like today – did you even do anything cool or was it just a dull summer's day where nothing happened?'

He clicks his tongue. 'I'll vlog anything. If I have nowhere fun to go or nothing cool to do then I'll just talk to my viewers.' He looks around, clearly wanting to change the subject. Meanwhile, I think I might feel bad for the pressures of a vlogger. Maybe not. 'Where's Mrs Kostas? It's not like her to not come over.'

'Rodolfo's in charge until Mrs Kostas comes back.'

'He's not doing a good job, is he, yarr?' Derek smirks. I can see my reflection in his sunglasses. He motions for me to sit but I shake my head.

'Nope. He's not a people person. Or a multitasker.'

'Definitely not. I hope he comes to take orders soon.' Derek rubs his stomach. Glances out the window. 'I'm supposed to eat with my little – oh, there he is.'

A younger version of Derek pushes open the cafe door. Bells chime. (Bells that Rodolfo should be able to hear from the kitchens, making him dash to the counter.)

'Frankster the prankster,' Derek greets his little brother.

'Derek the ferret.' 'Frankster' looks at me. 'You our waitress?'

Derek kicks him under the table. 'You're joking. Ani is your age. Hey, I bet you guys go to the same school.' I don't say anything even though just yesterday, Frankie asked Mx Henderson if we could leave five minutes early while I was telling everyone about the TUSC.

'Oh, I know you. We went to the same school. You're the brown Sherlock girl, right?'

I knit my eyebrows down. 'Is there a white Sherlock girl I don't know about?'

TUSC PROFILE

Name:	Mr Frank 'Frankie' Chase
Gender:	Male
Pronouns:	He/him/his
Age:	11 years old
Occupation:	Student

Physical characteristics:

1. Cauliflower ear
2. Shoulder-length locs
3. Wears braces

Observation: Is popular at school and everywhere else

Derek chuckles. 'Frankie, you idiot. Ani is a supersleuth. One of a kind!'

'Right.' Frankie's clearly not interested. He's staring at the menu. 'Surprised he hasn't asked you to work with him on his newest series.'

I blink, confused about who he's talking to, then meet Frankie's dark eyes. Oh, to me. Before I can ask, he says, 'It's a true-crime series based around old unsolved mysteries.' My eyes light up. Wow! 'Based on this guy's obsession with –'

'Ani!' My evil twin rushes over to me. 'Never ever take me out of this place because –' She looks at Frankie and her eyes widen. She blushes. 'Oh!' She smiles at Frankie. He's also smiling at her. Ugh, this is weird. 'I'm Riri. Hello.'

'Riri? Beautiful name. I'm Frankie. Your accent is so nice.' Frankie sounds smooth.

'Aw, thank you.' She blushes again. 'I'm from California.'

Frankie beams. Looks at Derek. 'I was about to say she has those California eyes.'

I gape at Frankie. 'What does that even *mean*?! Eyes can't be Californian!'

'OK, shush up, all of you,' Derek says. 'Ani, you and Riri look like twins.'

'Tell me something I don't know, *yarr*,' I snap. I definitely mean to snap at him, because he's such a traitor for not telling me about his newest series. He sees me at the cafe most days and he knows that this is right up my alley. I have a wealth of knowledge!

My evil twin taps my arm. Repetitively. Annoyingly. 'Ani, can I –?'

'Not now,' I bark. My eyes are on Frankie. 'We were in the middle of something. You mentioned Derek's newest series. What is it based on?'

'Huh? Oh, yeah. Based on his obsession with Cluedo and Sherlock Holmes: Consulting Detective. I prefer the Sherlock Xbox games myself.'

'Me too,' my Frankie-obsessed evil twin says airily.

Before I can whack her where it hurts, the bells of the cafe door chime. Mimi has returned. She smiles at all of us, except for Derek. They have a romantic past but before they could go social media official, Derek realised Mimi was using him for clout.

'I left my purse –' She stops. Her eyes widen. Has she seen a ghost? 'Uh . . . Ani? Someone's right beside you who looks *identical* to you. So freaky.'

'Mimi, how on earth are twins freaky?' Frankie's smiling eyes are still on Riri.

'The Grady sisters from *The Shining*.' Derek says, avoiding Mimi's stare.

'Anirbas, from *Sabrina the Teenage Witch*,' Riri adds. 'Ooh, Mia and Tia from *Cars*.'

Frankie chuckles. 'How are Mia and Tia freaky twins?'

'No loyalty to Lightning McQueen.'

'Oh, I know,' Frankie adds. 'Liquid Snake from *Metal Gear Solid*.'

'Dolly and Molly Preston-Grey from *Elephants Can Remember*,' I say. Everyone looks at me. Concerned. Confused. 'It's an Agatha Christie novel that – never mind.'

My phone buzzes. Dad's ringing me. Phew, I'm saved

from this conversation. 'Ji?' I ask. It's the respectful way of saying 'yes' in my native language.

'Assalaamualaikum. Imani, I'm finished. Is Noori with you still?' I tell him she is. 'OK, good. I'm coming to get you for ice-cream now. See if Mrs Kostas is free. I should treat her, you know, for helping me with the barbecue yesterday. Did you say sorry, I hope?'

'I will. But I need to find her first. Hudafiz.' He echoes my goodbye.

I look at the Chase brothers then at Mimi. 'It's been a pleasure, but we need to go.' I look at my evil twin. 'Dad's coming to get us. Move.'

I usher her out of Cafe Vivlio and she tuts and tries to get me off her. Obviously she doesn't want to leave Frankie. I didn't expect her to be the kind to fall in love at first sight but it's written all over her face. Sad.

'Dad wants to take Mrs Kostas with us to get ice-cream so I'll ring her,' I say. 'I'm excited to see her even though I only saw her yesterday.' Back when I stormed off.

'Yay. I'll finally meet the famous woman.'

I dial Mrs Kostas's number. It rings and rings. No answer yet. We sidestep some pedestrians. 'Stand on the side here so we're not in anyone's way.' I let my evil twin follow me to the side of the cafe. The Secret Garden is on the other side of the wall we're standing beside but we'd have to go back through the cafe to get to it. It's kinda fortified.

I sigh. 'Come on, Mrs Kostas. Pick up.'

'Why don't we go back inside the cafe and wait for her there?'

55

I give her a long look. 'Pretty sure all of Castlewick now knows that the visiting American girl has a crush on Frankie Chase. You're not helping yourself.'

'No! Do you think he noticed?! I thought I was discreet!'

'I'm so grateful you're not my sleuth partner because discretion is key.' I turn my attention back to my phone. Still no answer but I can hear her ringtone. I block out the faraway roadworks. The jingle of an ice-cream truck. Nearby cars revving.

The ringtone is coming from behind us. Through the wall. Is Mrs Kostas in The Secret Garden?

I glance around then dash through Cafe Vivlio, bumping into a few people. Someone's hip hits my pocket, which is full of TUSC supersleuth items such as a compact mirror, stain-removing pen, torch and wristwatch. You never know when such eventualities would require them. We're in the Secret Garden now. Suddenly I sniff the air.

The Secret Garden still smells like the BBQoBN from yesterday. And –

Oh no. Oh no, no, no, no. No!

'Mrs Kostas!' I scream.

She's unmoving. Lying on the grass. Face down.

6

ANI

I run over to Mrs Kostas – she's near the steps and the whole garden is a mess. She still smells of cinnamon, walnuts and cloves with lemon zest. The hose is on and water dribbles down the footpath. How long has it been running?

Think, Ani, think! There are things you're supposed to do to check if someone is alive. Can I remember what they are? If it was with anyone else that was hurt, yes.

But now, I'm not so sure.

'Oh gosh!' Riri exclaims behind me. 'I'm germophobic and something of a chicken so I can't be here! I don't know what the situation is over there but, Ani, I swear, I can't.'

I ignore Riri and her crisis. 'God, please make Mrs Kostas not be dead,' I pray. Then inhale. Slowly, slowly, I turn her over. She looks fine. She has to be fine. She has to be. My heart is a hurricane. I have to be focused to:

☑ Gently shake her
☑ Hold a compact mirror near her nose – does it fog up?

☑ Check for a pulse – neck and wrist
☑ Check if her pupils have dilated using a compact torch

I get some of my TUSC supersleuth items out of my pocket to do the checks. I've always wanted to use the items in emergencies but not like this. Not with Mrs Kostas.

Still warm but she's unresponsive. No fog forms on the mirror. No pulse. Pupils not dilating. No visible signs of injury but that isn't hopeful.

'Somebody help! Please! Oh God,' I wheeze out. Light-headed. I'm going to fall and vomit. 'Riri –'

'Oh my gosh.' She lets out a sob. 'Mrs Dimas?! I can't believe it!'

'Riri,' I slowly say. She's still my evil twin but saying 'Riri' is quicker. 'Her name is Mrs Kostas. Mrs Polina Kostas.'

Riri shakes her head. 'No, no, no. I remember her. *I remember her*, Ani. She is – *was* – she was Mrs Dimas, our school librarian. Sometimes, she babysat me.' She lets out another sob.

I'm confused. Mrs Kostas is Mrs Kostas.

Riri continues, 'She lived near us in California then moved to England, apparently to find a long-lost relative. She didn't go into details. Me and Mom never heard from her again.'

'What?' I squeak out. I'm . . . in shock. 'It can't be. How sure are you?'

Riri swallows. 'Her features are the same, except for one. The heart-shaped mole on her right cheekbone. I could never forget it. It must be covered up.'

'What?! I never saw a heart-shaped mole on her.' I peer at her right cheekbone. 'But anyway, now is *not* the time to be talking about moles. Help! HELP!' But no one's around and I can't stop looking at Mrs Kostas's cheekbone again. My hands are quivering. Even still, I reach for her to see where the mole should be.

'No, Ani. Don't touch it.' I glare at Riri. 'Fine, but wear gloves then.'

'My pockets can only fit so many things! There are no gardening gloves either.'

'OK, sorry. Just hang on.' My slit eyes watch as she tears a small piece of her hijab and hands it to me. Well . . . I wasn't expecting that.

Gently I wipe her cheek. Mrs Kostas feels like a living person, not a dead one.

Oh, but she's not moving.

She's not moving. Nonresponsive. And Riri is right – there's a mole there.

So she's not who I thought she was.

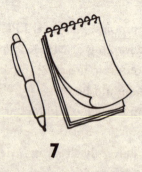

7

RIRI

I never thought I would ever see a dead body. But if I did, I knew I would freak out. It's good to know that I was right about that. I never could've predicted that on my first day in Castlewick I would see a dead body.

I saw Ani's shaking hands touch the mole to make sure it was real. My heart shatters at the possibility of Mrs Dimas covering it up every day. Who was she trying to be? Or trying *not* to be?

The fact that I even have to ask those questions has me second-guessing my semi-heroic moment of tearing off a corner of my hijab. What if my DNA is on the body now?!

'Calm down,' Ani says in a monotone voice, like she's in a zombified state of grief. 'Fingerprint elimination is a thing.' I blush, not realising I'd asked that question aloud.

Based on Ani's current expression I can tell that her heart

is shattering too. She holds Mrs Dimas's wrist affectionately, fingers grazing her Apple Watch.

'She told me to never hide anything about myself from the world. It helped me get through school.' Ani's chin trembles. I wait for her to continue because this whole thing feels outburst-worthy. But she doesn't. 'Ugh, I can't believe I'm saying this, but I wish it was yesterday and I was back at school. Back when everything was normal.'

I don't know what else to say, so I say what I know: 'In California, her hair was longer and red. And curly. She was fancy and – she mentioned belonging to a rich family.'

Ani firmly shakes her head. 'This doesn't match anything I know about Mrs Kostas.'

'You mean Mrs Dimas.'

'What I *mean* is that you're confused.' Ani lets out a long breath. 'And I don't believe she simply dropped dead.'

'That's just the first stage of grief. Denial.'

'No . . . Look around here.' She shakes her head and whispers, 'How did I not see this earlier? I need to be a better supersleuth. More observant. Not make it so personal.'

'Ani, don't be silly. A person you care for just died. Let's call the police.'

Ani scoffs and I now notice how red her eyes are. 'What for? I'm going to investigate before they get here. This is my crime scene. They'll just mess it up.'

My mouth widens. 'No,' is all I can say.

'The – look, Riri, the paper plates from yesterday's barbecue have been scattered all over the grass. Paper cups have been stepped on. Something's wrong. Could be signs of

61

a struggle. The hose is still running. One clay pot is broken, spilt soil opposite Mrs Kostas. I'm sure you've noticed the broken pot – it's so big.'

I did, and I wanted so badly to glue it back together.

Ani glances up at the hillock. 'Was Mrs Kostas going to the hillock or coming down from it? Look! A shattered mug.' Ani slowly goes up the stairs with wobbly legs. 'Riri, this mug is Mrs Kostas's. It's the *only* mug she ever drinks from.'

'So . . . ?' There's a chance Ani is onto something. But we can leave that to the police. 'We'll talk theories later. First, let's get help. Help!' I shout, ignoring the warning look Ani gives me. '*Help!*'

Before we know it, people with worried looks come through Cafe Vivlio to The Secret Garden.

'I'm a doctor,' one of them says. He runs over while dialling on his phone.

Cut to about ten minutes later. Mrs Dimas is confirmed dead and the police have arrived.

I can't believe she's gone. True, I hadn't seen her in years, but that doesn't make it hurt any less. Meanwhile, Ani walks away from the doctor, who is still kneeling by Mrs Dimas, and stops.

She has her back turned to me so it's safe to put a hand on her shoulder without her being mean. She doesn't turn. 'Do you need a hug?' The crack in my voice is the giveaway that I need one too. It takes almost a minute for Ani to respond but I don't let go. Slowly her red-rimmed eyes meet mine. But she doesn't say what I think she's gonna say.

'She might've fallen from the top of the hillock because

of her arthritis, maybe, but this place is a mess. And I can *feel* something wrong. This was a murder, I know it.' She turns away again.

'Wait!' I plead, enough for Ani to turn. 'How can you be sure?'

Ani opens her mouth, but she's cut off. A police officer with oversized sunglasses is near the hillock, waving a piece of paper in a plastic bag around. 'Look, a note!' I can see it from here – it's printed, not handwritten.

Another police officer takes it, his sweat-drenched forehead frowning. '"An open enemy is better than a false friend." Apparently it's a Greek proverb? Oh, what's this?' He squints. '"Come and find me. But she's where she should be."' The policeman's eyes widen as he looks at his colleague. 'Let's get this sent to the Forensic Linguistics team ASAP.'

'There,' Ani says to me. 'That's our proof that it's murder. I'm going to solve it. Bye.' Then she just walks away, leaving me with that bombshell.

'Young lady!' A police officer calls out to Ani. 'We need to take your statements. Stay here.'

Ani turns and walks backwards. 'I'm getting some air.'

'OK, stop there, please,' the police officer says, holding up his hand at her.

Ani stops a few steps away from me and I take the opportunity to go to her. 'I knew her too. Or . . . a version of her, at least. Maybe I have some skills to help solve this with you?' For someone who's trying to sell themselves, I sound unsure. But I hope she can see a spark in my eyes.

It feels like forever before Ani responds. 'You'll need to be eased into the TUSC. And you'll be a Sleuth-in-Training, so you *have to* listen to me. Always.'

'But Ani, I think sometimes my input would be good. Maybe? So, if I know that you've said something wrong, I won't feel right listening to what you say.'

'What?! Then investigate it yourself!'

I press my lips together. 'No, I think we'll be stronger together. Just . . . can't we be partners instead?' She opens her mouth to talk but I hold up a hand to stop her. 'I know you're more experienced in sleuthing –'

'*Super*sleuthing.'

'– but we need to be friendly and respectful. Please? What kind of an organisation would the TUSC be if everyone wasn't valued?'

Ani rolls her eyes, too stubborn to admit that I have a point. 'Fine, I'll hear you out if I think you know something I don't. But like you said, I'm more experienced *and* I know the way of this town. Plus, I'm in charge of the TUSC. OK, deal?'

I nod. Then Ani gives me a long look. Oh, I realise, a moment late. She wants me to say it. 'Yes, yes. Deal.'

We shake hands.

'The last – and only – people to join the TUSC were Helin and LaShawn, my best friends. It didn't end well for them. They had a good run. However they're both now on administrative leave. But once a TUSC sleuth, always a TUSC sleuth. LaShawn's currently on studying house arrest and Helin is babysitting her nieces and nephews.

You'll meet them soon. Although they both live quite a distance away. Sound good?'

Timidly I nod. I have only one friend – so that makes her my best friend – back home. Her name is Adora and she's great. Last summer, we worked on a comic book – my words and Adora's drawings. We also attended boxing classes, read loads of books and had sleepovers. Mom always encourages me to make more friends but it's so hard. But I think that joining forces with Ani on my first day here counts, right?

Ani proceeds to annoy the police officers with questions they refuse to answer, so I decide to do what's been at the back of my mind since seeing the body. I sanitise my hands.

But no amount of sanitiser can take back our deal. We're gonna solve this murder together.

8

RIRI

Two hours later, I'm not feeling so confident. In fact, I'm on the verge of freaking out even more. My body is sweat-drenched and I'm tongue-tied. I can't believe it's my first day in the country and I've seen a dead body and I'm now being interrogated by the police.

This means I'm having a double freak-out session!

The police did blood pressure and other checks on me and Ani when they came to the crime scene. I even got a silver shock blanket that I'm still wearing.

'No need to be afraid,' a friendly officer tells me. I'm in an interrogation room. Which is a sentence I never thought I'd say until, in the future, I'd be interviewing a criminal for the sake of justice.

Now, at the tender age of eleven, I'm on the *other* side of the interrogation table.

Thank goodness I'm not handcuffed.

The officer loses his friendliness as his brow crinkles.

'Why would you be handcuffed? Have you not been telling me the truth?'

I didn't realise I'd said that part out loud! I somehow sweat even more. Mom pats my back reassuringly. She sped back over to Castlewick as soon as she heard.

Mom lets out a small laugh. 'I – Officer, you know how kids are. Plus, she's still in shock.'

'Please don't speak on behalf of the witness.'

Mom gapes at the officer. If I weren't a bundle of nerves, I'd try to build a rapport with him. I'm shy but I'm also a teacher's pet.

'Noori Tariq, this is serious. You discovered a *dead body*.'

Mom tenses. We're all saving the who-was-she/who-wasn't-she conversation until we're back at Dad's apartment. *If* we get out of here, that is. Mom and Dad listened to me and Ani talk about Mrs Kostas and Mrs Dimas, through tears, all the way to the police station. They were confused and quiet, and the car ride was tense. 'I've told you everything! I-I mentioned Ani following the ringtone then us discovering the body –'

'And corrupting the crime scene by tampering with evidence,' the now-unfriendly officer says.

'Please don't speak on behalf of the witness,' Mom retorts.

'All I did was tidy up!' I defend. I simply gathered the scattered plates and cups!

'Young lady, that's not how crime scenes work.'

'Please don't deport us!' I blurt out. 'We're here for the summer and I've already gotten used to the weather and the smell.'

The officer looks offended. 'What smell?'

I let out a scared squeak. I've heard horror stories about how the US Embassy treats its citizens of colour overseas. There might be no saving us!

The officer sighs and glances at his notes. 'I think I've got everything I need. We'll be in touch at some point to follow up.' With that, he leads us out.

'I'm confused,' Dad says for the umpteenth time. He's tugging at his hair. It's been two hours since Ani and I discovered the body and we're back at his apartment. 'Was she actually Mrs Dimas or Mrs Kostas? Could they be twins?'

I'm wondering that too.

'Abderrazzak.' Mom sighs. 'We can try to fix our confusion later on. Right now, our daughters might well need therapy.'

'I already have a therapist,' Ani says. She still hasn't warmed up to Mom. But then, I haven't warmed up to Dad either, so we're even. 'Her name is Chandra.'

'Oh.' Mom clears her throat. 'Well, can we call Chandra?' She glances at Dad and he nods. 'Good. I think group therapy might be good. After all, we all knew Mrs Kostas or Dimas or whoever she was, didn't we?'

About forty-five minutes later, Ani's therapist knocks on the door. As Mom and Dad go to answer it, Ani hands me a pad of waterproof paper. I wonder what kinds of antics she gets up to, to own that. Bath-time ideas? Swimming pool stories?

'Waterproof paper is environmentally bad because it's

difficult to recycle,' I whisper.

'Hey, I got my Friends of the Environment certificate at school – I recycle everything I can. But sleuths use waterproof paper. Why? Because of accidents featuring rain, pools, puddles or juice. I speak from experience. Now shut up and read it before they come.'

I open it and glance down at the first page.

TUSC PROFILE

```
Name:        Dr Chandra Maheshwari-Robinson
Gender:      Female
Pronouns:    She/her/hers
Age:         45 years old
Occupation:  Child psychologist


Physical characteristics:
   1. The same shade of brown skin as me
   2. Wears pencil skirts
   3. Always has a bow headband in her black,
      straight hair


Observation:  Is the best sweet dealer in
              Castlewick (no, not because she's a doctor who
              prescribes stuff – she has a cousin in America
              who sends her Jolly Ranchers. Blues ones =
              best.)
```

While Ani's handwriting is messy, it's actually a helpful profile.

'Girls, I'm so sorry about what happened today,' Dr Chandra says. 'Talking about grief is a good way to accept the loss and let it go.'

Ani sighs. 'I don't want to let it go.'

'That's valid. Let's talk about Mrs Kostas in a way that allows us to let go of the *grief surrounding her loss* but not of the magical memories. OK?'

Ani looks at me. 'I can talk about it if you can.'

I think about this. No one I've ever known has died so I don't know what to do or how to react. Other kids might have experienced a loss in the family but Mom's parents passed away when she was young so I never even knew them.

I nod at Ani.

'Words, Riri,' Mom warns.

All eyes are on me and I wipe my sweating palms on my thighs. 'Yes. Thanks for asking. I'll go first.'

Dr Chandra smiles. 'Riri, go ahead.'

'So –' I start – 'me and Mom used to live in downtown LA before she got her promotion at NovaStarr Labs. That was about four-ish years ago. I was seven years old and Mrs Dimas was the school librarian. She taught me to speed-read and my love of books was thanks to her. Sometimes she babysat me when Mom worked late. Like I told Ani, she said she belonged to a rich family. One day, she just up and left.'

Mom nods, her hand over her chest as if she's sad to remember it.

'She said she was moving to England –' I continue – 'but

70

she didn't say where exactly, only that she was gonna find a long-lost relative. We tried to reach out but her number was disconnected and emails bounced back. Mom, do you still have that picture of the three of us on your phone?' It's the only picture we have of her.

Mom unlocks her phone. 'I must do.' A minute passes. 'Got it,' she says, and shows us.

Ani walks toward Mom but keeps her distance as she analyses the picture. 'That's definitely her. Even if she had an identical twin, they wouldn't have the same heart-shaped mole.'

Dad massages his temples. Clearly he's troubled by all this. 'Why would she live two similar lives with each daughter?'

I freeze. I hadn't thought of it like that. Was Mrs Dimas – or Mrs Kostas – a bad person? Did she maliciously target our family? If so, why? We're not millionaires.

If another word is said by any of us, Mom might cry. 'I don't know! All I know is that I trusted her. I swear, I didn't know her before.'

'I didn't either,' Dad says.

I think the 'before' they're referring to is back when they were engaged. Or even before that, I guess.

'Mum and Dad –' Dr Chandra frowns – 'am-am I missing something here? Has there been more than one death?' Dr Chandra doesn't know that Mrs Kostas used to be Mrs Dimas. She thinks we're talking about two different women.

'No,' Ani quickly says. 'No. Riri is grieving someone else.' Why would she lie? Mom and Dad are clearly too preoccupied to interject and tell Dr Chandra the truth. And

Ani clearly wants to hide the information that Mrs Kostas and Mrs Dimas were one and the same. I won't question her because I'm finally consistently 'Riri' instead of 'evil twin'. 'And she's traumatised because of the crime scene she stumbled upon.' Well, that's the truth.

'Can I talk about Mrs Kostas now?' Ani is surprisingly patient.

'Are you sure you can?' Dad asks her. 'You were close to her.'

Mom lets out an off-key, hysterical laugh that could double as a cry. 'What, and Riri wasn't? *I* wasn't?'

Dad whispers, 'I didn't mean it like that.'

Mom expels a harsh breath but soon crumbles as her voice breaks. 'I know.' Adults are incredibly odd. Parents are even odder.

As Ani looks from Mom to Dad, she frowns. 'Um . . . I'll say my bit now. Mrs Kostas was the best. We met when I was her first customer at Cafe Vivlio.' Her chin quivers. 'She was a mother figure to me.'

Mom wails then storms out of the room. I feel bad for both of them, Ani and Mom.

Plus, I can't help but feel a bit betrayed by Mrs Dimas.

Dr Chandra stares at where Mom was sitting. 'Dad, could you check on Mum please? Ani, sorry for interrupting. Please continue.'

With Dad gone, Ani rubs at her eyes. 'She lived in our building. Downstairs. Used to call me to help her find items that she'd misplaced. That made me love mysteries even more.'

I try to give Ani a small smile but she doesn't look at me.

'She spoke with a transatlantic accent. Never said anything about being from a rich family. Definitely wasn't fancy. Didn't have that mole. She used to teach me life lessons with Greek proverbs,' she adds.

'Oh, she told me those too,' I fondly remember.

'You're both grief-stricken and clearly have your own ways of honouring her.' Dr Chandra looks like she is trying her best to act like what we're saying is normal but she is clearly still confused. 'Whatever you need, you can tell me. Let yourselves grieve. Is there anything else anyone wants to say? This is a safe place. Anyone?'

'No,' me and Ani say together.

Dr Chandra goes on to tell us how to deal with grief. She gives us each a grief journal and wants to have another session in a week's time. After many questions we half answered, she leaves.

It's just me and Ani now, a million unspoken words between us.

Then she sighs and as she rubs her face she says, 'I can't believe I broke up from school just yesterday. And today, Mrs Kostas – someone super dear to me – was murdered.' She rests her chin on her hand, wrapped up in her thoughts.

'I'm sorry. Life can be wild sometimes. Where do we start?' I ask. Her eyes stare hard at the floor and don't move. 'Unless . . . you don't want to?' To be honest, I'm nervous about starting an investigation. What if we find out something bad? Still, whoever she was, she deserves justice.

Ani clears her throat then reaches into her pocket. I silently watch her place an assortment of items on the coffee table. Each item has a sticker of a tusk on it. I guess that's the TUSC logo? Her phone, a waterproof notepad, a compact mirror, a small torch, a pen, bubble-gum and a light that looks similar to the one I used to read my invisible ink-scribbled diary with. Then a little pot of black powder, white paper, a measuring tape, a magnifying glass and a wristwatch. Wow, she has big pockets.

Ani meets my eyes, hers red and unreadable. Then she sobs and runs off.

9

ANI

I've tried to block out everything but my mind wants to remember. All I'm letting myself remember is my time in the interrogation room on that awful day.

'No comment,' I say. That's all I've said in the interrogation room.

'Imani –'

'It's Ani. Your badge says your name is Police Constable Margaret Ribar. Am I going to call you Peggy like we're friends?'

PC Ribar blinks at me. 'I-I'm confused. You do want me to call you by your nickname but are saying you won't call me by mine? Nicknames are typically for friends so are you implying that you want me to be your friend? For the record –'

'You're the interviewing officer here, PC Ribar. You don't need to say anything for the record except for your questions or to answer mine.'

'I don't mind being called Peggy or Margaret.'

'Well, given the circumstances, I mind being called Imani. I don't mind being called Ani.' Brain-teasers = time wasters (that's a tried and tested TUSC tactic).

The sooner I'm out of here, the sooner I can begin my own investigation about Mrs Kostas. Who she was and who murdered her. I bite the insides of my cheeks. Push away the sadness of losing her forever. Deep down, I wish she would magically start breathing again. Maybe, just maybe, that was one of the mysteries she set up for me this summer. I hope that's the case. But hope gets a sleuth nowhere. Besides, I wouldn't be at the police station if it was pretend.

Peggy rubs her temples. Turns around to look at whoever's behind the one-way glass. She shrugs. 'This is my first time interviewing a kid who found a body and I didn't think it could be this hard,' she mutters. There are two taps on the glass. Peggy barely glances at me and Dad as she leaves. 'Stay here.'

Dad whispers to me, 'Please don't be complicated with the police people, Imani. They're only trying to do their jobs.'

'So am I. And I'm going to do it better and quicker than them.'

'I'm sure you will,' announces a voice I haven't heard in a long time.

Police Sergeant Chloe Li enters and smiles at me. Chloe Li who used to be a teaching assistant and helped me when I was diagnosed with ADHD before moving to Manchester to train as a police officer. I heard she'd moved back to Castlewick but I hadn't seen her yet. It's been on my to-do

list but I've been busy. I've missed her and try to smile back.
But I can't when I want to cry about Mrs Kostas.

TUSC PROFILE

Name: Chloe Li (Chinese name:
             Li Min Fang)

Gender: Female

Pronouns: She/her/hers

Age: 29 years old

Occupation: Police Sergeant (formerly
             teaching assistant)

Physical characteristics:

   1. Always wears her hair in a tight braid

   2. Has dewy skin that Mrs Kostas used to
   describe as 'radiant'

   3. Diamond-shaped face and bow-shaped lips

Observation: Currently the youngest Asian Police
   Sergeant in English history

Bonus fact: Won a plus-sized beauty pageant
   before she enrolled into the College of
   Policing

'Ani, it's been a while,' Chloe says.

'It has,' I say, cautiously. She's buttering me up to fish for information.

'I'm sorry for your loss. Mrs K was such a great part of Castlewick.'

'No comment.'

Chloe chuckles then looks at Dad. 'Abderrazzak! How are you?'

'It's been a difficult day, but we're OK, thank you, Chloe. And you?'

'I'm OK, thanks. Ani, is there anything you'd like to add before I let you go?'

I motion to the file in front of Chloe. The one Peggy had as well. 'Nope. Everything is in my written statement.'

Riri was a nervous wreck when the police officers who arrived in The Secret Garden told us we'd have to answer questions. I wasn't – I knew the procedure. Issue a written statement so you don't have to answer many (or any) questions. Genius. Besides, I'm working on an independent, private investigation for the TUSC. I can't clash with the Castlewick Police.

Also, my time in the interrogation room has had me thinking: Riri is too weak. How can she be a Sleuth-In-Training? I worry about her.

'Right,' Chloe says. 'I was wondering if you could explain why you corrupted the crime scene.'

'We were looking for clues.'

Chloe stretches her lips. 'I'm trying to not get you into trouble here, Ani. Please could you not pursue this case?

Let us – the Castlewick police – do our job so Mrs K gets justice.'

'On one condition.'

Chloe leans back to straighten her posture. Eyes focused on me. Clear tone and direct words. All of these things mean she's being serious as she tells me, 'The Castlewick police don't negotiate with anyone. Nor do any police in the UK, for that matter. That's the procedure.'

'Please, Chloe?' I hate to beg but what choice do I have?

'Fine.' Then she mouths, 'You're off the record.'

I mutter, 'Tell me if this is officially a murder investigation.'

A sigh leaves Chloe's lips. She works her jaw and then gives a single nod. 'Now off you go. And Ani? Don't get in our way on this case. Otherwise procedure will force me to do things I don't want to.'

I don't say anything. If I promise Chloe that, then I'd be lying.

```
TUSC timestamp
7 days since murder
0 days since TUSC investigation
  launched
```

My heart was breaking over and over again, but after endless snacks and phone calls with Dr Chandra, I'm no longer upset. I'm still sad, but now I'm motivated too. It's official: the

Bleak Week, AKA my week of mourning Mrs Kostas, is over. The last week, I'd only left my room to go to the bathroom. My time grieving was spent remembering Mrs Kostas. Dad told me to pray, so I did. Mum suggested writing about my fond memories with Mrs Kostas. Annoyingly, that worked. She's been trying to make me feel better but she's also so overly protective that I get annoyed. She's still worried that Mrs Kostas was targeting us. While I do appreciate that Mum asked for time off from work *and* managed to pull some strings with The Skyscape's management to take a vacant flat opposite ours to sleep in, I can't form the words to thank her yet. And no, Riri can't sleep with Mum in the flat opposite because sharing a room is apparently a good way for us to bond.

LaShawn and Helin tried to console me. So did Riri. I told them all to go away.

But now, I'm ready.

Riri walks in. She's wearing a turquoise jumpsuit that matches her hijab. I'm wearing a grey tracksuit. Helin and LaShawn are with her. There's a tray in Riri's hands. I peer over at it. Rashers and sausages (from the halal butchers). Baked beans. Fried mushrooms and tomatoes. Buttered toast. Fried eggs. An English breakfast. Well, brunch because it's nearing 11 a.m. The delicious smell nearly knocks me over. I shuffle to the end of my bed. Reach for the tray.

'Uh-uh-uh.' Riri angles herself and the tray from me. 'First, I want to know if you're OK. Dad said an English breakfast will make you happier if a Desi or Persian breakfast wouldn't.'

It's official: Dad *gets* me. Unfortunately the Desi breakfast from yesterday wasn't enough. Nor was the Persian one that Helin left outside my door. But I'm confident this one is.

'I'm fine, I'm fine.'

'Ani, you have to tell the truth,' Helin says, in her sweet voice. She's wearing a summer dress and flip-flops. 'We've been so worried about you.'

TUSC PROFILE

Name:	Helin Moradi
Codename:	Hgfdsa
Gender:	Female
Pronouns:	She/her/hers
Age:	11 years old
Occupation:	Sleuth-In-Training (SIT) and school student

Physical characteristics:

1. Light brown skin with dark brown eyes
2. Her straight hair is never out of place
3. Short for her age (apparently this makes her a good runner)

Observation: Always wears a charm bracelet. Charms include the logo of TUSC, a horse (she's obsessed with horses) and a pomegranate and a pen (to remind everyone that she's the school journalist)

'Yeah, we've been really worried,' LaShawn adds. He's wearing shorts and a shirt, with a chain around his neck. 'I thought I was gonna have to fly my drone in here and check on ya. Or straight up break in, *Three Little Pigs* style.' He steals a sausage from my plate.

TUSC PROFILE

Name: LaShawn Hart

Codename: Lkjhgf

Gender: Male

Pronouns: He/him/his

Age: 11 years old

Occupation: SIT and school student

Physical characteristics:

1. Black skin with light-brown eyes and dark-brown curls with a fade
2. A contagious smile
3. Wears T-shirts he designs himself that have pockets for Jawbreakers

Observation: Is obsessed with fairy-tales

'So?' Riri asks with a hopeful look on her face. Helin and LaShawn wait too.

I pause. Keep them all on edge on purpose. Then I look at Helin and LaShawn. 'Welcome back to the TUSC, Sleuths-In-Training Moradi and Hart. I'll debrief you on our current, high-priority case soon.' They both cheer. 'The investigation begins now. Sleuth-In-Training Noori Tariq, on paper your codename will be, Rtyuiop. Indecipherable. Uncrackable. Welcome to the TUSC. We'll begin by figuring out who exactly Mrs Kostas/Dimas was. After a brief induction of course.'

I eat all my breakfast and then it begins.

10

RIRI

```
TUSC timestamp
8 days since murder
1 day since TUSC investigation
  launched
```

So far, I've learned everything there is to know about the TUSC and nothing about the investigation we're supposed to be solving. Even though I said spending an entire day on TUSC induction was a waste – there's only a murderer to catch, after all – Ani insisted.

Typically I would say it's impossible for an agency like the TUSC to exist, but the light in Ani's eyes when she talks about it tells me that it will become a reality eventually. She has that drive.

Of course, the only illogical thing about the TUSC is that Ani keeps mental notes in her 'brainbook' instead of written or electronic ones. That is bound to throw up confusion down the line – which is why I'm going to fight for written notes. It's the only way forward.

Helin and LaShawn – who are so fun – were shocked when Ani debriefed them. LaShawn's mom called them both back home – Helin offered, earlier, to help LaShawn with some algebraic equations. Ani said she'll update them but thinks that me and her will be best suited to unearthing Mrs Dimas's true identity, seeing as we both knew parts of her. As a passionate puzzle-cracker, I'm excited about this. But also a bit nervous about what – if anything – we might uncover. And of course, working closely with Ani, my estranged twin sister, is enough to make me wholly nervous – I want us to be friendly and compatible. I want us to solve this case together.

'OK, Sleuth-In-Training Riri Tariq,' Ani starts as she paces. 'What we have before us is a murder investigation.'

I say a quick prayer. 'I can't believe there's a murderer in Castlewick!'

'There are murderers everywhere, Riri. Calm down. Now, one murder in this low-crime neighbourhood is enough for the Police Sergeant to start sniffing around. Lucky for us, I'm friends with her.' She smirks.

I hold up my hand like I'm still in school. She cringes enough for the both of us. 'We know the police are also treating this as a murder. Meaning, we have some competition –'

'Exactly. So, what have you got so far?'

'Oh . . . um . . . nothing.'

'Riri, haven't you been watching the news while I was in my room? I expected at least that from you during The Bleak Week.'

'No. Mom thought I would get distressed.' I don't tell Ani that I've had a hard time grieving too. The version I knew of Mrs Dimas back in California had gone the moment she left and never got back in touch with us. But seeing her body in The Secret Garden brought up some sadness from within. I had a few conversations with Dr Chandra and she helped. I've chosen to hide my therapy sessions with Dr Chandra from Ani in case it upsets her more. She's had it tough enough. Also, I had no choice but to tell Dr Chandra that Mrs Kostas was the same as Mrs Dimas and her mind was blown. I also fibbed and said that Ani wants to pass that information on to the police with parental supervision, so Dr Chandra doesn't pass it on herself.

'Oh, I know!' I say, remembering. 'I heard Dad talking about how the cafe is closed until further notice because of the investigation. The staff are out of work and people – customers, I guess – are huddled outside it, paying their respects.'

'They probably miss the karidopita like me,' Ani says then inhales a shaky breath. 'Just as well that it's closed. I won't be able to set foot there for a while. Or ever again.'

I swallow, surprised she's being so vulnerable. 'Me too.' Even though I only went there once, it would feel wrong to go there with the way things have happened.

She gasps, in her own world. 'I'll never have karidopita again. Not the way Mrs Kostas made it.' I think she's about to cry so I offer her a tissue. She swats it away, recovering remarkably fast. 'Back to our investigation. You have a pen and notebook?'

'Always.'

'Ugh, that's not as cool as you think. Now can we begin? Here's a list of questions. I call them *unanswerables* because only a supersleuth can truly answer them. No one else.'

UNANSWERABLES
- Who was Mrs Kostas/Dimas, really?
- Why did she have at least two identities?
- Was she in danger?
- Why didn't she tell Supersleuth Ani Tariq the truth?
- What time did she die?
- Who killed her?

11

RIRI

Ani says, 'Let's make a list of what we remember from the crime scene. Then we'll compare. I know I saw everything. You didn't, but it's fine because you're still a SIT.'

Is she trying to be nice? Maybe she's so unaware that she still comes across as condescending.

Even so, I listen to her and make a list.

What Ani saw:
- A mess of paper plates and paper cups
- Mrs Kostas/Dimas on the ground
- The hose still running

What Riri saw:
- A mess of paper plates and paper cups
- Mrs Dimas/Kostas on the ground
- The hose still running

Dad peers his head into Ani's room. 'We're ordering takeaway. What do you feel like?'

'Can I get a cheese burger with fries, please?' Ani asks.

Dad nods then looks at me. I can't get used to his eyes when they're mirrors of mine.

'Aloo gobi and naan, please,' I say. 'If the takeout place does curry, that is.' I hope the food comes on time otherwise my thoughts will feel scrambled. Or maybe I can convince myself that in vacation mode, schedules and routines get thrown out the window.

'They do.' Dad taps on his phone. 'OK, it won't be long, yeah?'

'Yeah, yeah, yeah, Dad,' Ani says. 'We're trying to solve something here.'

While Mom would've told her off, Dad simply stops and smiles. He glances between us as if our teamwork is something he's wanted to see for a long time. That's even though he knows nothing about the investigation – Ani told Dad she's reopening her Amelia Earhart case, and that I'm helping her. I don't think it's crossed his mind that there's an unsolved murder that sleuthing-obsessed Ani wants to solve – he's likely still too shocked from Mrs Dimas's – or, er, Mrs Kostas's – identities. Still smiling, Dad leaves.

Ani shakes her head. 'I hope I don't get interrupted again.'

Dad returns. 'Ani, you need to take medicine before the food. Let's go.'

'Oh yeah.'

She follows him outside and I take the opportunity to glance around her room properly. During The Bleak Week, Ani kicked me out during the day, leaving me to read books in the living room. The longest I was in her room was at night when it was too dark to fully look around. Movie posters of *Enola Holmes* and *Sherlock* are near her bed. She has a vintage-looking map opposite and another in her window nook with places circled in red. On her desk is a cut-out of an old aircraft.

I tiptoe over to it, the cold floor tingling my toes. Near the aircraft, a picture of Amelia Earhart has a list of theories about her disappearance scribbled on it in Ani's handwriting, plus sketches of an aeroplane crashing. I'm in awe of the messiness of Ani's room – I wonder what her brain is like. My hand runs over some of the pictures.

'Ahem.' Ani clears her throat. 'You don't have clearance to view any of that.'

'But . . . aren't I a Sleuth-In-Training? I should be exposed to this kind of stuff.'

'No, SIT. You shouldn't be.'

'O . . . K . . . But I don't want to sit.'

'I didn't ask you to, *SIT*.'

'What?'

Ani tuts. 'SIT,' she repeats, as if that'll magically make me understand. 'Sleuth-In-Training, S-I-T, SIT. Get it now?'

'I guess.'

'Now, shush – we need to get down to business. Part of your TUSC induction is learning that with murder, the gateway to solving it is by finding out as much information as you can about the victim.' I stare at her. 'We need to paint a picture of Mrs Kostas –'

'Or Mrs Dimas,' I say.

'– and her backstory. Her *real* backstory. Unless this was a random attack – which, by the way, is a possibility, because

Castlewick is classed as a big town. Big town, low crime rate. Mrs Kostas might as well be our poster person. Did you know that someone travelled all the way from Northern Ireland to visit Cafe Vivlio last year? That's how popular it's becoming. The Mayor of Castlewick knew Mrs Kostas and has eaten at Cafe Vivlio many times. In a few short years, Mrs Kostas helped Castlewick become the caffeine capital of England. Sure, the cafe's popularity might be to do with Derek's vlogs but Mrs Kostas's hospitality and coffee were something. We'll find answers in her backstory then we'll figure out the time of death. From there, it's a suspect list, interrogations, a confession and justice served. Easy peasy.'

'Ani, how do you know all this stuff? Like, all of this detective stuff?'

'"Sleuth stuff", *not* "detective stuff". And, I don't know how I know. I learned from my smaller cases. And from watching *Murder, She Wrote*. Now, while I've never solved the murder of a human before –' My eyebrows raise. *Of a human before?* Upon seeing my expression, she explains, 'I've solved the murder of three ants, half a dog, one pigeon and two rats –'

'Rats?' I screech.

'Relax. They're street rats. So harmless, they're part of the attraction here.'

'Whatever. And what on earth is half a dog?'

Ani shakes her head. 'That's confidential information that's the property of the TUSC. Become a sleuth and maybe you'll have clearance. Now –'

'But how do we find out her backstory?' It isn't like we can

91

simply google her names and see what comes up. From my inexperienced but logical standpoint, I'm sure we'd have to find birth records or newspapers that are in special restricted archives at the library. And I'm pretty sure Mom and Dad are not gonna be told about our investigation – not when Mom's acting like a loose cannon about all this because she thinks Mrs Dimas/Kostas was a con woman attacking our family and Dad's being overly nice.

'We google her and see what comes up.'

'Oh.' I'm unable to hide my surprise. 'I guess I do still have a lot to learn.'

Ophelia Polina Dimas. That was the name she told me and Mom and everyone in our neighbourhood in California. She said her family were from Greece and later on, she took the plunge of moving to California.

Polina Anastasia Kostas was the name she went by in Castlewick.

It's been three minutes since our first discovery and I kinda wish we could go back in time and not do this investigation. It's too intense, too much.

Even without googling, me and Ani came up with a list of the life of each pseudonym.

Here's my list:

Mrs Ophelia Polina Dimas

- School librarian that ran a Saturday book club for kids
- Occasional babysitter

- Loved going to the farmer's market. Sometimes mom drove her
- Never drove, possibly didn't have a license, never talked about it

'That's a weird detail to throw in there,' Ani says. It's not that weird – she probably only said it is because she didn't think of it herself.

Now it's time for Ani's list:

Mrs Polina Anastasia Kostas

- Owner of Cafe Vivlio
- Occasional puzzle and mystery master
- Worked at the community centre every weekend
- Takes arthritis medicine
- Never drove, possibly didn't have a license, never talked about it

I give Ani a sidelong look. 'You added that last point just now.'

'No, I didn't.'

I smudge the last word to prove my point – the ink is super wet. Even when it was dry, half of it was illegible, as if scribbled in a hurry.

'Shut up. I'm the Director of the TUSC. And by the way, this gets us nowhere. It's about as useless as a chocolate teapot.'

I splutter a laugh. 'As a *what*?'

'As a chocolate teapot. When you heat up chocolate, what happens?'

'It melts.'

'There you go. So, it's useless as a chocolate teapot.'

'The way you said that proves that *you* are a tempest in a teapot.'

'A *what* in a *what*?!'

'It means that you have a lot of unnecessary anger over an unimportant thing.'

Ani shakes her head at that. 'Moving on . . .'

Instead of counting on our memories, we google the names that we both knew her as. Here are our findings:

Mrs Ophelia Polina Dimas	Mrs Polina Anastasia Kostas
Born 18 May 1968	Born 19 May 1968
Born in Alexandroupolis, Greece	Born in Athens, Greece
Widow of businessman Barnaby Nikolaos Dimas	Widow of artist Ares Aloysius Kostas III

The information above is – I don't know, like a distorted reflection of the other, like:
- Born in May but a day apart
- Born in Greece but on opposite sides of the country
- The widow of a businessman and an artist –
  both occupations are far cries from each other
But this isn't substantive.

This information has come from pictureless, inactive Facebook pages and a brief mention in each of her husbands' death notices in the electronic archives of newspaper websites. Thankfully the archives didn't require us to sign up to view. Moreover, it's uncanny.

As Ani and I look at her laptop screen, wide-eyed, I find that I can hear the silence. And her breathing – it whistles. We're both too afraid to say anything.

Until I finally say, 'Well, you can't deny that this isn't normal.'

'No.' Ani sighs, unlocking her phone. 'Supersleuth's log –' she provides the time, date and location – 'we've made our first discovery. It doesn't make sense. Mrs Kostas/Dimas was definitely hiding something.' She exhales, shakily.

'Ani, we can stop right here, if you need to.'

She shakes her head one too many times. 'No. We're going to go all in.'

'But we've been all the way to page thirty of each name's Google search results.'

She shrugs. Then she does a handstand, near the fan that's trying to cool down the stuffy sunny air.

'Hey, what are you doing?' I ask.

'I'm thinking.'

'… OK.' I search online.

Ophelia Polina Dimas and Polina Anastasia Kostas 🔍

The same results come up. This is useless. No, it isn't – it's insanity.

Albert Einstein once reportedly said, 'Insanity is making the same mistakes and expecting different results.' Searching the same names is not only insanity, but illogical too. What's logical is looking at the variables of her names. Similar to how you crack a code, I need to search for all possible combinations.

Ophelia Polina Kostas. 🔍

Nothing.

Polina Anastasia Dimas. 🔍

Nothing.

Ophelia Anastasia Dimas 🔍

Nothing.

Polina Polina Kostas 🔍

Nothing.

Anastasia Ophelia Dimas 🔍

Something.

It's an article from an art magazine. Oh my gosh! Just skimming over the headline makes my blood run cold. 'Ani, stop handstanding and come read this!'

She rushes over then her eyes light up. 'What? No way!

Oh cool! This was written twenty years ago, so ten years before is . . . wait, Mrs Kostas had been on the run for *thirty* years. A lifetime! Wow!'

Meanwhile, my stomach stirs as we read the article.

World News

HOME   POLITICS   ECONOMY   WORLD   LIFESTYLE   SPORTS   HEALTH   TECH   CULTURE   OPINIONS   Search

International art thief still on the run, ten years later

A Look Back at The Uncatchable Bonnie and Her Catchable Clyde

Anastasia Ophelia Dimas was just 16 years old when she committed her first art crime with her beau, Nikolaos Aloysius Ares, also 16. They were two crazy kids in love . . .

It started with the theft of a small rock from an exhibition in the Benaki Museum in Athens, Greece then escalated to a bust, whipped from under the nose of the security guards in The Egyptian Museum of Berlin before continuing to rob galleries around the world of their priceless masterworks and statues . . . The first major painting stolen was *Athena* by Kostas Barnaby Dimas III.

Anastasia was the beauty who captured the Greek tabloids, with her heart-shaped mole on her face that she was poetically born with. Nikolaos was a handsome charmer with bright light-blue eyes whose slicked back hair and bright smile almost made him get away with murder. Almost.

Nikolaos was caught by police and arrested on the scene when he 'had no choice but to shoot and kill a security guard' at The Louvre. Since being imprisoned, he's gained a bad reputation and has ties to assassins and abductors.

Anastasia allegedly got away, but Nikolaos insisted throughout his decades-long prison sentence that he'd killed her first. He never revealed the location of her body.

Detective Larsson took over the case after the theft of Dimas III's *Athena*. Larsson doesn't believe that Nikolaos killed Anastasia. While he doesn't have any evidence – he alleged that Nikolaos said in prison, unrecorded, 'Anastasia and our child are in a better place' which another inmate confirmed hearing – Detective Larsson said he's never going to stop until he finds Anastasia and brings her back to Greece, to face trial for her crimes.

Nikolaos died in 2010 from a stroke. He died with the secret of Anastasia's whereabouts . . . if she's still alive, that is. Did she even have a child? Case experts say the rumour of her being pregnant at all is just that – a rumour. Barely anyone even believes it.

'She's out there –' insists Detective Larsson – 'and I'll find her. Even if it kills me.'

12

RIRI

Ani quickly types on her phone and then gasps. 'Oh my gosh, it actually did kill him!'

'What do you mean?' I hope she means that the search for Mrs Dimas/Kostas/Anastasia-the-beautiful-art-thief killed Detective Larsson morally or professionally, not literally.

'It. Actually. Killed. Him.' Ani shoves her phone in my face.

My hopes stand corrected – the investigation into finding Mrs Dimas/Kostas killed the detective. He followed a fake lead to her childhood home and died in an explosion in the car outside. 'Poor guy.'

'You don't think Mrs Kostas was responsible for blowing him up, do you?'

I shrug. 'No idea but it's a possibility. We need to separate ourselves from thinking we knew her because we clearly didn't. Every question we have, we have to answer with proof. OK?'

'Yep.'

'Oh,' I breathe, scanning the article. 'Look, Mrs Dimas/Kostas was allegedly seen in another car. The witness didn't take any pictures but he reported seeing a woman fitting Mrs Dimas/Kostas's description cry at the explosion and then run off.' I frown. 'Why would she have been there in the first place?'

'Maybe while Larsson was chasing her, she also chased him.'

'What do you mean?'

'Well, if I were an international art thief on the run and my partner was jailed, I would try to see how close the police were to finding me. Like cat and mouse.'

I nod slowly. 'That's still odd. I mean, she should've been running off into the sunset instead. What other reason could she have to be at the same place at the same time?'

Ani mutters, as if she's having a conversation with herself. 'Maybe she wanted to retrieve something from her childhood home? *Before* running off into the sunset.'

'Possible. It's still odd, though.'

Ani sighs. 'I know. Maybe she was trying to send him a message? To tell him to back off?'

I rub my face. 'I don't know . . . Why would she cry? If he was chasing her to imprison her, then she'd be happy when he died, right?'

Ani half shrugs. 'It's a standard human reaction? Plus, that could explain why she didn't drive in California or here in Castlewick. Painful memories, much?'

I can't believe any of this. Much less the fact that we're actually making progress.

Ani thinks. 'This detective – does he have any living relatives? Sometimes, they're so intense about investigations that they pass them down like heirlooms. If so, then we could speak to them, see if he was close to catching her. Maybe she had a rival. Was something about her worth killing for? Maybe she had kept the art she'd stolen all along? Nothing was ever recovered, remember.'

I google Detective Larsson. 'No. He says it himself here that he has no immediate family. His job, he said, is his life. Or, it was.'

'So, that's a dead end then,' Ani mutters.

Silence settles between us.

I continue searching for as much as I can about Larsson. There's a profile piece about him being on the stand at Nikolaos's trial. In the photograph he looks to be in a luxurious home. A maroon embossed wall is behind him with intricate gold details. Tendrils of a chandelier shadow his forehead. He's standing proudly in between a large Japanese Akita breed of dog and a vase, and he's holding up his detective card like it's a badge of honour. Behind him is a framed quote. I nudge Ani and she looks at it while I zoom in. The quote reads: 'At his best, man is the noblest of all animals; separated from law and justice, he is the worst.'

'Aristotle.' Ani sounds faraway. 'Mrs Kostas wanted that as the TUSC's motto. I declined.'

'Maybe . . . she said it before to Larsson, to taunt him? And he framed it to taunt her? Cat and mouse?'

'Or maybe *he* wanted to send *her* a message? Knowing she'd be keeping tabs on Nikolaos's trial and see his piece?' Ani shrugs. 'Or maybe it's a coincidence.'

We go quiet again for a few minutes.

'Hey, did you catch that?' I randomly ask, realising something. This information is like a puzzle clicking into place, although it's delayed – I should've noticed sooner. Ani follows my eyes to the article.

'The names of Mrs Dimas/Kostas's husbands – Barnaby Nikolaos Dimas and Ares Aloysius Kostas III – include some of the names of her lover/thief. *Nikolaos Aloysius Ares.*'

'Ohhhhh. Well, what does that mean?'

I shrug. 'Maybe we should see what it *leaves*, instead of what it means.' I tap my mouth with my pen and cross out the names Nikolaos, Aloysius, and Ares. That leaves Barnaby, Dimas, Kostas and III. 'These names must have been important if she used them as part of her alias.'

'I don't know,' Ani replies with a huff. 'Shall we try googling it?'

'Sure.'

> Barnaby Dimas Kostas III 🔍

Nothing.

> Dimas Barnaby Kostas III 🔍

Nothing.

> Barnaby Kostas Dimas III 🔍

Nothing.

Something.

'That's the name of the artist who painted the first painting – *Athena* – that "Anastasia" and "Nikolaos" stole,' Ani says.

'And?'

Ani smirks. 'The theft of *Athena* brought Detective Larsson onto the case. The guy who died.' She smugly unlocks her phone. 'Supersleuth's log. We've made a few discoveries. Mrs Kostas/Dimas was an art thief.'

'Which is a crime,' I cut in. 'She was a *criminal*.' I want to be the President of the United States so I have to believe in the justice system, and I've never heard of a *good* criminal. I swallow, my mouth suddenly dry. I could be getting nervous because of Ani's furrowed brows and narrowed eyes. It looks like she hasn't let it sink in that Mrs Dimas/Kostas was a criminal. 'We can't eliminate the possibility that she killed Detective Larsson, can we? Who knows how many aliases she's had?'

Slowly Ani nods a few times and I watch her rub her face. 'She was a *criminal*,' she whispers, more to herself than to me.

'Let's not forget that,' I say, for the purpose of the investigation being objective. 'Remember to separate yourself from thinking you knew her. Neither of us knew the real her.'

Ani nods again, this time faster, then claps and continues in her normal tone: 'Mrs Kostas/Dimas's lover, who was also her partner-in-crime, died in prison. He was caught, whereas

102

she went on the run.' She daydreams into the distance, lost in thought. 'Wait, that could explain –'

'What is it, Ani?'

'That might explain something else from Mrs Kostas's past. I'll tell you later. Now –'

'She had many aliases,' I add. Ani gives me a stern look. *No interruptions*, got it.

She puts her phone closer to her mouth, angling herself away from me so I don't interrupt again. 'The victim had more than one alias. For each alias, the name of her fake husband includes her lover's names. Remaining names are of a painter who painted the first work of art they stole. It must be sentimental to her, because of Nikolaos. Their first theft as a couple, right?'

I nod. 'That's poetic and romantic, her having a piece of him wherever she goes.'

'Yeah.'

There's more silence between us.

Ani rubs her face. 'OK. I think we've discovered enough about the victim. Let's create a timeline.' With that, she leaves the bedroom. I follow.

13

ANI

'Ani, I know your default setting is "speed-walk" –' Riri stomps on the floorboards as she tries to keep up with me. She could make a hole – 'but please stop and tell me what you're thinking.'

I stop. Turn quickly and waggle my eyebrows at her, mainly to taunt her. As a SIT, she shouldn't have been the one to find a lot of clues. Especially not this early – nine days since the murder and one day since the TUSC investigation launched. 'Basically, if Mrs Kostas/Dimas was an art thief, then she had enemies. Which is –' I shudder, still baffled by the truth – 'so hard to believe. Why else would she be on the run most of her life? Someone must've been after her and the only way to understand that is by looking at the timeline.'

'OK, but why?'

'It's a tactic as old as time! Someone pretended to be a regular at Cafe Vivlio to a) be a familiar face so as to not arouse suspicion and b) get her to trust them. Only six

Castlewick locals know of The Secret Garden. One is dead. Oh, and me and Dad have to be eliminated for obvious reasons. And –'

'You're really gonna accuse the cafe regulars then?'

'No,' I say, irked. 'I'm *gonna* blame the new American girl.' I take a step closer to her. 'Isn't it a coincidence that on the day you arrive in Castlewick, someone dies? No one dies here, Riri. No one.' I stare her down. She stares back. Who's going to back down?

Barely three seconds in Riri does a weird half-blink. 'I win,' I say, a smirk on my lips. I walk to the living room and hear her behind me.

Mum's sigh erases my smirk. 'Can we try to be nice to each other please? I heard you both arguing.'

'When's food coming?' I ask.

'Ani, can you try to be more polite to your mother?' Mum's bossy like a teacher, talking about herself in third person.

'Why?'

'Because I'm a superhero.' A smile pinches Mum's lips.

I glance at Riri. Glance back at Mum. It's uncanny, our resemblance. 'How?' I ask. Superheroes are in manga. In comics too. Not in real life though.

'I help make the medication for people to feel better. Your ADHD medication is manufactured by the company I work for, you know. Novastarr Labs.'

Oh, the funny star logo on the box. 'Cool.'

Mum smiles. Looks pleased at our 'progress'. Right now, progress with her isn't on my mind. I have a murder to solve. A mysterious woman to avenge. I don't think I'll ever get over the truth – was she a bad person? If so, then she was an exceptional actress, behaving like a good person all the time. I don't know how I'm supposed to feel about her. 'Food's ready, by the way.'

Dad comes over to say the same thing. He stands near Mum and even though he isn't close to her she still stiffens. Her smile falls. Dad clears his throat and goes away first.

'Great,' me and Riri simultaneously say. We both smirk.

'Dad?' I walk into the living room. 'What time is it?' I know exactly what time it is, as confirmed on my smartphone and wristwatch. Time is flying.

'6.30 p.m.'

'Because we're eating late and it's the summer holidays, do you think I could not sleep tonight?' I need to pull an all-nighter to solve this. Another rule I need to teach Riri is that investigations – especially murders – should be given everything we've got. Even if that means we sacrifice sleep.

'Absolutely not,' Mum and Dad say in unison. They're both too cross at my question to act awkwardly about jinxing.

'OK.' I open my box of fries and begin to devour my burger. Of course, I'm not going to listen to my parents about sleep – I can't. Not for the sake of justice.

The food is delicious. I burp. Out loud.

'Excuse yourself, Imani,' Dad says. So, I do, in Arabic.

'Ani –' Mum bites into her veggie burger – 'your dad said you enjoy laser tag. So does Riri.'

'Not that much,' I hear Riri whisper. I chuckle at that.

We continue eating in silence until Mum talks.

106

'I was researching this place in Leeds that looks great. Maybe we could all go there as a family. Take a train.' Mum smiles.

While I pick at my fries, I try to figure out Mum's ulterior motive. She's not the most discreet human being. My silence makes the room tense. Or tenser than it was before. 'I suppose we could,' I mumble.

Mum squeals. 'Wonderful! I'll arrange it.' She motions at Dad.

'Oh yes.' He clears his throat. 'Noori, I was wondering if you wanted to go to Waterstones Piccadilly in London. It's the biggest bookshop in Europe and so beautiful. Me and Imani went there, you know, and she loved it.'

'I did,' I admit.

'We could play Two Facts and a Fib on the journey.'

'Wow, really?' Riri exclaims.

'Really. We can have our first game now.'

'Oh!' Mum squeals. 'What a great idea, Abderrazzak.' I'm finally understanding Mum's ulterior motive. And Dad's. They want to get to know me and Riri better. They want us all to bond. How hypocritical when they have some unaddressed tension between them. I don't want to waste time while the murderer is evading the law.

Suddenly my stomach turns. I don't want to eat anymore. I barely glance at my half-eaten burger as I set it down on the table.

'Imani?' Dad asks. 'Done already? It's not like you.'

'Are you OK?' Mum asks.

I shrug. 'Yep. Can I go back to my room now?'

'Would you like to take your food to your room?'

'Natasha, I don't allow that –'

'Abderrazzak, I'm sure we can make an exception. Our girls have been through a lot. Go on, Ani. Riri, you can go too.'

Me and Riri are back in my room. 'Eat up . . . but not too much,' I say.

I know she's wondering why. I walk over to my desk. Inside is where I hide my key to Mrs Kostas's flat.

But right now, I focus *on* my desk.

I get my 500g ball of Play-Doh that's a weird brown colour as a result of mixing all the colours together. 'So, now that we've established Mrs Kostas/Dimas's backstory, we're going to learn her time of death. How? Well, look what I've got!' I tear apart the Play-Doh ball and safely inside is Mrs Kostas's Apple Watch.

'Is that what I think it is? How on earth do you have that?!'

I chuckle at Riri, who looks to be wearing a sweatband made of actual sweat. 'I took it off Mrs Kostas when we found her.'

'Oh my gosh, that's why you were holding her wrist! I thought you were being sentimental, Ani! But why do you still have it?'

'I can't give it to Sergeant Chloe without using it for my TUSC investigation, can I?'

'You're gonna get us both sent to jail forever.'

'Can you stop being so dramatic? It's like when you forget to pay for something at the store and head back after.'

'Ani, stop talking! This is wrong on so many levels –'

'But they all trump the fact that we'll get Mrs Kostas's time of death from it. Now take some deep breaths. Maybe drink some water so you don't vomit up your dinner. And mentally prepare. We're about to make a breakthrough.'

14

RIRI

TUSC timestamp
11 days since murder
3 days since TUSC investigation
    launched

Ani's troublesome idea of hacking into Mrs Dimas/ Kostas's Apple Watch to uncover the time of death ends up happening twenty-four hours later. After last night, Mom came to check up on us and decided that a family history lesson – one that I'd already heard – would soon put us to sleep. She was right.

But now, Ani's more ready than ever to hack into the Apple Watch. My insides are somersaulting. No, full on loop-de-loops, in fact. And with that, my food is turning too. And I ate over an hour ago!

'Ani, *please* reconsider!'

Ani scoffs. 'Whatever. I can do this myself then. You can hang out with Mum and Dad. Just so you know, as a SIT, you have to cover for me. It's legally binding. So, to not go to *juvie*, as you Americans say, and then adult prison, you need to make up an airtight alibi, OK?'

I can't answer her because I'm so gobsmacked. Tiptoeing out of the bedroom, I confirm that Mom and Dad are watching TV. All I can see is the back of their heads but I'm an observer so I can hazard a guess or two. The whole dynamic looks awkward – they're sitting on opposite sides of the sofa. Mom's on her phone, her screen illuminating the dim room. Dad is either asleep upright or really interested in what's on TV.

I'm beginning to think that we might actually get away with this. But after we hack into Mrs Dimas/Kostas's iCloud, then what? I'm not stupid. I know there will be a penalty for us having withheld evidence, even if Ani *does* know the police sergeant.

'Ani –'

'Would you shut up and join me? All you're going to do is be my lookout.'

I blow out a breath as if I'm meditating (I've seen Mom do it). The sound results in a low whistle that, in my peripheral vision, goes unheard by my parents. *No tension, just release.* I feel much better after that.

I'm a SIT. I can do it.

'Yes –' Ani hisses in a whisper – '*sit* on the floor and be my lookout!' She mimes the motion with her hands as well.

She must've misheard what I didn't realise I'd said aloud, but it still works. I do it.

'Riri, could you get my laptop please?'

'Here.' I stare at the watch before settling beside Ani on her bed. 'So . . . Mrs Dimas/Kostas died wearing that watch?' I squirm.

'Likely, and obviously, there's a chance it stopped working before . . . but only a tiny chance. I don't know . . . Hmm.' Ani's brow furrows and she curses. 'Oops. I haven't thought this through well.' If she means this whole hacking-into-Mrs-Dimas/Kostas's-iCloud, then she's right. But I have a feeling she's referring to something else. To demonstrate her point, she swipes the watch's screen.

It's password protected.

'Why wouldn't the murderer take it with them? To cover their own tracks or something?' I say.

'Because they think they're clever. It could be that they're sloppy. An amateur. First kill and all. I can guess her password. Well . . . I hope. I clearly didn't know everything about Mrs Kostas/Dimas like I thought I did.' She shakes her head, as if doing that will get rid of those sad thoughts.

'But is there still a possibility that we won't find her time of death on her iCloud?'

Ani pauses for what feels like infinity. 'Yes.'

'You need a magnetic charging cable, right?'

'Oh no! I knew I forgot something. Wait here and let me ring LaShawn to bring his over.'

'Why? Mom has tons – she made sure to pack four for our trip here, because she always loses them. I can get one.'

'Really? Great, go on then!'

I leave and come back with the wire in a flash. Ani logs into my laptop as she attaches the Apple Watch to the magnet then puts the USB in. Mrs Dimas/Kostas's Apple ID comes up and it's ffotsirk@cafevivlio.com

'Hmm,' Ani tilts her head, 'What's –?'

'It's "Kristoff" backwards,' I say without a thought.

'You figured that out instantly,' she mumbles, not jealous *at all*. How can I blame her? I'm good at anagrams. 'I wonder who Kristoff is . . .' Ani blows a long breath out, looking deep in thought. 'Kristoff could be a random person or maybe someone from one of her past lives. *Or* it could just be random letters strung together. Either way, it definitely isn't her Apple ID password – Dad strictly told her not to use easy-to-guess passwords like that.' Gentler, she says, 'Riri, you type. In case I accidentally make a typo. I'm not the best speller.'

'I'm good at spelling!'

'Meaning, we have no lookout. If our parents catch us, we'll improvise.'

'A-Ani, improvising makes me n-nervous,' I admit in a weird tone. It's high and off-pitch, which is how I sound when I have to give presentations at school. I clear my throat. 'Ple-please,' I try again, but my voice still sounds off. Also, I can't stop fidgeting and no matter how many times I wipe my palms on my jeans, they're getting sweatier!

'Whatever freak-out you're having, chill. The police are probably at the station, talking over theories. I bet they haven't even discovered Mrs Kostas's real identity. Thirty

113

years on the run, I imagine she had no fingerprints or dental records. So, they're not going to turn up outside my bedroom right this second.'

'Ani, your words aren't m-making me feel any better. This is the beginning of the end – all it'll take is a one-off job of you hacking into something to realise it's good money and boom, you will lead a life of crime.' I know I seem like a willing accomplice to Ani and yes, that's mainly because she's got a strong personality, but what is the problem in giving the un-hacked watch to the police? The difference between right and wrong is so obvious here.

'Do I need to remind you that *I'm* the Director of the TUSC? The longer we keep bickering about this, the bigger the chance of us getting caught!'

OK, I need something else to stop her. 'Are you sure you're well? What if this brings your grief back?'

'Riri, how insensitive! Why are you talking about grief like it's something I've lost? Grief is something I've overcome.' That last sentence is a direct quote from Dr Chandra – she said the same thing to me.

'So, you're OK? Definitely?'

'Yes, Riri! My mission is to solve the murder. I'm made of steelier stuff now.'

I frown. 'That's not the phrase. It's, "*I'm made of sterner stuff*".'

Ani chuckles. 'You're definitely not made of stuff, steelier or sterner. You're made of scaredy-cat nerves. Now, are you ready or not?'

I interlace my knuckles, aiming to crack them, but

unfortunately no sound comes out. Worse, Ani notices and laughs.

'OK, I'm ready. Any guesses?'

'Try "Anastasia". After all, that was what Nikolaos knew her as.'

I type that in with confidence, given that I'm in my comfort zone. So, when a message flashes on the screen, I flinch. 'Ack, that's not it. Only two attempts left.'

'Try my birthday.'

I smirk and look at Ani out of the corner of my eye. 'You mean my birthday?'

'Ha, I'll give you that one. Now type it in.'

'Uh-oh. That's not it. What made you think your birthday of all things?'

Ani half shrugs. 'She never forgot it and always gave good presents.' She taps her chin in an inconsistent beat that bugs me. I drum my fingers on the laptop in a consistent beat. 'This lead will either make or break the investigation. We *have* to find out the time of death. That'll help us with the suspect list, meaning we *have* to be sure. Otherwise, what will we do?'

'Hand this over to Sergeant Chloe, maybe?'

Ani ignores me. 'Oh, I've got it! Move over.'

'No can do. This is our last guess. We can try again in twenty-four hours but only with extra security questions. If we can't guess the password then we definitely can't guess the answers to the questions. We'd have to wait weeks or even months for the time of death from the autopsy. Ani, think about this.'

'Riri, move over. I've got this.' She cracks her fingers, and much to my embarrassment, sound comes out.

Then she types:

T-U-S-C

Ani cheers and I join in. 'It worked! Yay! OK, now we need to look at her heartbeat on the Health app. When it stopped.'

Neither of us move.

'Ani? I thought, maybe, you'd wanna do it? Unless you don't want to? I'm happy to. Ani, are you OK?'

She doesn't look at me. 'Give me a minute.' With that, she's gone.

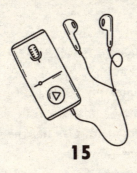

15

ANI

I'm in the bathroom. Something sad and dark keeps thrumming through my veins. I don't want to know Mrs Kostas's time of death.

It's cold here. Cool enough to calm me down. But my face is burning. My heart races and it doesn't stop. Panicking. Wobbly. Sad. I let out a squeak of a sob.

Dr Chandra's calming voice comes to mind: 'Deeply inhale and exhale. One, two, three times.' So I do. I feel less wobbly. 'If that doesn't work, repeat a mantra. *I will be OK*. While you're doing that, focus on what you can see, smell, hear, taste and touch.' I say the words to myself twelve times. My senses – I can't see anything because my eyes are closed. I can smell air freshener. Taste metal bitterness. I can feel the basin and the droplets of water in the sink. 'Don't worry if you're still panicking. Look around. Centre yourself. Find three things. Focus on them.'

Bathtub. Basin. Toilet. Weird as it sounds, focusing on

117

those things slows my heart.

I will be OK. I wipe a stray tear away, splash some water on my face and out I go.

As soon as I re-enter my room, I see Riri fidget. 'I've got the time of death.' She pauses. It takes me a minute to realise that she wants me to give her the go-ahead. I nod. '4.30 p.m. the day we found her.'

It feels like my heart is shattering all over again. What was I doing at 4.30 p.m. whilst Mrs Kostas was taking her last breaths?

I can't remember. Somehow, that's worse.

Riri must see me spiralling because she comes closer. Whispers, 'Bear in mind, this might not be accurate – the battery could've died or it could've glitched.'

'But it's close enough. Where are we with our to-do list?' I hand her my scribbled to-do list.

TO-DO LIST
- Find out the time of death then check footage
- Confirm who was inside the cafe at the time of death
- Create a timeline
- Create the suspect list
- Establish motives
- Begin questioning suspects
- Verify our timeline with each suspect

Unfortunately me and Riri finished something that *isn't* on our to-do list: chores.

But it's helped to unlock a memory.

I lay on my bed, spreadeagled. In my hands is my old iPad case that reminds me of what I was going to recount to Riri before. 'I might as well speak about the thing with Mrs Kostas's past I was going to "tell you later". Later is now.' It'll feel weird to share it as I had thought it laid the foundation of mine and Mrs Kostas/Dimas's relationship. Really it was a major red flag about her real identity.

'Two years ago, when Cafe Vivlio first opened, Mrs Kostas was becoming my favourite adult in the world in a matter of weeks – she was that great. Always happy and nice to me. Within its first month of opening, Mrs Kostas reported a theft of that day's money in the till. I sat at my table, reading manga and eating karidopita. Because she was insured she was promised the money back. She should've been happy but she closed the cafe early, which wasn't like her. She was still inside so I crept in to see if she was OK. Well, and because I had left my iPad in the cafe. With this case.' I hold up my old iPad case for her to see. 'Mrs Kostas politely told me to go away but I noticed a painting near the till, unhung. It was small and fancy. Frameless. A sneaky Google search told me that the painting was worth millions. It was *Poppy Flowers* by Van Gogh!' Riri gasps and her eyes widen as she fangirls over Van Gogh. 'I asked her about it and she said it was a ghost of her past. I didn't know what it meant so I left it alone. Anyway, my shoelace came undone so I tied it. Stuffed under the counter, far from anyone's sight, was a big wad of cash.'

'Whoa.' Riri gapes like a goldfish.

I pause to take in Riri's shell-shocked expression.

'Days later, the painting kept bugging me. I had a feeling it was real. If it wasn't, could it really shake her up so much? Maybe. I did more research and stopped by her flat. She tried denying it until she couldn't anymore. She admitted to me that it was real.'

'No way,' Riri whispers.

I ignore her and continue, 'I asked her where the painting came from and she refused to answer. Someone from her past must have planted that painting, to shake her up. Maybe to let her know they knew where she'd ended up. Friend or foe, I don't know. Or maybe she faked the robbery then called the police. The ghost from her past –'

'Ghosts don't exist so why don't we say *person* from her past?'

'Pfft, how boring does that sound?'

'And then what happened after the robbery, Ani?'

'A week later, I asked her what happened to the painting. Said she anonymously donated it to a museum. I'm sure I heard Rodolfo say something about *Poppy Flowers* but he was far away, in the kitchens. I didn't see who was with him.'

'Should he be a suspect?'

'If he was near the crime scene at the time of death, and we find a motive, maybe to do with this painting, then yes. Anyway, Mrs Kostas told me to never speak about it again. But promises expire after death. Except for the promises of twins.'

'You're referring to my TUSC induction, when you made me sign a waiver promising to not rise from the dead and

120

sue you if an investigation resulted in my death. Aren't you?'

I start pacing as I think back to the BBQoBN. 'The day before she died, she was uncharacteristically jumpy. I was just too angry to notice before.' I grit my teeth to suppress a sob. Riri mumbles to herself. 'Would you shush? I need to finish my log.' I pause as I resume recording. 'Supersleuth's log. I'm here with my Sleuth-In-Training, who can't be named due to confidentiality laws. Before we go further, let's go through our three main theories. Here, take this printout.'

```
Three main theories for Mrs Kostas/Dimas's
murder:
 1) Random
 2) Relating to Mrs Kostas's life in Castlewick
 3) Connected to her secret past
```

I point at Riri. 'Do you think we could eliminate one? What does your SIT gut say?'

Riri squirms, looking like she's been called out by a scary teacher. 'Um . . . it could be random . . . but then it might not be. And it might be about her life in Castlewick . . . but she might've gained a lot of enemies from her past.' She blushes, trying to think. Then excuses herself to go to the bathroom.

Now, I'm alone. How I like to be, with my thinking cap on. We have Mrs Kostas's backstory and her time of death. But I still need more information.

Only two people can get me that.

I unlock my phone. Go on my only iMessage group chat.

121

It's called ANImals. Get it?

> Yo, guys, I need you to bring your A game tomorrow. It's a matter of life and death.

> . . . Kinda . . . maybe more of a matter of death and justice? IDK

> All I know is that I can't say why. Especially over text.

Helin was my first ever SIT. But then I learned that she doesn't do so well under pressure. After that, I enlisted LaShawn. He's squeamish about death. And bugs, leaves, puddles and reptiles. Even so, they both have their strengths. In fact, they've helped solve a few TUSC cases.

My phone buzzes. LaShawn replied first, then Helin.

LaShawn:

Woo-woo, we're back, baby!

Helin:

Yay! Thanks, Ani. Unpressured is now my middle name 😊

I change the group chat's name to 'ANImals of the TUSC'.

Helin:

I can do anything!

LaShawn:

. . . Anything but get caught, right?

😄 LaShawn, you're funny. How are you? It's been a few days

LaShawn:

Eh, I'm OK. Mama's still got me on studying house arrest. I'll tell you all about it when we meet.

LOL no thanks.

Then I get in bed and fall fast asleep.

TUSC timestamp
12 days since murder
4 days since TUSC investigation
 launched

'Supersleuth's log,' I say, mid-yawn. '7 a.m. Director Ani Tariq and her SIT are in a state of FBFB. Meaning, we have fresh breaths and full bellies. Ready for the day ahead! The mission is to call in reinforcements.'

Riri nods. Then gets the notepad and starts reading.

'Shush, because I'm going to make one very important business call, so be quiet.'

Five rings later, it's answered. 'Hi, Helin.'

'Hey, Ani. How's the investigation going?'

'We're making progress.'

'When can you come over?'

'Hopefully soon.'

'Great. So, remember how you're the school journalist *and* our star runner?'

Helin makes an 'mmhmm' sound.

'Well, I need you to use your athletic insides –'

'I think you mean *instincts*.'

'If that's your inner athlete talking, then I'll accept the correction. I need you to prepare for an ultra-secret undercover mission.'

'Hmm. Will I interrogate people? Imagine me riding my future horse over to suspects and getting confessions out of them. Can animals be SITs?'

'Whoa, Helin, calm down. No and no – interrogation is my thing. You just need to start preparing your body – do some running and jogging. No horse-riding is required for this investigation. If your parents ask, say you're preparing for a *killer* race –'

Riri gasps, cutting me off. 'Excuse the pun.'

I glare at Riri. 'Helin, can you do this?'

124

'Yes.' Her mum shouts in the background. 'I've gotta go.'

'Is she calling you down for breakfast? If you have any leftovers, you know where to bring them.' Might sound gross, but I eat Helin's leftover Persian breakfast sometimes. Halim (porridge with wheat and meat!), flatbread, feta cheese, olives, eggs, cucumbers, adasi (lentil soup), honey and jam. Delicious.

'Deal. See you later.' Helin hangs up.

16

RIRI

TUSC timestamp
13 days since murder
5 days since TUSC investigation
    launched

Ani said our next mission is to look into retrieving the CCTV footage of Cafe Vivlio at the time of death. She's repeatedly said there's no other way into The Secret Garden except through the hallway of Cafe Vivlio.

Instead of our mission, however, we've done two other things:

1. Played Table Topics with Mom. Ani was being particularly difficult with her contributions to the conversations but I enjoyed it. (Every weekend, me and Mom play it over dinner and a movie.)

a. *Thought about how to get into Dad's computer to see the footage.*

'Why does Dad of all people have access to the CCTV footage?' I ask Ani again. The first time I asked was before we went to bed yesterday, after our twenty-something round of Table Topics. To me, it seemed significant that Dad would have access to Mrs Dimas/Kostas's computer. Was it only because he worked in IT?

'Because he helped her set it up, duh! Dad and Mrs Kostas were so close that he was the admin of all her accounts. Mrs Kostas wasn't crazy about technology, you see. She tolerated the Apple Watch because it counted her steps and she was on the brink of having high cholesterol.'

'Why not a Fitbit then? You do have those here, don't you?'

'Yes, we do. England isn't an alien planet, you know. Anyway, Derek insisted on an Apple Watch. He's super tech-savvy so I think that's why.'

'OK and how many CCTV cameras are there?'

'There's only one,' Ani says. 'A camera is hidden at the top of the doorframe. The entrance to Cafe Vivlio is the *only* way in or out. We'll have a full-frontal head shot of everyone going into the cafe at that time.'

'And a shot of the back of their head as they leave?'

'Yep. We can cross-reference the faces with backs of heads, pinpointing the duration of their stay.'

I can't help but ask, 'Um . . . do the police know about the CCTV camera?'

Ani shrugs. 'If they don't, we're one step ahead.'

127

'So, we-we need to hack into Dad's computer?'

'Yep. And I know the password. He locks the office whenever he's not in the building.'

I eye the door. 'But he isn't here right now and the door *isn't* locked.'

Ani smiles like she's a supervillain instead of a supersleuth. Sometimes, I wonder. 'I might have "lost" my ADHD meds. Mum and Dad have gone to get a new pack.'

'Ani, how irresponsible! I've read a thing or two about the NHS – should you be abusing it like this? Mom has to pay for my inhalers and antihistamines, even with health insurance.' I sniff, my nose stuffy. That reminds me, I should take an antihistamine. My hay-fever is stronger in Castlewick than it's ever been in California.

'What? I acted with good intentions! Nothing was wasted unnecessarily – my medicine pack will magically reappear after we've solved the case. Plus I haven't missed any doses.'

I massage my temples. 'Weren't there other ways to get Mom and Dad out of here?'

'Nope. This was a matter of urgency.'

'This doesn't ease my guilty conscience in the slightest, but I suppose we should just get inside before you do something worse.' I can do this. For the greater good.

I take one step towards Dad's office.

Ani leans against the door, clearly fine with sneaking into a forbidden room. 'Shall we?' She scurries inside, sliding on her socks.

Inside the spacious room, there's a comfy-looking chair and games consoles. Dad must relax here too.

I decide to kick-start this part of our investigation by sitting in Dad's chair. Ani leans over me to punch in the password. Our birthday.

Now it's my turn.

With shaky hands, I begin looking for the CCTV app.

'Ani, I've found the app.' I click on it.

'Good, SIT. Did you bring the case notes?'

'No.'

'Disappointing, but no matter – I'll go get the notepad. We'll video the footage from 4.30 p.m. No – 4 p.m. – for good measure.

I nod. 'Then we can look at it frame-by-frame.'

'Well done, SIT. Now, let's get videoing!'

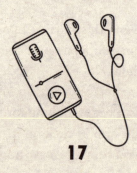

17

ANI

We've taken *loads* of videos. So many that I've used up all the memory on my phone. But I consider this mission a success. The conclusions are:

1) Rodolfo was there, going between the counter and the kitchens. Three customers were in the cafe (we visually confirmed that the bookshop was empty) at the time of death: Fred, Mimi and Derek. Derek technically wasn't inside the cafe at 4.30 p.m. But he also wasn't *outside* the cafe at 4.30 p.m. Basically he arrived at that exact time.

2) The murderer either came back to the cafe or was still there when me and Riri went in.

The Clio Trio is what Riri calls the suspects. Why, you may wonder? Well, me too.

Riri explains, 'Clio was the Greek Muse of History.' I don't know what that means. Google says Clio was the Goddess of History. 'And in history, like, from the beginning of time, murder is constant. In pretty much all cultures' folklore. So it not only fits because of Mrs Dimas/Kostas's ancestry but because of the way she was taken from this world.'

I give Riri a look that asks, *What on God's green earth are you talking about?*

'For poetic, historical reasons, can we please, *please*, call them that?' Riri pleads.

```
THE CLIO TRIO AKA Suspect List 1.0:
1) Fred Hunt (regular #1)
2) Mimi Bloodworth (regular #2)
3) Derek Chase (regular #3)
```

'What do they have in common?' Riri asks.

'. . . They all like coffee? I don't know. Electronics are their livelihood – Derek vlogs, Mimi records videos on her phone and Fred writes screenplays on his laptop. Because of that, all three of them are all too familiar with our flat, funnily enough. Dad sorts out their technical issues in his office. They pay him. Other than that, they share no common likes or dislikes. Except, I suppose, all of them like me. They all know about The Secret Garden.'

Riri's eyes widen. 'Permission to pitch a conspiracy?'

'No, Riri. Conspiracies are a pseudoscience. You of all people should know that.'

'OK, then call it a theory that will be proven in time.

131

Just hear me out? *You* are the common link between these suspects. Think about it – they knew *your* favourite person – Mrs Kostas – and they're familiar with *your* apartment. The place of murder? *Your* favourite place on earth – The Secret Garden. Am I onto something here? Tell me I am.'

That hadn't crossed my mind. 'You might be. Too soon to tell. Now, onto the next bit before we waste more time.'

I get my whiteboard-on-wheels out. Pass Riri the marker. The whiteboard is best for timeframes because, in my experience, timeframes require a lot of erasing and starting over. Once we come to a good enough timeframe, Riri will transcribe it to the notepad. But even then, things could change.

'Now, Riri –' I use my best serious face – 'this will need to be verified by the suspects. But first, let's lay out the timeline.'

Official murder timeline for Mrs Kostas/Dimas

Being an account of
The Tariq Ultrasecret Supersleuth Centre/TUSC
Produced by TUSC Director Imani 'Ani' Tariq

Transcribed by Sleuth-In-Training,
Noori 'Riri' Tariq

- 4.30 p.m.: Death of the victim, Mrs Kostas/
  Dimas. Location: The Secret Garden, behind
  Cafe Vivlio

```
- 5.45 p.m.: Ani and Riri enter Cafe Vivlio
- 5.50 p.m. (approx.): Ani chats with Fred,
  regular #1. Riri goes to the cafe's bookstore
```

I glance at Riri suspiciously. 'Didn't *you* see or hear anything in the cafe's bookstore? That's technically closer to The Secret Garden than the actual cafe bit is, you know. Sure, there are no windows but I'm sure you'd be able to *hear* something.'

'I was so wrapped up in all the books,' she whispers, 'I barely looked up and around. I didn't hear anything murdery. No screams or cries.'

'OK then. Back to the timeline.'

```
- 6 p.m. (approx.): Ani goes to the kitchens
  to (attempt to) find Mrs Kostas. Has a chat
  with Rodolfo, the chef.
- 6.04 p.m. (approx.): Ani leaves kitchens and
  bumps into regular #2, Mimi. Has a nice chat
  with her.
- Mimi leaves within this timeframe
- 6.10 p.m. (approx.): Ani heads over to Derek's
  (AKA regular #3) table and has a conversation
  with him.
- 6.24 p.m. (approx.): Derek's brother, Frankie,
  comes inside. Ani briefly chats with him
```

```
    before Riri comes over and drools and gives
    him her heart.
```

Riri's wide eyes are about to roll on the floor and out of the room. 'Ani, no!'

'What, Riri?' I mock her accent and high-pitched tone.

She attempts a glare. 'You can't keep that on the board! What if our parents see? Plus, that totally isn't what happened!'

I give her a lopsided grin. 'Then what *did* happen between you and Frankie?'

She blushes. 'Can we carry on before our parents hear us and we get in trouble?'

I tut but still amend my statement.

```
—  6.24 p.m. (approx.): Derek's brother, Frankie,
   enters cafe. Ani briefly chats with him before
   Riri comes over ~~and drools and gives him her
   heart.~~
```

Then I sigh. 'I hope you're happy now. If we ever get asked to present this evidence to the world, you know I can't withhold that this has been doctored.'

'Fine by me, as long as you don't disclose the original statement.'

'No promises. In fact, no comment. Moving on.'

```
—  6.29 pm: Mimi returns to cafe to get her purse
   (regulars #1 and #3 are still in cafe).
```

I check my phone log.

- 6.30 p.m.: Dad calls to tell Ani and Riri to
  find Mrs Kostas/Dimas for us all to go and
  get ice-cream.
- 6.37 p.m.: Ani finds Mrs Kostas/Dimas's body
  in The Secret Garden with pre-SIT Riri.

I glance at the note that Riri's just written in the notepad.

Conclusion: If the time of death was 4.30 p.m.
and we discovered Mrs Dimas/Kostas at 6.37
p.m. then she had been dead for 127 minutes/2
hours, 7 minutes.

I have to do deep breathing again. In . . . out. In . . . out.
In . . . out. Mrs Kostas/Dimas was all alone and in broad
daylight, dying or dead. That thought makes me want to
cry, but the thought of the murderer getting away is worse.

'Riri, we need more. Loads more.' A sigh escapes my
lips. 'So far, we've got the victim's backstory and supposed
time of death. We know for sure that a passerby wouldn't
be able to see what's happening in The Secret Garden. The
fence is too high with no access from outside. It has to
be one of the Clio Trio because no one else was there. We're
back to square one.'

I want to whine and stomp my feet. Instead, I look at
the to-do list.

TO-DO LIST

- ~~Look at the CCTV footage on Dad's computer from Cafe Vivlio's feed~~
- ~~Confirm who was inside the cafe at the time of death~~
- ~~Create a timeline~~
- ~~Create the suspect list~~
- Begin questioning suspects
- Verify our timeline with each suspect

I add two things:

- Uncover motives
- Get a confession

18

ANI

Update: Riri's handwriting is headache-inducing. We've been spit-balling motives for Fred, Mimi and Derek all day. But what we're coming up with is ridiculous. Too far-fetched.

My phone rings. This works in my favour, now becoming:

TUSC report: very important call #2

'Yo, LaShawn, what goes up but never goes back down?'

'What?' he asks.

'An exploding rocket.' I break out into laughter. So does LaShawn.

Meanwhile, Riri's eyes widen. 'How insensitive!'

My eyebrows knit down. 'It's a joke. Relax.'

'You're mad, son,' LaShawn tells me with a snigger.

'Mad enough to ask you for a favour. But is it *really* a favour if you're technically fulfilling your duty as a SIT for the TUSC?' I'm hopeful that this will be the year that

LaShawn and Helin qualify as sleuths. They have the skillset, for sure. Just not the stomach.

'Favour? Y'know Mama's got me on house arrest until I study my brain away. Mama actually asked the secondary school for the Year 7 curriculum so I could get ahead or whatever.'

'Sucks to be you.' Also, I hope Dad doesn't find out about that and get the curriculum for me – I have lots of things on my plate, and preparing for Year 7 is not on the agenda. 'I need you to use your drones for a super-secret TUSC operation.'

'Nice. You didn't ask me how I am, by the way.'

I hold back a sigh. 'How are you?'

'Y'know what? Not too good, man. Remember my dream of being a grime MC?'

'It's all you ever talk about. You want to be the first-ever grime MC who raps while he invents things for science. *The freestyling inventor*.' LaShawn has won many science competitions for his inventions. My personal favourites are his weather balloon and robo-ercoaster (his robot rollercoaster – the robot does your chores while you enjoy the mini rollercoaster in the back garden. The robot senses when parents are nearby, to disable the rollercoaster so you can act like you've been doing the chores the whole time. He's currently trying to program the robot to do maths homework). Between LaShawn winning awards for his inventions and Helin for her journalism, I'm starting to think I'm the unremarkable one of our friend group. But one day I'll win supersleuth awards.

'Well, I finally finalised my soundboard design. The LaSoundboard 5.0. Tryna make beats outside – for authentic, real-world sounds – and it went great. That bus in the background would sound epic, y'know?'

'Is there a point here or are you losing it because of your studying house arrest?'

'Pfft, patience. Let me huff and puff and blow your mind! So, sunset, about two weeks ago. *The day before Mrs Kostas got killed.* Streets weren't busy. I walked around, recording my audio and whatnot. Finally got round to listen to my slaying beats just now. Guess what? One had been disrupted. It picked up the audio of some angry folk arguing.'

'Who?'

'Patience, Ani. With a heavy heart, I had to put the LaSoundboard 5.0 to bed. And by "to bed", I mean "under my bed". And by "under my bed", I mean "in my archives".'

'And by this –' I yawn – 'I mean "I'm falling asleep". Did you call me to monologue? Cause I'm kinda busy here. Doing serious work.'

'Yeah, I did call you to monologue – Helin told me about your call to her. I felt left out, so what? I'm ready to help.'

'I know you are. Listen to that tape you're talking about – maybe you'll find something useful to our investigation.'

'That's what I've been trying to say – I already did. To both of those things.'

'What?'

'Listened to the tape, check. Found something useful to your investigation, check.'

'*What?!* Why didn't you start with this?!'

'For suspense! You're a supersleuth, aren't you? In sleuth movies, we always see the good guy do a big reveal *at the end*.'

I grunt. 'LaShawn.'

He laughs, nervously. 'Just listen to it yourself. I've refined the audio – stripped it of my rapping and background sounds so it's clear for you to hear. I'll send it over. Uh . . . not to bias up your thoughts but you will *not* like what you hear. 'Kay, bye.' He hangs up.

I turn to Riri. She probably heard that because she was dead silent throughout the conversation. 'OK, let's play it then we'll look at motives.' I hold my breath as I recognise the voices. Friendly voices – or so I thought: it's Derek and Mrs Kostas/Dimas!

Derek: Mrs K, listen to me for a sec!

Mrs Kostas/Dimas: No, young man, I won't. This isn't up for debate.

Derek: Actually it is! I'm your silent partner now, remember? I get a say in things about Cafe Vivlio now too. Don't forget that.

Mrs Kostas/Dimas: Don't forget your manners. Just give me time to consider it. And if you say you're a silent partner, then why go behind my back? It's unnecessary –

Derek: I've already explained to you why it's necessary. Our partnership won't work if you refuse to see my point-of-view, you know. Mine is current, fresh and successful.

Mrs Kostas/Dimas: It's costly and time-consuming. Not to mention an extra responsibility. Look, there's a lot to discuss but I can't right now. I've got to go to a barbecue with Ani soon. Tomorrow, I'll have an answer for you.

Derek: In the meantime, don't forget who helped people discover Cafe Vivlio on a bigger scale than Castlewick. On social media, you're the puppet and I control your strings.

Mrs Kostas/Dimas: I don't think you −

Derek: In life and in death, Mrs K. When you're six feet under, I'll fully own the cafe. If I'm six feet under before you, then you'll go back to fully owning it. But for now, it's ours.

Mrs Kostas/Dimas: Derek Chase, remember that the tongue has no bones but bones it crushes. You −

The audio turns static and then cuts off.

I'm dumbstruck but Riri must be clueless, so I explain: 'That was Derek talking to Mrs Kostas/Dimas.' Derek's words and his tone have chilled me. That doesn't sound like the Derek I know. And he was Mrs Kostas/Dimas's silent partner for Cafe Vivlio?! How did I not know this?

'Are you positive?' Riri asks in a husky voice, as if she's on the verge of tears. It was an intense exchange we just listened to.

I nod. 'I'm − I *was* − friendly with both of them, so I know their voices. Positive.' I know it's them and I'm so annoyed − my breathing is loud through flaring nostrils. I know my face is red and I'm glaring but that's not helpful for a supersleuth. No time for anger. But if I do focus on what else I'm feeling, then it's anger. 'I want to bottle up the sound of her voice. Even this angry voice.'

'Well, recordings can be forever . . .'

My shoulders droop. 'It's not like him to talk like that. I know people have different sides but . . . no.'

It's too painful. And now it seems like Derek might have *murdered* Mrs Kostas.

Riri turns to the board before we can dwell. I'm secretly grateful our investigation is still business as usual – it gives me something to occupy my mind from grieving Mrs Kostas/Dimas and having another Bleak Week. 'So, her silent partner has a fight with her the day before her death. They fight over the business. So it's obvious, right?'

'Wait,' I say. 'Let's prove it. Would he gain ownership now? Is there a law or something?'

Riri shows me this on my laptop:

According to the Partnership Act 1890 (Act of the Parliament of the UK), a partnership ends upon the death of a partner, unless a formal agreement is made prior to the deaths.

'Dead partner means dead partnership,' I deduce. 'So, he *would* lose ownership.'

'That settles it, right?' Riri says. 'Derek could've killed Mrs Dimas/Kostas because of greed – but only if there was a formal agreement made prior to her death about their partnership. All we have to do is figure out if there was one. But because he said if Mrs Dimas/Kostas dies then he'll own the cafe, let's assume there was an agreement.'

'Yep. Or that Derek *thinks* he'll get to fully own Cafe Vivlio,' I add.

'Yes, that's good.'

'I know, Riri. Now before I tell you about each of our suspects so we can figure out their motives, I need you to wait in the living room.' I send Riri on her way so she doesn't see what I have up my sleeve. Then, I create the invention of a lifetime, sticking out my tongue as I concentrate cutting. Writing. Tacking. After about ten minutes, I call her back.

'SIT, welcome to The Motive Board.'

'Is that my corkboard and its stand? And my thumbtacks and cards?'

'Yes. Why you decided to pack them for a summer holiday is beyond me. But I'm happy you did because, well, when I first searched your things –'

'Hey!' she protests, eyes wide.

I continue, unfazed, 'I thought it was odd. But now it's worked out perfectly.'

Riri motions to my invention. 'And what exactly is this?'

'The Motive Board,' I repeat, wondering if she has a concussion. 'I've cut out pictures of Derek and Mimi from old issues of *The Castlewick Chronicles*. Fred is a ghost online so I've drawn a face. We're going to talk about The Clio Trio and see which motive best fits what I know about them. Once we've talked through each motive for each suspect, we will have a clearer picture. You can offer a different perspective because you don't know them.'

'Ooh, so I'll be the deciding factor?'

'No, Riri. Get off your high horse. See, I didn't say you had the *right* perspective. Just that you have a *different one*. Now without further ado . . .'

We've finished going through The Clio Trio and The Motive Board. My ingenious idea was to write notes/theories about potential motives for each suspect:

MOTIVES	
Fred	
DESPERATION	**LOVE/OBSESSION**
Desperate to be a successful screenwriter	Could be obsessed with fame/success? Loves Mrs Kostas/Dimas? Hates Mrs Kostas/Dimas? Meticulous and a perfectionist (takes ages writing scenes)
JEALOUSY	**REVENGE**
Is jealous of the cafe's success?	Wants revenge for something Mrs Kostas/Dimas did in the cafe — maybe spilled his drink or stopped making his favourite pastry? Maybe she laughed at something she read on his laptop? Revenge for something Anastasia did? But how would Fred have known her? And what — or who — would he want to be avenged?
GREED	**CRIME OF PASSION**
Greedy for fame/success Greedy for the unlimited internet the cafe provides	Argument/misunderstanding with Mrs Kostas/Dimas that led to a random murder

MOTIVES

Derek Chase

DESPERATION	LOVE/OBSESSION
Desperate to be the sole owner of Cafe Vivlio (but what about his YouTube channel? That's a full-time job. Can he juggle both without the quality of one decreasing?)	Loves money and fame? Obsessed with making Cafe Vivlio successful but only according to his vision
JEALOUSY	**REVENGE**
Jealous that Mrs Kostas/Dimas was doing a good job on the cafe on her own	Revenge for the argument he had with Mrs Kostas/Dimas the day before she was murdered? Revenge for Mrs Kostas/Dimas not listening to his suggestions about how to run Cafe Vivlio? Revenge for something Anastasia did? But how would Derek have known her? And what — or who — would he want to be avenged?
GREED	**CRIME OF PASSION**
Wants to be the sole owner of Cafe Vivlio (again: what about his YouTube channel? That's a full-time job. Can he juggle both without the quality of one decreasing?)	Maybe he couldn't shake the argument he had with Mrs Kostas/Dimas and his anger took over OR maybe he was regretful and went to apologise but something triggered him to hurt her

MOTIVES	
Mimi Bloodworth	
DESPERATION	**LOVE/OBSESSION**
Desperate to get her big break Desperate to have more followers and views So desperate she tried to use Derek for clout	Might be obsessed with Mrs Kostas/Dimas's popularity in Castlewick and on Instagram Might be obsessed/in love with Derek – maybe she wanted to hurt him by killing Mrs Kostas/Dimas?
JEALOUSY	**REVENGE**
Jealous of Mrs Kostas/Dimas's popularity in Castlewick and on Instagram	Revenge for something Mrs Kostas/Dimas did/said as her boss when Mimi was a barista? Revenge for something Anastasia did? But how would Mimi have known her? And what – or who – would she want to be avenged?
GREED	**CRIME OF PASSION**
Greedy for followers/fame	Maybe she got in a spur-of-the-moment argument with Mrs Kostas/Dimas in The Secret Garden?

I think we did well. Sure, there are loads of unanswered questions and lots of uncertainties. But it's something.

19

RIRI

TUSC timestamp
14 days since murder
6 days since TUSC investigation
   launched

Ani says motives are the key to solving murders.

'Motives reveal secrets. Secret gambling problem? Secret child? Secret trafficking ring run by our suspect?'

'*What –?*' We hear Mom outside Ani's room. Ani's eyes widen and my face burns. Ani goes toward The Motive Board one second too late – Mom bursts in with Dad. I didn't even hear Mom call Dad but they must've been wondering what me and Ani have been working on together. '*The Motive Board!* Abderrazzak, I thought you said Ani's teeth grinding was due to her reopening her Amelia Earhart case!'

While Dad scratches his eyebrow, I remember the rough night I had last night due to Ani's teeth grinding. Dad told me and Mom that Ani grinds her teeth in her sleep when something is majorly bugging her. The thing that's bugging her has to be this investigation. She's determined – maybe obsessively – to solve it.

'No more investigating.' Mom takes The Motive Board off the corkboard stand. 'Girls, let's leave the investigating to the police. This isn't negotiable.'

'I agree.' Dad's eyes linger on Ani. Like me, he's expecting her to object. Instead, she says nothing. Dad goes on, 'We can do ice-skating.' I'm starting to like him. We've been bonding with small talk and snacks. He has good ideas too – I love ice-skating.

'Excellent idea, Abderrazzak,' Mom says but I notice something. She can *sound* like she's one-hundred percent fine with him – it's part of her job to do presentations and meetings so her communication skills have to be strong. But she never looks at him when she talks to him. And her posture is always so wooden around him. He's in the same boat – he tries to stay a healthy distance away from her as possible. 'Let's keep the girls busy and far from anything to do with murder.'

TUSC timestamp
15 days since murder
7 days since TUSC investigation
   launched

'Supersleuth's log,' Ani utters into her phone as she squirms in the theatre chairs, 'I've been forced out of my private TUSC office. They want me to watch a movie on a large screen with strangers because I "need to relax". The mystery of the murder makes me cranky but so what? Investigation obligations have stalled. An unforgiveable order from the adults.'

After ice-skating yesterday, we were forced to watch a National Geographic documentary. I say "forced" but that's Ani's word – I rather enjoyed it. Then, Mom played board-games with us until Dad was done helping Fred update his laptop for the second time in fifteen days. After dinner, and with The Motive Board still hidden away, we fell asleep.

I lean closer to Ani's phone. 'I'm in the theatre too.' However, I soon regret both leaning and speaking because Ani roughly taps me on the arm. I yelp; my dress has thin sleeves, so I felt it fully. Ani, on the other hand, wears capri pants, a shirt and a denim jacket.

'How many times, Riri? It's a *cinema*. Learn *Eng*lish of *Eng*land, would you? Moving on. Mum's attending a Zoom meeting for work and Dad's doing some errands. My SIT and I are watching Disney's latest creation.'

'Shush,' some grown man tells Ani. He's not here with any kids. 'Can you not talk?'

'No.' Ani stands. Oh no. Why does she always have to make a scene? There are already plenty of scenes in a theatre – or cinema, whatever! You know, on the screen.

'I paid for a ticket too,' Ani defends. 'Consumer rights –'

I cover her mouth with my hand. She squirms and I reach

for my hand sanitiser with my other hand. But it works. She stays quiet. Yay.

An hour later, the movie has ended. Ani and I are in the foyer. It's loud, busy and bright. The whole place smells of blue raspberries from the ICEE machine. I'm eyeing it, desperate for a refill, and Ani's gawking at the arcade.

But we have strict instructions from Dad: wait here after the movie ends.

'Ani,' someone says. Even though it's loud, we both heard that voice clearly.

It's Sergeant Chloe! Oh no – a police officer here for Ani in a public place. I'm sweating so much I have to wipe my shaking hands on my skirt. Are we in trouble?

'Chloe?' Ani squints, confused. 'Are you even allowed to watch movies in your uniform?'

'I came to tell you something, but we need privacy.' Chloe's eye travel to the growing crowd. The foyer has become significantly quieter than before. 'Let's let these people continue on as they were and you both can come with me.'

I take a step in Chloe's direction because this is clearly *the* Chloe. As in, the Police Sergeant Chloe Li who knows Ani. As an upstanding citizen, I plan on doing the right thing.

Ani comes close to me. I feel her warm bubblegum-smelling breath as she murmurs, 'Riri, we've been made. Don't listen to anyone, trustworthy as they seem, until you know their true intentions.' I have so many questions but there's no time – Ani now loudly addresses Chloe. 'Is this to do with my investigation?' she asks. 'They're after my evidence because they're all useless, I knew it.' Now I kinda get why Mom insisted Ani keep a healthy distance from this investigation; it is turning her paranoid.

A sombre look crosses Chloe's face. 'It's about your dad. Let's go. Now.'

I've been in Castlewick for fifteen days now. I'm growing to love Dad. And now something has happened to him? My heart does the biggest beat ever. It worsens when Mom comes bursting into the foyer. She's crying. 'Has he been hurt?' I don't know if anyone hears me over Mom's crying and Ani's rambling.

'You want to exchange my dad for my investigational findings? Unbelievable!'

'Ani!' I hiss. 'Can you stop thinking about your investigation for one second?!'

'No, Riri, I told you –'

'Dad might be hurt!' I shriek. 'Or worse! She said it's about Dad, Ani, not *you*.'

It takes her a moment to get it. When she does, her eyes fill with tears, mixing with her anger. 'Dad can't be dead too! NO!'

'No, he's fine.' Worry wrinkles Chloe's forehead. What is she hiding? 'Your dad is under arrest. I'll explain everything once we're at the station. Let's go.'

Then, we both cry.

20

RIRI

'Chloe, please release my dad!' Ani begs.

Me, Ani, Mom and Chloe are inside a cold interrogation room. I flash back to when we discovered Mrs Dimas/ Kostas's body and have concluded that each interrogation room is as unremarkable and unpleasant as the next.

'Yes! Please!' I add with streaming tears.

Chloe shifts in her seat and can't meet either of our eyes. 'Girls, the evidence is –'

'He's being framed!' Ani yells.

'Miss Police Sergeant –' I try to be polite – 'excuse me but we don't believe that our dad is responsible.' To make matters worse, the local news has already caught wind of Dad's arrest. On the car radio on the way over here we heard about him being arrested on suspicion of Mrs Dimas/Kostas's murder. It's likely that everyone has heard.

'Let him go!' Ani screams. 'You know how they treat

people of colour in prison! There's absolutely zero chance that my dad *killed* Mrs Kostas. Zero. Negative one million.'

'Please consider Ani's valid points,' I add. 'Minus her tone.'

Chloe gently says, 'Ani, listen to me, I will fight tooth-and-nail to free your dad but I must follow the procedures. The evidence is there.'

'What evidence?!' Ani screams.

'Please could you tell us about the evidence?' I ask Chloe.

After a long pause, she answers, 'There was a man's bootprint in the soil on the hillock that matches your dad's. The note we found – your dad's fingerprints were on the paper. It looks to have been printed from his printer. The last piece of evidence we got was an abruptly ended call. Rodolfo rang Mrs Kostas just before our estimated time of death which is between 4 p.m. and 5 p.m. He mentioned it and had it on loudspeaker so Derek, who was sending a voice note, had the call running in the background. With all that, it was easy to get a warrant.'

'Can we h-hear it?' Ani's voice cracks.

Chloe rubs her face. 'Mum, do you think that's all right?'

'It depends.' Mom's posture is so rigid. 'What will they hear?'

'Mrs Kostas says, "Rodolfo?" And then, "No, get away from me! Abderrazzak –!" After that, it cuts off.'

A shiver goes up my spine, making me fidgety. 'Well, we –'

'How does that mean he killed her?!' Ani screams. 'It proves nothing! It could mean she was calling out to a friend for help!'

153

'All it proves is that this doesn't look good for him right now. Sure, everyone is innocent until proven guilty, but he's still a suspect right now. That doesn't mean I won't try my hardest to do my job. If I can't, then I'll ensure he gets a fair trial. But I can't let him go just because I know him. Once we're done questioning him, pre-charge bail will happen. He won't be charged as of yet, and his bail can last for three months so, if new evidence comes to light, there's still time for the investigation's focus to shift. And you know I can't control the local news.'

'What's his alibi?' I ask.

Chloe swallows. 'He doesn't have one. Fifteen days ago, he said he was waiting for you two to come from the airport.'

'HE WAS!' Ani declares. 'At 4.30 p.m. he was on the phone to Mum and Riri. I came in and disrupted the call.'

Chloe shakes her head. 'That was at 3.30 p.m., Ani. Your dad can't remember if he was at the shops or The Skyscape, but no CCTV footage corroborates him being at either.'

Ani groans and covers her face. 'I was supersleuthing and sulking in my room after the call. I didn't see him.' She cries and Mom rushes to console her. 'But he didn't do it!'

'Ani, I'm sorry,' Chloe says. 'We'll get to the bottom of it.'

Suddenly Ani bangs her fists on the table. Mom and me flinch. 'What about – I don't know – Fred?!' I think she just said Fred's name off the top of her head. 'His relationship with Mrs Kostas was awkward and that could be a motive. He always tried so hard to talk to her and she found it too eager and creepy. Why isn't he here being questioned?! And he was in our flat because Dad's been updating his laptop!

Fred could've framed my dad! Taken his boot and gotten Dad's fingerprints on the paper he'd print the note on!'

'I've confirmed with them both that Fred was at your flat the day *before* Mrs Kostas died. Not the day of. Your dad updated his laptop but then today, Fred noticed a virus so your dad took it back. Fred has it back now and we've found nothing incriminating on it.'

'So?! Fred could've taken Dad's boot before *Fred* killed her!'

'Ani, you're not helping any of us by being like this,' Chloe warns.

'*Chloe*, something isn't adding up! Fred has always been –'

'Fred was at the cafe, sure, but he was writing between 4 p.m. and 6 p.m.'

'This sucks! I bet your people wouldn't even give my dad a chance to explain his innocence!'

'Not everyone,' Chloe admits. 'But I would. You're forgetting that all of us in this room are people of Asian diaspora. Me, from the East. You three, from the South. I'd like to think I've got this far in my career because I've brought about change in policing processes for the police stations I've worked at. Marginalised people can be as innocent or as guilty as non-marginalised people, mind, but I make it my mission to prove that fairly. I'll do the same for your dad. You have my word.'

'So, Fred just gets away with it?!'

'He's not getting away with anything, Ani. We searched his house and found nothing. That's the fact.'

Ani curses under her breath. I catch Mom giving her a

reprimanding look. 'Well, you should be questioning Mimi Bloodworth and Derek Chase as well,' she mumbles. 'I just thought of Fred before as my first example.'

'It's already on my to-do list. Look, I'm sorry –' Chloe winces – 'I know how hard this must be and I would love to advocate for Abderrazzak's innocence. But we need a miracle at this stage. And that's me sugar-coating it.'

Ani glares. 'What even prompted you to search our flat?'

'We've been investigating everyone who had contact with Mrs Kostas during the last twenty-four hours of her life, which includes your dad. Then, we received an anonymous tip-off. Matched with the DNA evidence at the crime scene – the fingerprints and the bootprint – we had no choice but to focus our investigation on him.'

Ani grunts then retorts, '*This* is the thanks we get for doing our own investigation into the death Mrs Kostas?!'

'Or Mrs Dimas,' I say out of habit. Bad habit, it turns out; I freeze. Ani shoves me.

'Ani, can you behave?' Mum snaps. 'And I've told you, you can't investigate that.'

'Wait,' Chloe says. 'Rewind. Riri, who's Mrs Dimas and why did you say that name straight after Ani said Mrs Kostas?'

I open my mouth, feeling my nerves set my bones on fire. I'm certain I resemble a goldfish, opening and closing my mouth. Helpless, I turn to Ani.

'I'm willing to negotiate, Chloe. I'll give you some intel in exchange for you giving my dad full immunity.' Ani crosses her arms, not budging.

'No, Ani, this isn't playtime. We're at a *police station*. Do as I say.'

Ani and Chloe are stuck in a stare down. It's odd, being an onlooker in such a tense situation. I feel like I too, can't blink.

'I have Mrs Kostas's Apple Watch. She was wearing it at the time of her death.'

Chloe's eyes widen and she gapes, trapped in a frozen expression. Suffice it to say, she looks livid. 'You what?! Ani! Did you –' she leans over the metal table and whispers – 'did you take it off Mrs K's body?'

'Ani!' Mom screeches. 'Do you know how many levels of wrong that is?!'

'I did what I had to do. No wait –' Ani says – 'let me rephrase that. I took it as a memento.' I've gotta admit that Ani's a good liar. I could never be that smooth.

'Nice try,' Chloe tells Ani. 'But I know you took it for investigative purposes.'

Mom stands, fanning herself. 'Oh God. My daughter's a grave robber!'

'Mom, stop,' I say. 'Ani's not a *grave* robber.' She's a robber of the dead.

Chloe's got her unwavering gaze on Ani now. 'If I know you, I know you've got the Apple Watch with you. Hand it over.'

'Miss Police Sergeant, could you please tell us about the lead you had to search our flat? Then we'll tell you all about Mrs Dimas without bragging about making the discovery *before* fully qualified and resourced professionals.' Ani gapes at me, surprised, while I sweetly smile at Chloe and continue, 'From an American ally, thank you for your service.'

'Good one, SIT,' Ani whispers.

'Ani will give you the watch first of course.' I nudge Ani. Cursing, Ani gets it out of her pocket and shows it to Chloe. 'I believe we're ready now.'

Chloe clears her throat and glances at all of us but her gaze stops on Mom.

'I'd like to know the answer to this too,' Mom says. There's an edge in her tone that she usually uses when I'm in the principal's office for having an intellectual duel with someone who scruffs up my hijab. It's always me, the victim, who gets in trouble. Luckily Mom defends me.

'We were searching the victim's flat,' Chloe reveals. 'It's directly beneath Abderrazzak's flat. There was a knock at the door. We found a note on the floor that said your dad did it, from an alleged eyewitness who was anonymous. No fingerprints were found on the note. Anonymous tips are hard to take seriously but we have other evidence that points to your dad too. That's as far as we've got.' Chloe clicks her fingers, prompting Ani to hand over the Apple Watch.

'Your turn, Riri,' Chloe commands. 'Tell me about Mrs Dimas.'

21

RIRI

It hasn't been the easiest time. The day Dad was at the station, I hadn't expected the apartment to feel *so* empty without him in it. Mom's been on the phone to lawyers for days. Dad is on bail, now back at the apartment, with the following conditions:

1) A tracking anklet to remain on him at all times
2) A curfew to be home (at his apartment) by 10 p.m. every day
3) He must sleep in his apartment (no other place) every day

4) He must check in with Chloe at the station once a week
5) His passport in police possession so he doesn't leave the country
6) All for three months

The police told Mom they released Dad on pre-charge bail 'to allow for further enquiries'. Ani told me that means they will still keep Dad under investigation while they're looking for more evidence, which will hopefully come to light soon to reveal the true murderer.

It's midday and Dad hasn't left his room. Mom gave me and Ani a hushed order to leave him be, so we've been trying hard to do just that. Mom left his breakfast – bought from a local bakery – outside his door. No one saw or heard him open the door to take it.

'To make sure Dad isn't framed for murder –' Ani looks like she's gonna have another Bleak Week – 'we need to get some concrete motives for our suspects.'

To be honest, I might have a Bleak Week too. I think of everything I know of Dad from mine and Mom's visits to Castlewick and how he has been during this vacation. He isn't a murderer. He's far from it, in fact. 'I wish we could simply magic all this away.'

'Riri, listen to yourself. There's no such thing as magic. The closest thing to magic is finding the real murderer's motive.'

'OK but how good would we be as sleuths –' Ani clears her throat – 'or *super*sleuths, if we didn't play devil's advocate?'

Ani grits her teeth. 'What are you suggesting?'

'I think you know.' I wince, despite myself. I might be

the worst daughter ever for saying this but at least I'd be a thorough SIT. 'Could Dad have done it?'

Ani glares at me but it soon crumbles into a sigh. 'I-I suppose we need to see what his motive could be. Because I know him better than you, let's see . . .' She paces and thinks. 'It could've been a crime of passion. Dad knows – *knew* – Mrs Kostas/Dimas's passwords for her phone, emails and CCTV cameras.'

'So . . . maybe they had a disagreement.'

Ani looks like she's tasted something bitter. 'No. No! He is gentle. Even when he's super angry, he doesn't hit things or people. He isn't like that. He never kills flies or spiders.'

'But accidents happen,' I whisper.

'Even if Dad *accidentally* killed her, he would've admitted it to the police.'

'You're right. Mom always said he honoured his word.'

'Stop talking about him in the past tense. Now, let's make some real progress.'

'Fine.' But I decide I could always just ask Dad. I have a feeling he'll open up to me because of the distance between us.

But I still wish we could magic all this away.

'The TUSC's robust investigation and my keen eye –' Ani starts.

'And my assistance.' I raise my hand.

'Fine, yes, your assistance. All of that has helped us possibly even beat the Castlewick Police's investigation.

Because we have a suspect list of three. The Clio Trio. Derek Chase, the vlogger who doesn't bother telling the resident supersleuth about his newest series. Fred Hunt, the wannabe screenwriter who is off the grid online. Mimi Bloodworth, the viral sensation who has yet to go viral or sensational.' Ani claps once. 'Derek's motive is the strongest, so let's start with him.'

'He's the silent-partner/part-owner of Cafe Vivlio. It's super plausible for him to want Mrs Dimas/Kostas out of the picture if, as we heard on LaShawn's recording, they couldn't agree. Derek said some nasty things.'

'You're learning, Riri. Well done. Now, Fred. He used to study and work at Columbia University as a professor. Maybe he knew her when she was your librarian and babysitter.'

'Columbia University is in New York and that's six hours away from California by plane.'

'Oh. Maybe they met online for some educational thing? Or maybe in a university chatroom or something?'

'Unlikely. Mrs Dimas was as un-tech-savvy as Mrs Kostas was. She could barely work the library computers.'

'Maybe she was faking it?'

I shake my head. 'Speculation. How would we prove that?'

'OK, never mind that then. She hand-wrote all her Instagram captions and Derek typed them, anyway. Fred did say he left the university to become a full-time screenwriter. Obviously that didn't work well because he still hasn't sold a script. What if he moved to California to try and make it in Hollywood?'

'There's a possibility.'

'But they acted like they didn't know each other at Cafe Vivlio.'

'. . . Well maybe that was part of the plan. To cover up their paths crossing.'

'What for? Fred definitely isn't an art thief on the run – he's clumsy even when no one's looking. Why would he keep her secret? Fred might take bribe money. Riri, you'll get a sixth sense about people when – or if – you become a sleuth. Mine is tingling.'

'Bribe money isn't enough. Maybe Mrs Dimas/Kostas didn't want Fred to reveal that he knew her under a different name with a different accent and a different backstory, so they ignored each other.'

'Wouldn't he get a reward for turning her in?'

'In the article –' I remember – 'Anastasia had dual-citizenship. She was American-born but lived in Greece. The statute of limitations for her art crimes would surely be over, thirty years on –'

'So, no reward money from the FBI?'

'No reward money from the FBI. Legally, if she came out with a memoir or interview, she can't be tried for her crimes.'

'Then why would she stay on the run?' Ani wonders. 'Seems like hard work.'

'Once on the run, always on the run? Maybe she realised that she'd come so far on the run so would ride it all out.'

'Maybe. Let's not forget about Detective Larsson's murder.'

I nod. 'There's nothing online to say that Anastasia was a suspect for Larsson's murder, *but* it might be that she stayed on the run because she killed him.'

'Or maybe she stayed on the run because she was afraid of being blamed for his murder,' Ani adds, and I agree.

I remember something. 'Anastasia was notorious – she'd never live a nice quiet life in Greece after coming out of hiding. Enemies might crawl out of the woodwork.'

Ani strokes her chin in thought. 'But Fred could've known the real story all along. And he wanted to kill her to bring her story full circle – her life in crime, life on the run then death. *Inspired by True Events* – that was the name of his latest screenplay!'

'That's not a compelling title at all.'

'Agreed. But Fred isn't a compelling person.' I tell her that's mean and she replies, 'What? A fact is a fact. So, could we sum up Fred's motive as desperation?'

'Yes. Let's move onto Mimi. So, I was thinking –'

'Jealousy.' Ani cuts me off. 'What? It's obvious. Mrs Kostas wrote weekly captions on the very popular Cafe Vivlio Instagram account. In a day, her captions would get thousands of likes and hundreds of comments. Mimi has fewer followers on all her socials combined and how far would she go for fame? I mean, she dated Derek for online fame. How messed up is that? Plus, people buy accounts with loads of followers every day. Helin's sister told me.'

'So why wouldn't Mimi *buy* an account instead? I mean, if she killed Mrs Kostas and got caught then she'll be in prison, unable to enjoy her thousands of followers.'

'She'll still be sensationalised so it could be win-win either way. And Mimi isn't well off. She doesn't work, her parents don't talk to her. She thinks being on benefits will hurt her brand, which is silly – benefits saved me and Dad. She relies on freebies and scarce savings.'

'Won't the police notice that someone has taken the Cafe Vivlio Instagram page?'

'Nope. She can change the handle so it'll be like that account never existed. The cafe's followers might notice but do nothing other than unfollow. Most can't be bothered.'

'Yikes. Ani, this is wild. What a world we live in. First, Fred potentially killing Mrs Dimas/Kostas due to his desperation. Then, Mimi potentially doing so because she's jealous. What's next?' I go back to The Motive Board.

'What's next is Derek. I can't lie, SIT, but looking for Derek's motive puts me in a compromising position.'

'How so?'

'Well, I consider us chums. Now, I know you're head-over-heels in love with his brother and everything – not new information – but you'll have to lock up your heart and guess Derek's motive.'

'Can't you lock up your chumminess then? He did, after all, have an argument with Mrs Dimas/Kostas *the day before her murder*.'

Ani works her jaw and slits her eyes. 'Just do it. Consider it a SIT test.'

'OK. By the way, I'm not in *love* with Frankie.' I clear my throat, uneasy with all the Frankie talk. Why does she always have to bring him up?

'Yeah, yeah, keep telling yourself that. Now, let's put LaShawn's recording of the argument aside for a moment. Look at the facts. Derek is super famous. Well, for a vlogger

165

who isn't living in London, Los Angeles or New York. His content is anywhere from "A Day in The Life" to him discussing unsolved mysteries.'

'Isn't that confusing? What's his brand then? How does he know what his fans want?'

Ani shrugs. 'They're loyal enough to watch whatever he does. Their loyalty is the reason for him being experimental. *Or* he's experimental because of their loyalty. Personality wise, he's great. Friendly, fun, fashionable.'

'Ani, act like he's a stranger otherwise it's a conflict of interest. What else? What was his relationship like with Mrs Dimas/Kostas? Other than what we heard on that recording.'

'They were friendly. Derek treated Mrs Kostas with respect, like she was his grandmother.' Ani goes to her dresser and starts rummaging about. I watch her carefully pull apart a stick of mostly-melted string cheese. Before long, she makes a mess. With half of it on the floor, she offers me some. I decline, trying hard to ignore that her floor definitely has double the amount of dirt as the average floor. 'Of course, I need to reassess the Derek I thought I knew. Your thoughts?'

'Uh . . . Derek helped to boost Cafe Vivlio. He had a financial stake in the cafe and with its rising popularity, maybe he changed.'

'Yes, of course. A testament to his loyalty to it and her. Good job, SIT. I think we're ready to start questioning our suspects. Are you sure you don't want some string cheese? It's delicious.'

22

ANI

TUSC timestamp
19 days since murder
11 days since TUSC investigation
    launched
4 days since Dad got arrested

'OK, Riri, we're going to spend today getting all of our interrogations done on The Clio Trio. Don't be scared, OK? Yes, we'll be looking a murderer in the eye. Follow what I'm doing. In fact, sit there and don't talk. Make note of anything you find interesting but don't worry, we will be recording everything.'

Riri nods.

'Chloe implied that our investigation is silly. We'll prove her wrong.' I nod, more for myself than Riri. 'The aim is to not be too firm. If I go in too deep, pull me out, OK? I can be persistent when interrogating.'

Riri nods again.

Before I can walk out, Dad comes in. I turn silent and can't swallow away the lump in my throat. It's been four days since I last saw him. His hair is messy. He has dark purple circles under his tired eyes. His face is shadowed with facial hair. He *appears* small. 'Girls?' His voice is weak. I feel like crying.

'Dad, a-are you OK?' I ask, my voice also becoming weak.

He tries to smile but it's broken. 'I-I thought you both had gone, you know, outside.'

'Not yet,' Riri whispers. 'We were about to.'

'Oh.' Dad manages to smile this time but it doesn't reach his eyes. 'I was going to tidy up your room while you were gone. Ani, I did it for you every day.'

My chest aches as if my heart has just shattered. Tears well up in my eyes and my vision goes blurry. Before I can buckle over, I run over to Dad and hug him tight. He crouches down and hugs me back tighter. He really is the World's Best Hugger.

'I love you, Dad,' I say between sobs. I don't care that I'm wetting his hoodie with my tears. 'I'm sorry you're going through this. Thanks for always cleaning my messes. I'll fix the one you're in.'

'I love you too, Imani.' I swear, I feel a teardrop of his run down the back of my neck. He loosens his hold and turns slightly away. 'I love you, Noori.'

I nearly lose my footing when Riri joins the hug. 'Love

you too.' Her words are muffled. 'We know you didn't do this . . . Right?'

The tears dry from my eyes and I step away. Glare at Riri for being so insensitive.

'Imani, calm down,' Dad soothes. 'Noori, you have the right to question. But no. I would never hurt a fly. I was very fond of Mrs Kostas. Framed, I think I am.'

'I knew it!' I proclaim.

'But it's been tough.' Dad's words make me gloomy again. 'Please, patience with me. Girls, I hate for you to be seeing me like this.'

I continue hugging Dad until his phone rings and he disappears into his office. Then I look at Riri. She has red eyes. 'What are you waiting for?' I ask with the aim of uplifting both of us. 'Let's go find the real murderer.'

We've headed over to our outdoor location, the part of the park that's opposite Cafe Vivlio to meet our first suspect: Fred Hunt. Along the way, we pass people fanning themselves while eating ice-cream that dribbles down their arms. Wow, morning ice-cream. But there's no time – we're here now.

Flowers from the public line the cafe's exterior, nearly three weeks later. Police tape is still at the entrance. This is tough to look at.

'Supersleuth's log,' I say into my phone, removing my sunglasses. 'The time is 8 a.m. Two days ago, we finalised our suspect list. Due to family obligations –' I'm referring to

Mum taking us to Yorkshire Wildlife Park and then Jorvic Viking Centre the day after. She ignored my tantrums and protests against joining her and Riri for a 'good time'. It was unfair that Dad could stay home but I couldn't – 'we had to postpone our interrogations. The discovery of the victim's body was made about two hours after the assumed time of death, to be exact.'

'That's not exact,' Riri whispers to me. 'Not if you can't give a specific number of hours after the body was discovered.'

All I can do is sigh at her and roll my eyes to the bright blue sky. I continue, 'Fred, you're being recorded. Do you understand that?'

'Yes, but that doesn't mean I consent to it.'

I kiss my teeth. Glare at him. 'Why? You hiding something?'

'No!'

'Then let me record you.'

He huffs. 'Fine.'

I clear my throat. 'I am here with one of the three regulars who were at the cafe at the time of the incident –'

'That's me, Mimi and Derek. Right, Ani?' Fred asks. He's already sweating buckets and the sun isn't even at its hottest yet. He knows he's about to be interrogated by a masterful sleuth. 'You're a regular at Cafe Vivlio too. And you discovered Mrs Kostas's body.' He motions to the closed cafe, police tape flapping along the perimeter.

I smirk. 'I'm not including myself as a suspect because that would be a conflict of interest, don't you think?'

Riri sniggers at that. 'Good one.'

'Thanks. Now, developments in the case are unfortunate –'

'It's so sad, isn't it, about your dad?' Fred says. 'I don't believe he did it.'

I slit my eyes. He's trying to build a rapport with his interrogator but I'm no fool. 'Fred, this'll be harder than it needs to be unless you answer honestly.'

'You do know I'm not legally obliged to be sitting in this park at your mercy, don't you?'

With gritted teeth, I say, 'I'm trying to save my dad.'

'Let the police do it.'

'No! Because Mrs Kostas meant something to me and I have to try my best here. And obviously my dad is innocent and I have to prove that. Give me a chance.'

'Yeah!' Riri adds. Her nose is red. 'And if you don't tell us anything but lies then that means you're hiding something.' She sneezes.

'Riri, pipe down now. And did you take your antihistamine?' She shakes her head. There's no time for this so I turn back to our suspect. 'Fred, tell us what we want to know we can eliminate you from our list of suspects. That's all. Don't make me get out my little pot of black powder, white paper, sewing measuring tape and magnifying glass,' I threaten, remembering my unused sleuthing tools.

'That's good,' Riri tells me. Nods at me like she's grading a test. Like *she's* the Director of the TUSC and I'm a SIT. Pfft.

'Fine, whatever,' Fred mutters to himself. 'I've already said all this to the police but what do you want to know?'

'We've pinpointed that Mrs Kostas –'

'RIP,' Riri whispers.

'RIP,' Fred echoes. He looks overly sad.

I work my jaw. 'RIP. We've pinpointed that the time of death was roughly 4.30 p.m. the day she was found. I have confirmation that you were at Cafe Vivlio between 4 p.m. and 6 p.m. Tell me everything you did within that timeframe. Spare no detail.'

Thirty minutes later, I'm brain dead. He doesn't stop talking. Spares *literally* no detail. Talks about how he spent two and a half hours on one scene for his latest screenplay. Apparently he barely noticed the time go by. 'I don't need to know about your toilet breaks.'

'Toilet breaks might be a diversion for when he did the deed!' Riri whispers to me.

'Oh yeah.' Under my guidance, she's getting good. 'Fred, do you remember who else was in Cafe Vivlio at the alleged time of death?'

'Around 4.30 p.m.? Yes, only because I had to remember hard for the police interrogation. That left me, Derek and Mimi inside. Rodolfo had gone out for a smoke break. Quiet day.'

Riri tugs my sleeve like a lost child. I widen my eyes at her, hoping to scare her. 'Why didn't we see Rodolfo on the CCTV footage? If he came out, the doorframe camera should've shown us him?' she whispers.

That's a good point indeed. I whisper back, 'We'll have to question Rodolfo and see what he says. The smoke break could've been a smoke*screen* for him to kill Mrs Kostas.'

'Uh, excuse me?' Fred snaps.

'Shush, Fred,' I snap back. 'In this interrogation, you listen to us, OK? Now, do you remember anything else when Rodolfo was out?'

'Not much. Same as I told the police. Me, Mimi and Fred don't even talk to each other. I would say we've got nothing in common but we've never spoken long enough to find out.'

'Huh, OK.' He's kinda got a point, based on what I know they'd be an unlikely trio of friends. Bar the slight similarities of their career paths – a vlogger, a wannabe influencer and an aspiring screenwriter – they don't share the same interests and their personalities are so dissimilar they're incompatible. Even when Derek and Mimi went out, I heard there wasn't a lot of small talk that wasn't shop talk.

I show Fred a rough sketch of our timeline and he verifies it. We need to add in his toilet breaks. 'Where were you born, Fred?'

'Sh-uh-Sheffield. Why?'

'No reason. Where was Mrs Kostas born?'

'. . . Athens, I think.'

'Did you know Mrs Kostas by any other name?'

'She never let me call her by her first name, that's for sure.'

I exchange a curious look with Riri. 'Fred, can you answer the question?'

Fred pauses, all pale with a wrinkled forehead. 'I –'

I repeat the question. He's clearly hiding something. In my peripheral vision, I see Riri eagerly jotting down notes.

Fred still doesn't say anything. But he does fidget about.

'Fred –' I say, smoothly – 'I know of her by at least two other names now. Did you too?' An interrogation technique

I've learned from crime shows I'm too young to watch is to show the suspect your soft side. Make them think what they're about to say is all right.

Fred finally caves in. He keeps dipping his head in a weird nod like it's repeating on a broken loop. 'Yes. Fine. I knew who she really was. Anastasia Dimas, art thief on-the-run.'

'Fred, we have reason to believe that your motive for killing Mrs Kostas was to write a killer – excuse the pun – screenplay. Finally get your big break. What do you think?'

He grimaces. 'Very creative but *no*. I know I've said I'd do anything for my big break but not that. What kind of a person do you think I am?'

'Well, you're in debt, Fred. I heard you telling my dad. And apparently you know Mrs Kostas's real identity. That's an expensive secret and yet you've only written a school play. You want to write award-winning indie movies and Hollywood blockbusters. Fair to say you have big dreams. You've been trying so hard for years and it hasn't been paying off.'

Fred pouts. 'Look, I was inside the cafe between the times you said. I swear. I didn't kill Mrs Kostas.'

'How can you prove that? Don't answer that – it's a hypothermic question.'

'Hypothetical question,' Riri obnoxiously corrects in a whisper. What's her problem?

I focus on Fred. 'Prove it by going to the properties of the folder where your most recent screenplay is saved. "Previous versions" will show us if you made any progress fifteen days ago, at the date and time of the murder. You could've had it open but not typed a word. You know, while you were off *murdering* Mrs Kostas.'

'That could check out,' Riri says, 'because you mentioned that he's a slow writer.'

'See? I know him – we were friendly before. Now talk, Fred, tell us everything.'

'No!' he shouts. 'I don't owe you anything. I'm entitled to my privacy!'

'OK, fine.' I hold up one hand and put down a finger as I count up the facts. 'Fred, here are the facts: one, Mrs Kostas was found dead in The Secret Garden. Two, it looks like she was pushed to her death. Three, she didn't really like you.' Of course, we'll get the actual cause of death when the autopsy report is done – but that'll take weeks or even months.

'That's mean,' he mumbles.

'Well, it's true. Four, the only way to The Secret Garden is through Cafe Vivlio and you're one of the only people who knows that. Five, you knew who she really was.'

'. . . So what? That is all coincidental, because I didn't kill her!'

I lean forward. 'Did she know that you knew who she really was?'

'No.' He's more animated now. 'No, she did not.'

I don't believe him. 'Out of curiosity, who would you kill for?'

'Hypothetically.' Riri adds with a shaky voice.

'My grandma or my mum.' But Fred's never, ever mentioned any family.

'OK, thank you for your time.' I stand. So does Riri.

'Ani, are you thinking what I'm thinking?'

'That he told Mrs Kostas/Dimas that he knew she was an international art thief and bribed her? Yep.'

We head to the next stop.

'Mimi lives close by,' I say as I speed-walk over the cobblestones. The sun burns down on us. My sunglasses slide down my nose. 'Try to keep up!' I chide Riri. 'So far, we've got Derek's compromising audio recording and Dad's DNA tying him to the crime scene. We can't eliminate Fred from our suspect list. He's acting too weird and he knows about Mrs Kostas's secret past. It's not enough to go on . . . yet. What will we find from Mimi?'

I march toward a little cottage-like house.

'Wow,' Riri whispers. 'This looks like a smaller version of Barbie's Dreamhouse.'

I sigh. 'What did I say about being objective?'

'What? I can't admire her house?'

'No! Because then you're going to be lenient with her in the TUSC notes. Like, "Oh, the suspect with the nice house totally killed the victim but I'll disregard that because her rug is awesome".' I ring the doorbell. 'You're questioning her, by the way. Let's throw you in the deep end and see what you've got.'

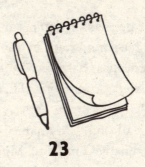

23

RIRI

The door opens and we see Mimi again. I look behind her, confirming that the rug in the foyer is indeed awesome. A tripod on the rug supports her phone. Based on Ani's TUSC profile, I'm guessing that Mimi was filming a TikTok video.

'Hi, girls.' Mimi has a nice, friendly smile. The décor is straight out of a fairy-tale – Mom would love it. Maybe when all of this is over we could show Mom the interior designs. 'How sad is the news about your dad?'

'Not that sad, if you were filming a video,' Ani utters under her breath. She also isn't smiling. For that, I un-smile.

'It's so sad to lose a family member. My uncle – well, I was pretty young when he was killed – but it devastated my whole family.' Mimi shakes her head then tries to smile. 'I find it so sweet that your family has reunited. I think –'

Ani holds up a card that acts as her TUSC credentials, which is a library card covered over and with her picture stuck on.

Mimi's smile falters as she squints at Ani's card. 'Oh. Are you trying to solve the mystery of Mrs K's murder?'

'Yes,' Ani abruptly says.

Mimi's eyes wander over to me. 'Hi. I'm so sorry, I didn't get your name.'

I give her a small smile. 'My name is Riri.'

'Oh, I love that name! I'm Mimi. Mimi, Riri.' She giggles. I giggle back, something I didn't know that I could do. Human beings, it turns out, can change.

'Can we come in?' Ani grumpily asks.

'I thought I'm supposed to be asking the questions here,' I tell her through gritted teeth.

'If you can wipe the drool off your chin, then by all means.'

Shaking my head at Ani's silliness, I follow Mimi into the house, Ani behind me.

The house's interior is quirky. It's a mix of neon and furry fabrics, with horseback riding influences – there are a few horseshoes hanging on the wall, and some pictures of a younger Mimi posing with a horse in front of the brightest greenery. I've always wanted to ride a horse. The entire house smells of vanilla and oranges. It's beautiful!

Well, except for the hole in the middle of the floor.

'Uh, Mimi?' I ask. 'What's with – uh that?' I point at a glass vase with detailed overglazed decorations painted on it, positioned on a stand above the hole in the floor.

Mimi groans. 'Oh, is it that obvious? I thought covering it with the vase would hide it. Basically I was dancing with some friends on a creaky floorboard. It was the worst night ever because then there was a leak and next thing I know, there's a hole in the floor! It'll be fixed soon. Well, I hope so. I drilled some feet over the hole so the vase can hide it, just in case.'

'Oh.' What else can I say?

'So, how can I help you girlies?' Mimi motions for us to sit on her pink furry sofa. She sits opposite us, on a neon green armchair.

I clear my throat. 'Mimi, can we ask you a couple of questions about Mrs Kostas?'

'Of course. Anything to help. Sorry again about your dad.'

Ani turns to face me, giving me my cue, which is off-putting but I power through and tell Mimi, 'We have some routine questions to ask.'

'Fire away.'

'First, please be aware that you are being recorded.'

'Anything for the TUSC,' Mimi says. 'By the way, I love the accent.' I don't mean to, but I blush at that. I try to control myself from full-on fangirling over her.

'What did you think of Mrs Kostas? Like, how was your relationship?'

'Aw, Mrs K was the best. She gave me a casual contract to work at the cafe last summer. Big help for me to get some extra cash.'

Ani says, 'You only did about five shifts though, right?'

'Six. She was the sweetest; she knew I was struggling financially and she offered.'

I ask, 'So why weren't you called to cover when the baristas were off sick?'

She winces. 'Because I quit. Unavailability. No animosity.

179

I just need more time to upload and edit my pictures and videos.'

'Where were you between around 4 p.m. and 6.30 p.m. nineteen days ago?'

'Nineteen days ago?'

Ani answers, 'The day of the murder. We're going to solve the murder and save Dad.'

'Go, girls! So first, I went to the cafe for my morning coffee, at around 9 a.m. It was so busy. Then, after a whole day of shooting, I went back there to have a late lunch. Probably around 3.30 p.m. I stayed until around 5 p.m.'

'Then you went back for the third time that day, coinciding with me and Riri. That's why you said to Rodolfo, "*See you, Rodolfo. Maybe for the fourth time today.*"'

'Yes! What a day – I was so exhausted that I went to Cafe Vivlio *again*. This time to get a green tea latte, something to calm me down. That was just after 6 p.m. I finished my drink quickly then dashed out. After that, I returned.'

'Returned from where?'

'The newsagents next door to the cafe. I picked up a magazine subscription.'

I revisit my memories of when I first met Mimi. It wasn't long after meeting Derek and Frankie. 'But you weren't carrying anything in your hands,' I remember.

'Right. It's because I forgot my purse. I needed to transfer money from the card in my purse to the card on my phone. That's why I went back to the cafe. What a faff! Derek's footage will show me going in and coming out of the

180

newsagents. Thank goodness he vlogs *everything*. Do you know how many boring days he's vlogged where he's done nothing?'

Ani chuckles. 'Yep.'

I shake my head and say to Mimi, 'But Derek was facing the window inside the cafe during his live vlog.'

Mimi presses her lips into a thin line. 'Not his vlog. I'm talking about the videos he records on his phone in his other hand. Don't ask me why he does it – "for posterity", or something. But I'm definitely in that shot when I was out of the cafe before I saw him enter.'

'OK.' Ani takes over my questioning. 'Did you pay on cash or card?'

'Card.'

I try to catch Ani's gaze of steel. She's cornering Mimi with her words so I'm gonna take over. I think I know what Ani's trying to get out of Mimi. 'Mimi, would you mind showing us the time that you paid for the magazine? From there, we can amend our timeline.'

'Sure.' Mimi unlocks her phone.

'No, Riri, wrong question,' Ani says. I raise my eyebrows, confused. I was certain it was the right one. 'Mimi, can you tell us the time that your first attempt of payment *failed*?'

Ohh, I see my questioning fault. Hats off to Ani because that's ingenious.

Mimi scrolls. 'Here . . . the attempted payment was at 6.13 p.m. Then, I tried again at 6.15 p.m.'

'How about at specifically 4.30 p.m. that day?'

Mimi smiles at us both, her pearly-white teeth gleaming.

'I was editing some clips on the most amazing app ever, SparxPix.'

'Prove it,' Ani challenges, sounding rather friendly.

'I'll do just that.' Again, Mimi unlocks her phone. And she proves herself, yet again. Mimi chuckles at me and Ani. 'You two are prying hard. No stone unturned. I like it.'

'It's a formality.' It sounds like Ani is well practised with the textbook things to say in these situations.

'So, you're questioning the others?'

'Who exactly are the others?' I ask her. Of course, I know who "the others" are – I just want to hear who they are to her. Even Ani looks impressed as she turns her lips downwards at me. Maybe I am meant to be a sleuth, after all.

'Oh, you know. Me, Derek and Fred. The police asked me who was in the cafe between 3 p.m. and 5 p.m. I'm pretty sure I remember it being only me, Fred and Derek. Rodolfo had gone out for a quick smoke break but was otherwise busy in the kitchens and at the counter. I only remember who was there then because it was unusually quiet in the cafe.'

'Did you ever get your purse back?' I ask. 'When you came back in after leaving.'

She smiles and blushes. 'Yes . . . Derek helped me find it after you two left.' Looking down, she bites her lip. Then, she lets out a lovey-dovey breath. 'We might still be in love.'

'Oh. Congratulations?'

'Well, I don't know for sure. Nothing's ever plain and simple with Derek.'

I smile then look over at Ani. 'Is that all?' I discreetly ask her. (Well, as discreetly as I can be).

'Quickfire round. Then motive,' Ani whispers back.

'Oh yeah,' I say. 'Where were you born, Mimi?'

'London.' She looks and sounds like she's giving a television interview as if she's a famous person.

'True or false: Mrs Kostas was born in Athens.'

'True. Love Athens. I want to go some day.'

'Did you know Mrs Kostas by any other name?'

'Other names?' She does another nervous giggle. I don't know why but I echo the giggle again. Ani sharply clears her throat at me. 'I don't know. Polly? She never let me call her that. It was nice though, made me feel like a child again.'

'Out of curiosity, Mimi, who would you kill for? You know, to protect. If you were hypothetically in that position.'

'Oh, intense question. My family, for sure.'

'Right. And-we-so . . . we were thinking about . . . well, a couple of –'

Ani covers my mouth with her cold hand. It smells of bubblegum. 'Mimi, we have reason to believe that your motive for killing Mrs Kostas –' Mimi gasps – 'is for you to become a viral sensation that lives forever on the internet.'

I carefully watch Mimi's emotions and by our accusation alone, she's upset.

'Not to mention the fact that your videos are not going viral and that you desperately want to be famous,' Ani adds. 'And Mrs Kostas's social media accounts for Cafe Vivlio had way more likes and followers than any of yours.'

Mimi kicks us out of her house, citing outrage at our accusations as her reasoning.

As we're walking on the street, Ani sniggers. 'Well, that was eventful. Let's interrogate our last suspect.' She leads the way.

'Our last suspect out of The Clio Trio,' I whisper when she's out of earshot.

I just know we're going to prison before we've even solved this case. How? Well, Ani is practically begging for someone to see us and call the police because she's *publicly damaging* Derek's window!

'Ani!' I hiss with wide eyes. Holding her wrists, I try to shake the pebbles free from her hands. 'You can't throw pebbles at his window!'

'I can too. Derek says he's a deep sleeper and it's the only way to wake him.' Ani blows in my face. Cool, bubblegum-flavoured air throws me off-kilter – I let go of her wrists.

She throws one pebble at Derek's window. Then another. One more before it works.

'What-what-what, yarr?' Derek hollers, pointedly looking down from his window at Ani. 'You do know that I have to get my beauty sleep, don't you?'

'Derek, Toby broke up with you because of your vanity, remember,' Ani reminds him. My mouth widens at her cheekiness. 'People don't like vanity.'

Derek scrunches his face up at Ani. 'Yarr, why are you always in my business?'

Their weird big-brother-little-sister bond is a peculiar one, but it's both entertaining and heart-warming to watch. They're definitely solid with each other.

She smiles at him. 'I'm about to get even further in your business. Let us in?'

'Fine, whatever. First, let's clear the air. I didn't tell you about my new series because I wanted to surprise you. You're gonna be the guest-of-honour of the first ever episode, yarr.'

Ani's eyes show that she wants to jump up and down at that. Instead, she nods once, keeping her cool. 'I always knew you were one of the real ones. Now, let us in!'

He mutters something under his breath then shuts the window. Next thing we know, he opens the door. I find it hilarious that he doesn't wait for us to enter – he's already past the foyer while we've barely set foot in his home. I look around, taking in the guitars hanging on the walls and the framed vinyl records. Why does Derek have the house of a rockstar? I have to clamp my mouth shut at the spiral staircase. *Wow, two loops like a rollercoaster!*

'So, how are we gonna do this?' I ask Ani as we walk in sync through the foyer. The house smells of his cologne that is a combination of vanilla and tobacco.

'It takes a while to get used to the smell,' Ani says, and I realise that she can see my nose wrinkling.

She raises her eyebrows at me as if she's wondering where I got the audacity to ask that question. '*We* are doing nothing. I'll be questioning Derek. You keep your trap shut.'

'Why? I did great with Mimi.'

'Frankie stays over at Derek's house in the summer. He

185

might arrive mid-questioning and I can't have you losing your cool. Like you did with Mimi.'

I blow out a breath – I kind of did, but it was my first interrogation so she should cut me some slack – and look around so I'm nonchalantly looking at my reflection in the mirror in Derek's kitchen. My reflection tells me to smooth out the crinkles at the top of my hijab, but other than that, I don't look so bad. On another note, why does Derek have a mirror in his kitchen? 'Fine.' I follow her through the foyer, ignoring the fact that Ani is familiar inside Derek's house. It makes me so jealous, how close she is with people in Castlewick. In California, people are nice but we're not that close. Maybe it's because it's bigger or just the way most of us are. Without a doubt, me and Ani have lived opposite lives. I wonder how that's shaped us into who we are today.

'Derek, Derek, Derek.' Ani sounds disappointed as she looks around his kitchen. She opens the fridge and reaches for the mango juice. I wish she offered me one. But then she slides something over to me that's wrapped in a paper towel. The smell – cumin – gives it away – jeera biscuits! I grin at her and take a few bites.

'What, Ani? You and your twin think I killed Mrs Kostas? Yarr, do I even have the guts to kill someone? Seriously, do I? You tell me.'

Ani shrugs. 'It's always the ones you least expect, isn't it?'

'Fine. Then you owe me for the mango juice.' Derek glances at me and then at the crumbs of my jeera biscuits. 'And you owe me for the crumbs. Another thing – can you control Ani? I'm weirded out by your kid sister acting so familiar in my crib.' Ani rolls her eyes. On the way over here, she mentioned she'd be overly friendly with Derek so he wouldn't suspect her accusations. Basically, Ani's supposed to be good cop and I'm bad cop. She said she wants Derek to feel the betrayal Mrs Dimas/Kostas would've felt during the argument.

'Can we talk business now?' I ask.

Derek motions for me to hang on while he puts a couple of ingredients in his blender. He's standing at the island in the middle of his huge kitchen. 'Protein shake. Great for the bones.'

'Stop stalling,' Ani snaps, standing opposite him at the island. I slowly walk over to be beside her. 'How did you know what we were coming here to accuse you of?'

'Mimi texted me.'

'Why would Mimi text you?' Ani asks. 'You're not together anymore.'

Derek shrugs and sips his shake for a suspiciously long time. Me and Ani both watch him, waiting for his answer. 'We had a nice chat while I was helping her find her purse that day. Since then, we've been talking like friends.'

Ani is glaring at Derek. Clearly she doesn't think Derek with Mimi will make a good couple. I have no opinion.

I say, 'Who do you remember being in the cafe on the day of the murder at 4.30 p.m.?'

Derek looks up as he recalls: 'Me, Fred, Mimi and Rodolfo. But Rodolfo left at that time to take a quick smoke break.'

Ani looks suspicious. 'Derek, can we see the footage from

your live vlog and your other video on the day Mrs Kostas was murdered?'

'Oh, you know about my posterity shots? Long after I'm gone, those'll be sold at auctions, yarr. Timestamped and dated.'

'*Motive?*' me and Ani mouth to each other, synchronously. Greed indeed.

'Like behind-the-scenes of my live videos as I film a couple of scenes to know which to cut,' he explains despite us not asking.

I frown. 'Doesn't that imply that they're planned? I thought lives are supposed to be, you know, unplanned . . .'

Derek gives me a funny look. 'California, don't overstep.'

I look over at Ani, unsure if Derek's joking or not.

Ani chuckles. 'Can we watch them? And try not to scare "California".'

'My name is Riri,' I say.

Now, it's Derek who chuckles. 'Yarr, there's only one Riri and that ain't you.'

'Just show us the videos.'

Wordlessly Derek leads us on his huge leather sofa to show us them.

Ani says, 'Fred can be seen typing on his laptop through the window. He doesn't do email because he's weird. That typing energy doesn't look like research so it's safe to say he was writing his screenplay.' She curses. 'Would it have killed Fred to have told us that?! Why does he have to be so complicated?'

'Well, Mimi told the truth.' I point to the paused shot of

her focused on her phone. She was on SparxPix, editing. 'No sign of Rodolfo leaving to have his smoke break, though.'

'Hmm.' Ani thinks. Me and Derek look at her, expectantly. 'Your videos stop at –' she squints, focusing on the timestamp – '4.29.59 p.m. That is one second away from 4.30 p.m., so the murder might've happened without any preparation.'

'Or remorse,' I add. 'But we knew about Derek entering the cafe within the minute.'

'And the time of death is allegedly 4.30 p.m. – other things could've happened. It could've stopped working or lost connection. Maybe the battery died. It was off when I you-know-what.' She refers to when she removed Mrs Dimas/Kostas's Apple Watch from her body.

I sigh. 'So, we're back to square one.'

'Because any of the three could've done it. How long does it take to push someone down a hillock? It can't be very long.'

Derek is busy scrolling and double-tapping on his phone. He literally looks so preoccupied that I'm certain he didn't hear anything we said.

Ani whistles at him and he frowns, stubbornly. 'Where were you born, Derek?'

'On this street.'

'Did Mrs Kostas tell you where she was born?'

'Athens. But, listen to this, I went on holiday to Greece last year, do you remember?'

Ani thinks for a beat. 'Oh yeah. With Toby, right?'

'Yeah, I was going to do some modelling for this Grecian

fashion brand, no big deal. Their headquarters is at Alexandroupolis, right? She told me she was born there. Then I told her I thought it was Athens and she quickly corrected herself.'

Ani and I exchange a glance. *Interesting*. So, she sometimes mixed up her aliases.

'Why did you come back to Cafe Vivlio that day? Twice in one day is a lot for a busy person like you,' Ani says.

'Yarr, can we plead the Fifth in the UK?'

'Nope. Now spill.'

Derek spends an alarming amount of time humming and hawing before admitting, 'My live vlog didn't upload. So . . . I rerecorded it.'

Ani frowns so hard that it turns into a glare. 'You *rerecorded* a *live* video?'

Derek takes another sip of his protein shake. He's clearly stalling. Does that mean he's hiding a big, bad truth? Groaning, he said, 'I – not all of my lives are live. I . . . prerecord them and there's a mirror recording the recorded video when I go live. I-it's getting too much. I can't always be live for my viewers. Life, you know.' He rubs his face.

'I've lost a lot of respect for you now,' Ani admits. 'How did you become a silent partner for Cafe Vivlio?'

He visibly freezes at that information. 'How – what makes you think that?'

'Maybe be careful when you're arguing over secret things in public,' I suggest.

'Riri, let me handle this.' Ani turns to Derek, glaring. 'You were silent partners with Mrs Kostas for Cafe Vivlio and we have audio of you arguing with her the day before she died. You were so mean! Explain that! And tell the truth, unlike your inauthentic vlogs, otherwise I'll give the audio to the Police Sergeant.'

'Calm down, Ani, geez! We were just talking shop. Nothing wrong with business partners disagreeing and losing tempers. If anything, it's normal.'

'So, you admit that you are – were – Mrs Kostas's silent partner?'

'Oh yeah, so as my viewership was growing, people came from all over to see the place where DerekChasesThe-Globe gets his daily coffee from, yeah? Because I was responsible for the growing tourism at the cafe, I asked Mrs Kostas about owning half of it.'

'How did that conversation go?' I ask. 'And how long ago was it?'

'It went well. In fact, she seemed relieved. And, California, I became her silent partner – officially – about six months ago.'

'Did you know Mrs Kostas by any other name?' Ani asks.

He chews his lip in thought. 'She might've mentioned that her old surname was Dimas.' My eyes widen. She was close with Derek then. 'Can't remember if it was her maiden name or her ex-husband's name.'

'Talk to us about that argument, yarr. And if you don't remember, I can play it.'

Derek licks his lips then clenches his jaw. 'Ani, I remember what I said. I have a great memory. What's there to know? It was between two business partners. Sure, harsh things were said, but I can't go back in time.'

'If you could –' I speak slowly – 'would you?'

'Yes.' He swallows. 'Yes, I would. It was about opening up a Cafe Vivlio branch in London. I even spoke to a team there who were happy to manage it –'

'Without her permission?' I ask.

'Ugh, no wonder you got burnt with her words,' Ani utters.

'That's true.' I look at Derek. 'But what are the chances that you talk about Mrs Kostas's death the day before she's murdered?'

'I'm not a gambling man but I'd say that's a one-in-a-million chance and obviously not the good kind.' Derek's voice sounds firmer. 'I shouldn't have said it.'

Ani looks at me. She mouths something so fast I miss it.

'What?' I mouth back.

She sighs before mouthing it again, faster than before.

'Ani, just say it normally, *please*.'

'So, you're a speed-reader but not a mouth reader? I said, "I think we're done here."'

'Cool. Can you two get out now?' Derek finishes his protein shake. 'Might have some company coming round.'

'Not yet, yarr.' Ani changes her tactic. 'Now I remember what I was going to say. Out of curiosity, who would you kill for? You know, to protect.'

'My followers.'

'Ugh, you're so cheesy. You're aware we were voice recording all this, right?'

He clicks his tongue. 'I'm most comfortable being

recorded. That's where I live. Yo, what else is new?'

'What's new is your motive for killing Mrs Kostas,' Ani smoothly says. 'There's so much information from that recorded argument. Your threats, mentioning her death, abusing your role as a silent partner – should I go on?'

Derek looks like he's trying to find the punchline. 'Uh-uh. Don't be accusing me in my own crib.'

'Then come out in the street. Because there's a whole law about this. The Partnership Act 1890. Dead partner means dead partnership. But that's not what you said in the recording. You thought you'd get full ownership upon her death. But you won't. Instead, it'll be the beneficiary or beneficiaries of her will. Unless you had a written formal agreement. Did you?' Derek briefly looks panicked.

Then I loudly accuse, 'That would make for a great first episode of your unsolved mystery series!'

Derek laughs us all the way out of his house.

'This is almost conclusive,' Ani says. I can hear the dry grass crunch beneath her feet. The warm air whistles and messes up her hair. The strong smell of wildflowers greets my nostrils, making me sneeze.

'Almost?'

'Let's dig deeper in Fred's alibi first. Then Derek's.'

'Why Derek second? He's the silent partner *and* we have the audio of the fight!'

'I'd like to think that the police can easily find out he was Mrs Kostas's silent partner. That makes him the biggest suspect. That's too obvious and I have a hunch about him.'

I tilt my head. 'Are you sure you aren't fixating on Fred because you're friendly with Derek and Mimi and you *don't* want it to be either of them?'

Ani glowers at me. 'No! I'm trying to be unbiased here. I have a hunch about Fred. It's in my gut.'

'Fine, then what about Mimi?'

'Inconclusive. The call log and online banking check out. But you can manipulate timestamps on some phones.'

'Have you ever heard that story about her uncle before?'

Ani bites her thumbnail. '. . . I don't think so.'

'She sounded like she wanted to talk more about it. You cut her off when you showed her your credentials. Should we go back? Maybe we should apologise to her as well.'

Ani gives me a long look. 'You just want to go back to her house, don't you? For shame, Riri – you were just trying to paint me as a biased supersleuth a minute ago. There's no room for favourites in a murder investigation.'

I roll my eyes, wondering how she can sometimes be spot-on and sometimes so laughably off-target. 'Are you saying it's nothing?'

'Everything is something, Riri.' I don't realise that she's ringing Mimi until she puts it on speakerphone. 'Hi, Mimi. TUSC Director, Ani Tariq here.'

Mimi sounds sad, 'To what do I owe the pleasure again?'

'We're sorry –' I quickly say, before Ani makes it worse – 'for our behaviour.'

Mimi's quiet for a few long seconds before she answers. 'It's all right. What's up?'

'My associate wants to express her condolences about what happened to your uncle.'

'Aw, thank you.'

'So . . .' I say. 'What happened?'

Mimi lets out a shaky breath that crackles through the phone. 'My uncle's death was a shock. Everyone coped in their own ways. We used to be rich, but my childless aunt drove herself mad and bankrupt trying to find the truth and it ruined my dad to watch her do that. Then my dad drank to cope with all the responsibilities. He ran away, leaving just me and Mum. She spent what was left of our money on parties, clothes and cars. We fell out and I wish I could have the reunion you're having. I hope I become famous. Maybe that will give me and my mum a reunion too. Until then, I'll keep wearing this necklace to remember my family, the good and the bad.'

I remember her amethyst necklace. 'I'm sorry.' I thought we had it bad in our family, but that's nothing compared to what Mimi's been through.

'Oh, it's OK,' Mimi says, although she sounds emotional, sniffing a few times. 'It was nice telling you both. Is there anything else?'

'No.' Ani hangs up. She tells me, 'We're far from closing this case but at least the interrogations are leaving us further from nothing.' I've realised that she's got a signature focus face – eyebrows knitted down, lips moving but no words coming out, eyes looking off into the distance. I watch Ani walk in front of me and follow with a small smile on my face, appreciating and amazed by her.

24

ANI

'All this chatter about Rodolfo's smoke break is bugging me,' I admit to Riri as we walk through the warm streets. Since Mrs Kostas/Dimas's murder, everyone's been afraid to go outside. But the sun still shines and sunflowers are around, so there's that. My T-shirt and shorts are sequined, sparkling in the sunlight. 'We shouldn't have been so dependent on the CCTV of those entering *and* leaving – we forgot to consider who was *already inside* the cafe.'

'How so?' Riri fails to catch up with my quick strides. It's funny watching her try.

'Well, it wasn't mentioned by Fred. Only by Mimi and Derek.'

'Oh, that's true. Similar phrasing as well – "quick smoke break". Rehearsed together, maybe? The Clio Trio could be working together to tell that lie. To throw us off their scent. Maybe they're covering up the murder together.'

'Good work, Riri. It's possible. And Mimi texted Derek

about our interrogations.' I stop walking. Tilt my head sunward. A butterfly of confusion flutters in my stomach. A real butterfly flies around my face too. I waft it away. 'But how does it have anything to do with Rodolfo?'

Riri answers, 'Rodolfo's motive is that he didn't want to be replaced. Mrs Kostas/Dimas wanted to hire another chef and they weren't getting on.' She fiddles with the sleeves of her dress.

'We can ask Rodolfo about that. So, he's officially a TUSC suspect in this investigation.'

I find a bench and start scribbling. I say, 'We'll put this on The Motive Board later.'

MOTIVES	
Rodolfo Espinoza	
DESPERATION	**LOVE/OBSESSION**
Desperate to keep his job with 12-hour shifts 7 days a week – for money? Or maybe loneliness	Loves being a chef? Obsessed with work?
JEALOUSY	**REVENGE**
Jealous that another chef would get the praise he gets from Cafe Vivlio's customers	Revenge for Mrs Kostas/Dimas putting up the chef vacancy?
GREED	**CRIME OF PASSION**
See above: Desperation	Maybe he tried to communicate civilly with Mrs Kostas/Dimas and she wasn't having any of it. So, he threw her down the steps in The Secret Garden?

'So, Riri, Rodolfo has his call log showing that he rang Mrs Kostas/Dimas at the time of death. But, if he's the murderer, then he would've been in The Secret Garden at the time of death. We need an electronic trail – proof – just like with The Clio Trio.'

Riri nods. 'The police might've officially ruled out Rodolfo but the TUSC is incoming!'

```
Suspect List 2.0
  1) Fred Hunt
  2) Mimi Bloodworth
  3) Derek Chase
  4) Rodolfo Espinoza
```

Rodolfo is a difficult man to find. He's difficult in general – like I said, he still hasn't warmed up to me yet. I imagine this interrogation won't improve that.

Sweat glistens on Riri's forehead. My underarms are sticky. I'm thirsty with all this roaming around. It's like Riri can feel my thirst because she gets a water bottle and starts chugging. I stare, half amazed and half astounded. How is she not drowning? She hasn't taken a breath and has nearly finished the bottle! All the while still walking!

'You done?'

Panting, Riri nods. Then she offers me the drop that's left of her water. 'No, thanks. I'd drink my own sweat before I drink your water.' I snort, half joking – I wouldn't want to drink Riri's water because she's a germophobe and I've seen how flustered she gets about germs and anything disordered. I think she only offered to be nice. Besides, I'm not *that* thirsty.

Riri shrugs, unaffected. 'Either way, both have fifty per cent of the same DNA.'

'OK, no need to get all biological. You're a germophobe so are you telling me you'd actually drink from *my* bottle?'

Her hesitation is answer enough for me. I walk off. Three seconds later, I feel a breeze and see her shadow nearby. 'Ani, wait up. To answer your question, I would never be in that situation because I'm an organised individual.' She doesn't look down as she steps closer.

'So organised you stepped in dog dirt? Ha! You bring something to clean that up?'

Riri grimacing and pinching her nose as she lifts her leg is funny. I step away from her. I bite my lip, realising I've been mean so I say, 'Luckily for you –' I fish around my deep pocket – 'I carry travel wipes.' I hand one to her. A peace offering. 'They're lifesavers. The things Dad doesn't find out about because of them. Phew!'

Riri sets the wipe on the ground. Don't ask me why but I'm intrigued. She wiggles her shoe on the wipe like how you sometimes see people put out their cigarette butts. I fight every instinct I have to mock her. Why? Because I've noticed a few things about Riri recently. Her and Mum haven't labelled it out loud in front of me but I know Riri has a routine. Even though Mum's firm with her, I see and hear her faffing over Riri. I've seen Riri get flustered when her routines are jumbled up and things are dirty.

Just like now.

A feeling overtakes me as I crouch on the ground. Of course, it could be sickness from the smell but I ignore that. Take out another wipe. Hold her leg in place so I can clean her shoe. Well, as best as I can – I'm not going to scrub in each part of the tread.

'Stop moving,' I say through gritted teeth.

'Sorry.' Riri is a squirmer. When I'm done, she says, 'Thanks, Ani.'

'Don't mention it. Literally never mention it to anyone ever in your life.' I bin the wipe I've used to clean my hands. Speed-walk back on the path of the last place I can imagine Rodolfo to be. I don't wait for Riri to catch up to me.

'It's OCD and autism, by the way,' Riri calls out from behind me. I stop walking. Swallow. I don't know much about OCD or autism so I don't know how to react. 'I have OCD and autism.'

I turn. She's shaking. Her smile wavers as if it wants to run off her face. 'Look, if there's anything I can do to support you then I will,' I say. I don't think she has a therapist like Dr Chandra in California. Having Dr Chandra to talk to really helped me. 'Even if it's simply to listen. OK?'

Riri nods one too many times. 'OK. Thanks.'

I squeeze her shoulder and she smiles. 'You're welcome, now hurry up. We're nearly there.'

We walk the rest of the way in silence, but it's a comfortable silence. Soon enough, I see the sign of our destination: CASTLEWICK PARADE.

Riri's nose crinkles. 'Why is this a parade? Where are the people and the costumes?'

200

'A parade also means a row of shops. Now reprioritise yourself. I believe in you, SIT. You're quite the asset to the TUSC and I'd hate to let you go. Our murder suspect might be in that shop there. Edna's Elite Entertainment. 'EEE' for short. Now, I'll be interrogating him because Rodolfo isn't the most forthcoming dude. I mean, he pretends to hate me but deep down, he thinks I'm cool.'

'Whatever you say.' She's fighting a smirk and I know exactly why – she's happy I said that I believe in her and that she's an asset to the TUSC. It's like getting praise from your boss so I get why she's happy. Both things I said are true anyway.

'Your role will also be important,' I tell her, sternly but also praising. 'You'll be notetaking and observing.'

She nods. 'Two things I excel at, perfect. Lead the way.'

I've never actually been inside Edna's Elite Entertainment before. But I know Dad likes to come here. Well . . . maybe not anymore. My stomach feels funny now. No, I can't feel things now – I have to be an unemotional supersleuth. I scan my surroundings. Stacks of DVDs and VHS films. Ancient stuff. Books falling apart at the spine. Video games displayed in no order. A thin carpet with dark dry stains. Sixties music plays quietly. I subconsciously sway. I only realise when I grimace at the smell – mothballs and pine. Not a nice combination.

We're greeted by an overenthusiastic cashier. 'Can I help you, girlies?'

'We're doing an investigation.' My tone lacks all emotion.

Her smile dips. 'Oh! That sounds fun. A school summer project?'

'Where's Rodolfo?'

'Ani,' Riri whispers. 'Maybe try to be pleasant to this kind woman.'

The cashier beams at Riri. Not at me. 'Rodolfo!'

'Annie?' Rodolfo emerges from one of the far aisles. 'What do you want?'

'Rude much?' Riri whispers under her breath. 'Excuse me, but it's *Ani*. Please learn how to pronounce her name.'

'Fine,' Rodolfo grumbles, to my surprise.

I jut out my chin and meet Rodolfo's stare. 'I need to ask you a thing or two.'

Riri chuckles, nervously. 'Excuse me, miss? We'll have a glance around this amazing shop and call you if we need any help.'

'Aw, so polite. I must say, it's great seeing you young people in a shop like this.'

I turn to look at the cashier. 'No need to listen,' I say and march toward Rodolfo. 'I'm questioning you, Rodolfo Espinoza, on behalf of the TUSC –' I stop when he sighs – 'What? Am I keeping you from something? Your place of work has closed down due to the murder of your boss and I'm investigating. Meanwhile, you're – uh, what are those?'

'Floppy discs,' he answers.

'Well, get back to your floppy discs later. First, do you consent to being recorded?'

'Yes, whatever. You should know, everything I have to say, I've said to the police.'

'Do I look like I work for the police? Now, let's begin.' I glance at Riri. The notepad is in one hand in a way that makes her look like a chef bringing a tray out. Her free hand has her pen at the ready as if she's armed. 'Rodolfo Espinoza, where were you on the day of the murder?'

'Come on, seriously?' His gruff voice is annoyed. 'You know where I was.' I give him an expectant look, not intimidated. 'I was manning the counter and kitchens at Cafe Vivlio.'

'And was that difficult?'

'Yes, I was doing two jobs. It wasn't busy but it's still hard to take orders and payments and then make the food.'

'I can imagine. And how did that make you feel?'

He shrugs. 'I don't know, I was exhausted.'

'So, it didn't make you feel angry? Maybe like hitting something? . . . Or someone?'

'Nice try but no. I'm a practising Buddhist – I can let go of any anger or frustration with meditation.'

'That's interesting, Rodolfo. But murder has no religion. How many serial killers have been devout in their religions?'

His lip curls in a sneer. 'Are you accusing me of killing Polly?'

'I remember you being angry with her for the last few weeks. More so the day before she died. Remember? She'd put up the vacancy for the new chef. Against your wishes.'

Rodolfo pinches the bridge of his nose. 'I was stupid. I overreacted with my *words*, yes, but I didn't kill her.'

'How many smoke breaks do you take on average?'

'As many as I need.'

Riri lets out a squeak that makes me look over at her. Rodolfo also stares at her. 'Sorry, it's just – smoking is so bad for your health. And for other people too. And the environment!'

I meet Rodolfo's eyes and point at Riri, showing him I agree with her. 'I'm asking for a number,' I tell him. I don't flinch or give into the games he's playing.

He sighs, acting like he's under duress. 'Around two. Three max. But I didn't want Polly to feel like I was taking advantage of my job. I'm grateful for it.'

'OK. How many smoke breaks do you recall taking on the day of the murder?'

'Two.'

'And what time were they?'

'11 a.m. and 2.30 p.m.'

I freeze. Feel Riri's confused eyes on me. 'But . . . you took one at 4.30 p.m.'

He chuckles. 'Are you asking me or telling me? Either way, I didn't. I'm sure about this. I was the only person working that day so I *couldn't* leave for three smoke breaks. The first two were only taken because Polly covered the counter.'

My shoulders tighten and my mouth feels dry. What does this mean? Riri waves at me. I look over at her. 'Mimi and Derek are working together,' she indiscreetly stage-whispers. 'He was at the cafe twice that day and she was there three times!'

Alarmingly, Riri has a point. I release a breath. Try to

hold my composure. 'Rodolfo, we've heard that you *told* people in the cafe you'd be going for a smoke break at around 4.30 p.m. Did you tell them that?'

'Maybe. But I wasn't smoking. I hadn't even left the cafe.'

'Then why tell them that?'

'Because.'

I grunt. 'Rodolfo, do you have to be so complicated?! This is a *murder investigation* I'm trying to solve here. All I'm asking is for you to be honest.'

Rodolfo works his jaw. 'I don't know why – probably just a force of habit. Or maybe I planned to and then decided against it. I actually went to the hallway toward the kitchens to ring Polly. I lingered within earshot so I could hear any customers coming in the cafe.'

Within earshot – so that's how Derek's voice note picked up Rodolfo's call. 'How can you prove it?' I ask. 'No cameras in the kitchens. Everyone thought you were outside smoking.'

Rodolfo unlocks his phone and shows us a screenshot. 'Find my iPhone shows I was inside Cafe Vivlio at 4.30 p.m. that day.'

'But that isn't specific. You could've been outside the entrance or outside in The Secret Garden. This isn't good enough. Can you *actually* prove it?'

'No –'

'Aha!'

'Let me finish. I wanted to ask her how long she was going to be. It was getting a bit too much.'

'Of course it would be. Every other staff member was off sick. But did you at least try to ring them?'

'No, I didn't. Mrs Kostas rang all the baristas that morning to see if anyone could cover. None of them were well enough.'

'So, it was getting too much for you and Mrs Kostas was AWOL. When you rang her, what happened?' I bite my lip to prevent nausea from rising. I'm referring to the call where Mrs Kostas said Dad's name. AKA one of the three pieces of evidence against him.

Rodolfo scratches his head and winces. 'I don't know if I should – I'm sorry, by the way, about your dad.'

He's buttering up his interrogator with a fake apology. But I don't fall for his silly attempt. I repeat the question: 'When you rang her, what happened?'

Rodolfo shakes his head. I ask again. He ignores me.

I sigh – fine, he's beaten me here. But I *will* get the answer eventually. 'Anything else?'

Rodolfo nods and says, 'One thing – you can't prove I was at the scene of the crime. My footprints don't match those found in the garden. It wasn't my paper that printed the note. The police know that, and that's why I'm not a person of interest.'

I curse and look at Riri. 'What did you hear in the call?'

Rodolfo lets out a breath before he recounts, 'Polly screamed and called your dad's name. Sounded like shock . . . but could've been excitement? I don't know. Sorry.'

'And this was at 4.30 p.m.?'

'Thereabouts, yeah. Why?'

'I'm the one who's asking *why*. Can I see your call log? Please?'

Mumbling something under his breath, he shows it to

me. 4.30 p.m. is correct. The conversation responsible for arresting Dad was only seven seconds long.

'Why didn't you report it to the police sooner? Why wait weeks?'

'Because I wasn't sure what it was. I know you and your dad sometimes hung out with her so . . .' He shrugs. 'Polly's body was discovered when I was still at work, the cafe was open. I was questioned that day, closed up early but I couldn't give the police any information. It wasn't until I was waiting for a taxi after my interrogation that I checked my voicemail. There was only one – of Mrs Kostas screaming your dad's name. I showed it to the police there and then. It was on loudspeaker in front of Fred, Mimi and Derek –'

'So why didn't they seem concerned? The voicemail was distressing enough to make the police think my dad *killed* her.'

'I don't know. Because they were all doing their own things? I wasn't in sight so the call was in the background. Maybe they thought they heard it from outside, thinking I was on a smoke break.'

'OK, we're nearly done here. Where were you born?'

'Seville, Spain.'

'Did you know where Mrs Kostas was born?'

'She said she was born in Athens.'

'Did you know Mrs Kostas by any other name?'

'Polly?' He tries to chuckle. I'm not amused. 'That's it.'

'Your motive is that you and Mrs Kostas had a disagreement. She was in the process of hiring another chef. That would mean shorter shifts and less money for you.'

'We were coming to an arrangement,' he utters. Sounds like a growl.

'I assume you're sad about not having a job anymore?'

'Of course. It's been a sad summer. I-I might head back to Spain, relax a bit. I could go back to being a security guard, I guess. Not sure.'

'Well, stick around here until the investigation is complete. In case we need to ask you more questions. Thanks for your time, Rodolfo.'

I walk out of Edna's Elite Entertainment store. The breeze is humid. I continue walking back home, feeling Riri close.

'We should rename The Clio Trio, The Upset Quartet.' She snorts a laugh.

I don't laugh back because I'm confused by a few things. My phone chimes with a message from Dad.

> Why are you all the way at Edna's Elite Entertainment?

> Don't worry about it.

> I'm coming back home now.

Of course, he tracks my phone. Also, I kinda didn't tell him what me and Riri would be up to today. Bonus also: with his position at Ellextrus Tech now under review because of his arrest he has a lot of free time. He has enough to worry about as it is.

Findings after interrogating The UPSET QUARTET

1) FRED HUNT

Motive = desperation

Fred was secretive about his screenplay progress. However, we've confirmed that it looks like he was writing on his laptop at the alleged time of death (4.30 p.m.). This was visually confirmed.

Breakthrough (note: <u>without</u> Fred's help) = He was seen in Derek's posterity shot to be typing *one minute before* the time of death.

2) MIMI BLOODWORTH

Motive = jealousy

Mimi was cooperative with showing us her online banking and call log, proving she was inside Cafe Vivlio during the killing and discovery times and *not* in The Secret Garden. She's shown in Derek's posterity shots up to one minute before the time of death.

3) DEREK CHASE

Motive = greed

He had an intense argument with Mrs Dimas/Kostas the day before her death. He even mentioned how he'd be the full owner after her death. He was more interested in the money. Plus, his vlogs are not as authentic as he's stated, so his word means nothing. Maybe it doesn't matter that he didn't confirm or deny anything about the formal agreement between the silent partners...?

4) RODOLFO ESPINOZA

Motive = hatred

He had public arguments with Mrs Dimas/Kostas because she planned to hire a new chef. He didn't want her to. His Find My iPhone says he was on the premises at the time of death — but that doesn't specify when he was in the kitchens, at the counter, outside smoking or in The Secret Garden. He said he was exhausted from being the chef and the counter person of the cafe on the day of the murder and can't remember. Exhausted after murdering an old woman?

UNANSWERABLES

- When and how did Fred find out about Mrs Dimas/Kostas's real identity?
- Why didn't he publicly reveal this information? He was in debt and a failing screenwriter — he had a lot to gain if he told the world what he knew!
- Was Fred faking all his laptop technical difficulties just to get into our flat/close to get Dad's DNA?
- Why has Fred never mentioned his family before now?
- Why has Mimi never told that sad family story before?
- The necklace: why would she want to remember the bad as well as the good of her family?
- Could she have accidentally learned about Mrs Dimas/Kostas's real identity while working at Cafe Vivlio?
- Would Mimi really kill to get social media famous?
- Why and how is Derek suddenly closer to Mimi?

- Could they have murdered her together?
- Could Derek have accidentally learned about Mrs Dimas/Kostas's real identity when they got closer as silent partners?
- Is this all a publicity stunt for his unsolved mysteries series?
- Would Derek really kill for the cafe — and money?
- Would Rodolfo really kill over a job?
- What are Cafe Vivlio's employee benefits? Are they so good that Rodolfo would kill to keep his job? What other reason could there be for him to love his job so much? There has to be something bigger than a wage.
- Why is Rodolfo always secretive and cold? Does he even have the spiritual capacity to care about anything?
- Did he stage the phone call to Mrs Dimas/Kostas at the time of death?
- Who killed Mrs Kostas/Dimas???

25

ANI

TUSC timestamp
21 days since murder
13 days since TUSC investigation
    launched
6 days since Dad got arrested

For the last two days all we've done is go over what we've learned from the interrogations of The Upset Quartet.

And we've got nothing.

It's like a big unsolvable puzzle – who's lying? Who isn't? Why can't people just be truthful in murder investigations?!

Ugh, I feel like a fraud – I can't face the town of Castlewick in the name of the TUSC Director and Supersleuth Ani Tariq ever again. But I have to.

Our investigation is now insanely personal – Dad is still

on pre-charge bail. Mum and Dad haven't told us much so we've resorted to eavesdropping – last night, I heard them talk about Ellextrus Tech disliking all the negative press Dad's getting. They might fire him. He's already on leave without pay. I'm working hard to stop spiralling but it's hard.

I need to solve this.

TUSC breakthrough #1: The long-lost relative theory

Mum has Dad's permission to go through his things to build good character evidence about him. I got even more worried for Dad, because I was told he hadn't been charged. Mum said that's true, but Chloe rang to say it isn't looking good and that we should be prepared. The Castlewick Police – good for nothing – can't find any evidence that'd prove his innocence.

Mum's also on the phone with her boss. After all, she's only supposed to be in the UK to set up the office of NovaStarr Labs, for the entire summer. Her body language is stiff, voice hushed. She's had to extend her time off work.

Because I've offered to help get good character evidence for Dad (for my own investigative gain, as well, of course), I form a mountain of mess on the coffee table. There's a card:

Dearest Abderrazak,
Hope you have the happiest of birthdays. You've been like a son to me.
Polly

'Would she write this to the person who *killed* her – to Dad?'

Riri shrugs. 'Maybe the police are thinking it was a betrayal on Dad's part. Or an argument that could've quickly turned things sour.'

I tense as I hear my heart pounding. 'This again?! Whose side are you on?!' How could she even think that Dad could actually kill someone?

'I'm trying to think like them!'

'Well, you – oh, Riri, I've just remembered! Mrs Kostas came to England to find the child she once lost! In the article, Detective Larsson reported Nikolaos saying, "Anastasia and our child are in a better place," which some prison guards confirmed hearing.'

Riri nods.

'Mrs Kostas never spoke about any relatives to me in Castlewick –' I push down my rising sadness about that. It's hurtful that Mrs Kostas hid so much. If anything, this investigation has shown me how little I actually knew of her – 'but she did to you and Mum.'

'We need more. But consider that she could've lied.'

'Maybe but we can't leave any stone unturned. Age-wise, Fred or Mimi could be her long-lost kid, according to the date of the article. Derek is younger so he could be a nephew? Rodolfo's the same age, so a cousin?'

'Maybe, but we'll need loads of evidence to prove that. It'll be tricky.'

Even still, seeing the birthday card makes it a bit better that past the lies, Mrs Kostas/Dimas was human deep down.

Loads of whining and guilt-tripping later, Fred agreed to show me the previous versions of his screenplay document – the one he was working on between the time of death and discovery.

'If your dad wasn't in prison, I wouldn't be doing this.' He gives me his laptop.

'Good to know.'

I quickly scan the laptop screen. I cheer. Reflexively look at my side for Riri. But she isn't here because I didn't want to spook Fred. She's rereading the case notes at the flat to ensure nothing has been missed. If we're lucky, there'll be an obvious clue there somewhere.

Before, I updated a table I've been working on.

It's time for me to utilise my other SITs.

Suspect	Alibi at the time of death	Technological proof	Time between next update
Fred Hunt	Writing his screenplay in Cafe Vivlio	'Previous versions' on file explorer	59 seconds
Mimi Bloodworth	Editing videos	The SparxPix app (note: SparxPix is NOT like Apple's Photos that can alter date and timestamps of when pictures and videos were taken.)	30 seconds
Derek Chase	Rerecording a live video	Posterity shots with incorruptible timestamps and dates	39 seconds
Rodolfo Espinoza	On a call with the victim	Call log and Find My iPhone	Nil

Fred has the longest time between his update.
So, are 59 seconds enough for a murder? 39
seconds? 30?

I'm going to test them all.

TUSC timestamp
22 days since murder
14 days since TUSC investigation
   launched
7 days since Dad got arrested

It's good to be back at mine and Dad's old house. LaShawn's mum gave it a beautiful makeover. Super cosy. Music always playing. Bright walls and furniture. I can smell my favourite dish of hers – flying fish, cou-cou *and* baigan choka (roasted aubergine). She's made it especially for me. Well, and Riri too.

LaShawn keeps uttering, 'Twins,' every time he looks at us. I suppose it's jarring, especially with us sat together on the sofa. But I'm happy to have her around.

'Thanks again for your lead with the soundboard,' I tell LaShawn. The plan is for us to eat dinner (quite early, mind – it's 5.30 p.m.) and then we'll meet Helin.

'No probs, yarr. I'm just glad the LaSoundboard 5.0 could

help someone out, y'know? Still sorry to hear about your dad. So unfair.'

I take a bite of cou-cou, tasting its okra flavour. 'And untrue. I'm not that worried because I'm going to get him off the hook.'

'Yeah, you are, with the help of my drone! Speaking of which, it's officially ready to be the lookout for Operation Cou-cou. After dinner, that is.'

I smile. 'Excellent.'

TUSC tactical plan #1
(Operation Cou-cou)

- Operation Cou-cou involves measuring the time from Location A (each of The Clio Trio's tables at Cafe Vivlio) to Location B (The Secret Garden behind Cafe Vivlio). In Rodolfo's case, it's from Location C (the kitchens), Location D (the counter) and Location E (the outside smoking area of Cafe Vivlio) to Location B.

- Team: Director Ani Tariq and Sleuths-In-Training (SIT) LaShawn Hart, Helin Moradi and Riri Tariq.

- Pre-mission mission: Director Tariq stood in the street with a weighing scale, urging the residents of Castlewick to check their weight for health — and secret sleuth — reasons. She got the body weight of The Upset Quartet.

- They spent the day monitoring the behaviour and analysing the gait of The Upset Quartet using footage from a kite drone made by SIT Hart.

- TUSC has measured each average step of The Upset Quartet by staging an accidental soil spillage on pavements. Then measuring each step of theirs.

- A mini mission prior was in association with the local pharmacy and the ruse of a summer project.

- SIT Moradi, an award-winning runner with award-winning journalistic skills and equestrian ambitions, will run from Location A, C, D and E to Location B.

- SIT Hart, an award-winning inventor, will be positioned in a nearby bush, manoeuvring the 'Heli-Drawn' (a helicopter drone, named after 'heli' from 'helicopter', 'dr' from 'drone' and 'awn' from 'LaShawn').

- SIT Tariq, a bookworm and esteemed boxer, will serve as security/backup.

- The Heli-Drawn will record visuals in sync with LaShawn's phone.

- In the event of Operation Cou-cou being compromised, the pigeon-sized Heli-Drawn will outstretch its robotic arm to tap on the window of Location A. The taps will spell out 'SOS' in Morse code.

26

ANI

'Darlings, I know the situation with your daddy is unfair –' Miss Monique, LaShawn's mum, looks at me and Riri as she shovels more food on our plates – 'but right now, you must focus on food. Eat or else you're not leaving my house.'

'This is like reverse *Hansel and Gretel*,' LaShawn whispers, eyes on his fork.

'Yes, ma'am,' I say.

'Thank you,' Riri mumbles.

'Your mum seems nice,' Miss Monique says. Her and Mum exchanged niceties in the doorway earlier.

'Sh-she's OK, I don't know.' I fill my mouth with mouth-watering flying fish and cou-cou, same as Miss Monique. Riri eats the roasted aubergine. Or 'eggplant' as Mum and Riri call it. Or 'baigan' as Dad and LaShawn's mum call it. So many names for a fruit that looks like *Barney*. LaShawn eats fish fingers and fries, much to his mum's disappointment. 'How's LaShawn's studying going?'

LaShawn lightly pinches my arm. I smirk.

Miss Monique laughs, off-key. 'I caught him with his invention kit and had to hide it.'

'He's getting distracted? Why? I love studying.' Riri sounds shocked. I expect to roll my eyes but instead, I smile at her. Her quirks are what make her. I can finally appreciate our differences.

'Studying is boring because I already know everything,' LaShawn defends. Did I mention that he's a bit of a bright boy? High IQ and all. Well, apart from maths.

'Well, kid, until you can rule the world, you follow its rules. I want you to be prepared for secondary school. Smart is one thing, distracted is another.'

There are at least three more scuffles between LaShawn and Miss Monique before we're done eating. I offer to help her clean up but Miss Monique looks like I've insulted her. That's my cue to hug her thank you and get going with LaShawn. She knows nothing about Operation Cou-cou.

We meet Helin at the end of the block. 'I hope you're ready,' I tell her.

'Ready as I'll ever be. I've eaten two-and-a-half bananas so I don't cramp up.'

LaShawn laughs. 'Yo. Helin, man, this isn't a marathon.'

'It might as well be,' I say. Turn so they can see my rucksack of wearable weights. Helin and LaShawn nod and we talk on. Riri trails behind.

'*I'm* not,' Riri blurts out. We all stop. 'Ready, I mean. I-I don't think I am. The first and last time I set foot in the cafe, I saw a dead body.' Her hands shake. I ask her if she wants to sit this one out but she refuses.

'It'll be tough so if you need to, go whenever. Be a big help if you stick around but you're still super cool even if you can't do this.' I reach out to stop her hands from shaking.

She looks down and smiles. Nods her head and announces that she's ready.

I jog to Cafe Vivlio. The sun is on its highest setting. I'm already sweating and Riri is bright red. Beads of sweat blot LaShawn's forehead. Helin looks normal. I say, 'You know the drill, Helin. You'll have these weights strapped to you so you can have Fred's weight, Mimi's and Derek's. Otherwise, it won't be a true reflection of if they could've killed Mrs Kostas in that timeframe. Now, the time taken to push someone to their death depends on the weight and strength of the pusher and the pushed. Oh, and how long it takes to go up and down the steps leading to the hillock. We'll have to rely on good old-fashioned mathematics.'

LaShawn sighs. Riri, meanwhile, cheers at that and LaShawn gives her a friendly shove with a mocking look of disapproval.

Helin asks, 'What if the police are guarding or searching Cafe Vivlio and The Secret Garden? It's still an active crime scene, right?'

'The police aren't keeping a watch on the crime scene because they've got all the forensic evidence they need. Helin, stop pulling that face! We're here now and no one's around. If you make a scene then we'll be compromised – ousted by an adult and marked as failures – and we'll all go to a young offenders prison. Do you want that? I thought not.

Besides, I thought your middle name was now *Unpressured*.'

'I lied –' Helin whispers – 'it's Bozorgmehr-Mazandarani.' Of course, I already know that but it isn't in her TUSC profile because I'm a terrible speller.

'OK, let's go. LaShawn, get in position.' He salutes and dashes off. 'Riri, are you OK? Are you sure?' She nods once and I give her a thumbs-up. Then I open the doors of Cafe Vivlio for Helin, using the keys Mrs Kostas/Dimas gifted me. It was a secret surprise, *a symbolic gesture*, she said, of how much I meant to her. Because the possibility of us getting caught by police or pedestrians is high, I run inside before her. It doesn't take her long to join me.

I focus on the counter to ignore the dark despair that's growing inside me. Cafe Vivlio has a shadowed stillness that sends shivers down my spine. It'll never be the same again. Especially with the stuffy air – the AC is disconnected. Everything feels wrong.

'Ani?' Helin's gentle voice snaps me out of my sadness. 'Is the stopwatch ready?'

'Yes, let's start. Fred's weight first, right?' Helin nods then puts them on.

After doing a perimeter check – making sure no one is inside the cafe and The Secret Garden – I show Helin where Fred typically sits.

'What if he decided to sit someplace else on that day for this very reason?'

I tap my chin. 'To throw us off his scent so we're getting the wrong data? Interesting. Let's time how long it takes from table-to-table. We'll use the table closest to the hallway as the minimum distance. Then we can deduct that from Fred's usual table to The Secret Garden.'

Helin gives me a thumbs-up. I nod once I start the stopwatch. She goes table-to-table. Each table is on one side of the cafe and the hallway is opposite. I scribble my notes. 'It's only a matter of seconds between each table. Maximum, ten. Our findings could be either give or take ten seconds. Let's begin.'

Update: Helin was remarkable. She adopted the entire body language of Fred, Mimi and Derek. No one could've done what she did – and without breaking into a sweat. Each trip from the cafe's seating area to The Secret Garden was done three times. Same results each time. Averages identical to each set of readings. No errors. Even Riri's jaw dropped.

I look at my results, lit up by my phone in the dim Cafe Vivlio.

Suspect	Alibi at the time of death	Technological proof	Time between next update	Time taken from suspect's table to The Secret Garden
Fred Hunt	Writing his screenplay in Cafe Vivlio	'Previous versions' on file explorer	59 seconds	15 seconds
Mimi Bloodworth	Filming videos	The SparxPix app (note: SparxPix is NOT like Apple's Photos that can alter date and timestamps of when pictures/videos were taken)	30 seconds	19 seconds
Derek Chase	Rerecording a live video	Posterity shots with incorruptible timestamps and dates	39 seconds	17 seconds

Rodolfo Espinoza	On the phone with the victim	Call log and Find My iPhone	Nil	C	60 seconds
				D	40 seconds
				E	131 seconds

'Fred had a total of thirty seconds of going to and from The Secret Garden. Leaves him with twenty-nine seconds to kill Mrs Kostas. Walking, not running.'

'He could've left his laptop open and done the deed?' Riri says.

'Possible. Mimi would've taken nineteen seconds from her table to The Secret Garden then back again. That's a total of –'

I'm bad at mental maths. Helin helps me out, 'Thirty-eight seconds.'

'Thanks. Thirty-eight is eight more seconds than the gap in her SparxPix update.'

'Unless she ran, she couldn't have done it,' Riri adds.

'Based on the numbers and technology, you're right. Would she have run?' There's no evidence either way. 'From each of Rodolfo's possible locations, he had the most time. Bearing in mind, he doesn't have a technological update at around the time of death. Then Derek – seventeen seconds from his table with his gait and weight. Another seventeen back . . .'

'Totalling to thirty-four seconds,' Helin says.

I rub my face, frustrated. 'Leaving Derek five seconds to kill Mrs Kostas.'

'So, what does that mean? Who did it?' Helin looks between me and Riri.

'With enough time to kill her, based on the numbers and motive –' Riri starts.

'It was Rodolfo,' I finish. 'Look at all that time *and* Mrs Kostas/Dimas could've been calling Dad for help. Maybe he staged the call, right in front of her. Fred's the runner-up.'

'Now what? Can we leave this former crime scene now?' Helin asks.

'Yes,' I say but we're already too late. The situation worsens.

LaShawn's Heli-Drawn taps S-O-S on the window. He's in danger?

Before we can act, the door of Cafe Vivlio opens.

Chloe enters, a cross look on her face.

Operation Cou-cou has been compromised.

27

ANI

I don't need a reflective surface to tell me I look like I've seen a ghost. *Why did this have to happen?!* We were *so close* to walking out of here with every adult none the wiser. My shoulders droop. Helin pales and gasps. Riri yelps. 'Chloe –'

'No, Ani,' she says. 'No excuse will be accepted.' She narrows her eyes at Helin and Riri too. 'From any of you. There's no way you can excuse trespassing onto a crime scene!'

I wince. 'We were following a stray cat? Right, Helin?' I scratch my head. She isn't standing beside me anymore. 'Helin? Yo, where are you?'

Me, Riri and Chloe move our heads, looking for her, like we're trying to dodge a wasp. It's so quiet, it doesn't even sound like she's still here. Has she managed to escape? What a traitor. She swore the TUSC oath so she should know better.

'Found her.' Chloe motions to the statue of Athena. Helin's hiding behind it.

'Please, please, don't arrest us!' Helin is seconds away from wailing.

'I'm not going to arrest you, any of you. But I do have cause to do so. It's illegal to unlawfully enter a crime scene on the grounds of obstruction. You're lucky all I'm going to do is drive you home and tell your parents.'

How unfair. 'Please, no!' Riri squeaks.

I clear my throat, embarrassed that I thought she could be our backup with her boxing background.

'Right, yes. I-I know how to box?'

I shoot Chloe a smile, no choice but to step in. 'The only way we'll learn a lesson is for you to trust that we'll tell our parents ourselves, as soon as we get home. If you'll excuse us . . .' I motion to Riri and Helin to go to the door. 'Besides, this is a *former* crime scene.'

'Ani, pump your breaks – there could be a murderer on the loose. And even if not, how do I know you won't trespass another place where you shouldn't be?'

And then, me, Riri and Helin are escorted home in a police car.

A quick look through the car windows confirms that LaShawn ran off, out of sight.

Mum almost faints with shock and Dad's forehead vein protrudes. I get shouted out and have to promise never to do that again. Riri's tears started to fall even before she put her seatbelt on in Chloe's car. She's so apologetic to Mum and Dad. I hate that I have to pretend to cry when Dad says he'll ground me all summer long and will ban me from sleuthing forever. Although, the sadness of that thought came from a very real place.

The things I have to do for justice.

```
TUSC timestamp
24 days since murder
16 days since TUSC investigation
    launched
9 days since Dad got arrested
```

'Pass the ketchup,' Riri says as I fiddle with the greasy chips in the paper on my lap. She keeps talking but it turns to background noise in my mind. 'Hello? Earth to Ani?'

'Huh?'

'I'm asking for ketchup and want to know what you're thinking about.'

I pass an unopened ketchup sachet. Don't look up from my food.

We're sitting on a park bench. The park near The Skyscape. Near enough that if I squint hard, I can see Mum watching us from the window. That's because I'm technically grounded and have broken a few rules this summer. The only reason she's let me and Riri out is because I gave her a speech for the sole purpose of sympathy.

I'm now eating fish and chips – a treat I bought with my secret pocket money (being grounded means Dad confiscates my un-secret pocket money). Riri's just eating chips because of her lifestyle-enforced dietary choices. Mum must know we're eating this and hasn't stopped us, so maybe she's decided to cut us some slack. 'I'm thinking about who did this. Whoever they are, they're better than me. The murderer is –'

'Fred,' Riri says.

'I think it's looking to be Rodolfo but we need solid evidence. Could be Fred.'

'Ani, shush. I mean that Fred's right here.'

I look at where Riri's pointing. Fred is here. 'We don't take bribes to eliminate you from the suspect list. You are still a person-of-interest, Fred.'

He gives me a look. 'That isn't why I'm here. I-I'm here to talk to you about . . . well, about my interrogation.'

Interesting. I look up at Fred. Lean back against the bench's backrest. Raise my eyebrows. 'If you wish to recant your answers, then there's a process.'

'I do want to recant *some* of what I said.'

'Riri, do you have the notepad?' My eyes stay on Fred.

'Always.' She wipes her hands on a serviette then uncaps her pen.

'Fred, can I record?'

He blows out a breath. 'Yep. So . . . the reason my document modifications were so spaced out was because . . . at 4.30 p.m., me, Mimi and Derek weren't at our tables doing our own things like we said to you and the police.'

'*What?!*' I stand and throw away my food. I see red. 'You're a liar *and* a murderer?'

'No, no. Listen for a minute –'

'Have you told the police?' Riri murmurs.

'I was going to. I saw you two here on my way so I thought I'd tell you first.'

'So, the three of you murdered Mrs Kostas together?' I scream the accusation. 'Was Rodolfo part of it too? Oh gosh, this is like *Murder on the Orient Express*! This was planned group project! Mrs Kostas was Cassetti!' I'm starting to hyperventilate.

'Nothing like that happened.' Fred seems calm for a murderer who's just given himself up. 'We had a chat. Derek called me and Mimi over to his house before the police questioned us. We were all away from our tables and were scared it would look like we were guilty. So, we lied to cover our backs.'

I clench my fists. 'You lied? I knew it. Riri, didn't I know it?'

'You had a feeling. Fred? Where exactly were you at 4.30 p.m. then?'

'I went to the toilet.' He goes bright-red. 'IBS. The cafe's facilities are near the entrance of The Secret Garden. There was an OUT OF ORDER sign but the toilet worked.'

'You must've heard something,' I say.

He presses his lips together. 'No. Sorry. I swear I didn't.'

I groan and rub my face. 'So we did Operation Cou-cou for nothing?!' Riri looks at me so I explain: 'We thought that in the times between the next updates of their devices, they were murdering. When really, in Fred's fifty-nine second window, he was on the toilet!'

Riri pats my shoulder. 'We still have some useful information from our investigation . . . even though it seems to be slipping away from us.' She squints at Fred. 'Where were Derek and Mimi?'

'Derek was taking a call near the snack bar.'

I frown. The snack bar was only added to the cafe because of Derek's insistence. Now, I realise that his nagging was as a silent partner. It was a nice addition where you could just grab a snack (after paying, of course). 'A call near the snack bar? That must've been what happened in his thirty-nine-second window. But why would he when it's opposite to where his table is? And Derek doesn't snack – I know this because Mrs Kostas/Dimas always tried to get him to eat one of her snacks. Sure, Frankie does but he didn't enter the cafe until hours later. There's no bad phone signal in Cafe Vivlio – it's good everywhere, so why? For privacy?' Also, the snack bar is closer to the entrance than The Secret Garden. So is the toilet. And the bookshop isn't too far.

So, any of them could've done it.

Especially now that the data from Operation Cou-cou is not an accurate representation – we didn't take the readings of the distances from the facilities, the bookshop or the snack bar. Shouldn't I have prepared for this?

'He didn't tell me. To be frank, I didn't ask – I only took his word for it.'

'Well, he'll tell me when I ask him. What about Mimi?'

'Now, this sounds superficial for anyone else but Ani, you know her. It's on-brand for her to dash back into the cafe's bookshop to retake an accidentally deleted picture.'

'OK, so her deleted folder? Her phone should be able to recover it for us, providing the timestamp. And that explains what she was doing in her thirty-second window.'

'No. She uses that app, Sparks-something. You upload your picture and then, Mimi says, edit and save. Once it's posted on socials, it automatically disappears from the app. There's no way of recovering it. Apparently it's to do with their privacy policy.'

Fred is right that it does sound like something Mimi would do. However, there's one huge problem. 'But you didn't *see* them doing these things, did you, Fred? If you were in the toilet. They just *told* you. No inside CCTV camera to verify their alibis either.'

Fred gapes, looking hopeless. 'I-I know. That's why I had to go to the police. I don't know if they're in on it together – they are both acting strange, secretive, though – but I can't keep lying any more. Someone killed Mrs Kostas and she deserves justice.'

I make Fred run along, then I eat Riri's leftover chips. Between bites, I say, 'What a breakthrough. The Clio Trio lied! That's why Rodolfo never went for a smoke break – they planned to say that to cover their backs and pin it on him! And the police are too busy with Dad, instead. For shame.' My chest tightens. I don't like that the suspects lied to me. I thought they liked me enough to tell the truth. More urgently, 'This throws the focus of our investigation so far out of the window.' I groan at that.

'Lying is nothing to a murderer, Ani. It's expected. But we can try to salvage our investigation and solve it. Now, let's see if we can piece together what actually happened at 4.30 p.m. that day.'

28

ANI

I'm outside the police station.

I can't go inside because I'm representing the TUSC. Instead, I take a seat on the bench. It's called *The Waiting Game*. I'm waiting for Police Sergeant Chloe Li, but I imagine I'm still in trouble from Operation Cou-cou. I'm waiting for her to take a break or go to her car so we can discuss some things, as fellow justice-seekers.

'Ani?' I hear after sixteen minutes on the bench. It took me nineteen-and-a-half minutes to walk from home to the police station.

I smile, looking at her uniform and her bursting bag. 'Chloe, hi! Been a long time.'

'Ani. You're acting like I didn't catch you committing a crime four days ago. Why?'

'Consider it payback for imprisoning my dad.'

'I don't believe Abderrazzak did it. But following procedure means I have to have solid evidence that someone else is the murderer. So let us do our jobs, yeah?'

I nod.

'Thank you. I must say, it's rubbing me the wrong way, letting you get away with breaking into an active crime scene. And for withholding evidence. Now that I've got time, give me one good reason why I should *consider* not reporting it.'

I can't help but smirk. This is exactly what I wanted – a negotiation. In a sense, at least – she's giving me the chance to apologise. She isn't expecting me to give her a major breakthrough in the case. 'On behalf of the TUSC, I have reason to believe that Mrs Kostas AKA Mrs Dimas AKA Anastasia was being taunted by someone who knew something about her past.'

She sighs. Looks around. A group of police officers acknowledge her. She acknowledges them back. Walk on. But still in earshot. 'Come on, I'll drive you home. I was going to fuel up. Lucky for you, the petrol station is before your flat, so jump in.'

She opens the door that leads to the seat *behind* hers. 'Why can't I sit shotgun?'

'There's a height requirement, Ani. And a safety law.'

'I know but *you're* the law.'

Shaking her head, she watches me put my seatbelt on and settle into the seat behind her. 'Keep it on. You know I would never stray outside my professional duties.' She starts the car. 'Text your mum to tell her you're coming back home, although I can't imagine she knows where you are.'

I pretend to type on my phone. She looks at me through the rear-view mirror. I give her a thumbs up. She can't be that gullible – she must know I'm faking. Maybe she's ignoring it as a professional courtesy.

'You were saying . . . ?'

I tell Chloe about the *Poppy Flowers* painting turning up at Cafe Vivlio years ago and how it links to Mrs Kostas/Dimas's past and murder.

'*What?!*' Chloe asks in such a loud tone that I think she might crash the car. 'How –'

'I know about *Poppy Flowers* because I was there. You're welcome.'

'Thank you, Ani,' Chloe says as we approach a red light. She briefly catches my eye in the rear-view mirror to nod her head. 'This will certainly help our investigation.'

I shrug like it's no big deal. Obviously I didn't give her this information for no reason – I want some in return. 'So, who's your prime suspect?'

'. . . We don't have one just yet. Other than your dad.' We're at the petrol station now. 'Stay here. Promise you'll be good while I'm gone.'

I cross my hidden fingers. 'The goodest, I promise.'

I scroll on my phone while Chloe goes to the petrol pump. I can feel her eyes on me. She might be fond of me. But that doesn't mean she wholly trusts me right now.

It also doesn't mean I wholly trust her right now.

I depend on my peripheral vision to confirm when she goes inside to pay. Then, humming, I grab her bag from the front passenger seat.

It's a black laptop bag with no laptop in it. Instead, it's stuffed with case files. Loads of papers like budget plans, performance management documents, audits. But I'm only interested in one. Investigational intelligence information.

About the murder of Mrs Kostas/Dimas.

There are crime scene images of The Secret Garden. I scan the pictures of Mrs Kostas/Dimas's body, transported back to that horrible time. Then I put a stone over my heart. Blink it away. Look on. Loads of shots of Cafe Vivlio. Close-ups of the walls, doors and windows.

The last document contains a partly redacted copy of the autopsy report. It's an inquest by the coroner's court. It has only the deceased's initials – AOD. Anastasia Ophelia Dimas. I skim through it. It says Mrs Kostas/Dimas died from blunt-force trauma to the head. And her positioning and bruises were consistent with being pushed from the back.

So, she *was* pushed down the hillock's stairs. *I knew it!*

I gulp at that realisation. I know it's been real all this time but this makes it official.

More so with further information about the time of death.

This makes me sad. I wonder what I was doing during those hours. While Mrs Kostas/Dimas was dying. I would cry but something catches my eye.

Item number	Description
1	Sack of postcards, some addressed to Nikolaos Ares and ███████
2	Torn clothing
3	Suitcase full of belongings
4	Handbag full of belongings

The evidence log from Mrs Kostas/Dimas's flat.

A heavy feeling hangs over me. *Mrs Kostas was going to run away?* Maybe the murderer set up her flat to make everyone assume that?

I can hear my heartbeat. I rub the back of my neck, trapped in a daze of sad thoughts.

But I can't react because Chloe will be back any minute now. I put everything away as it was. As best I can. Then twiddle my thumbs and wait for her.

Less than twenty seconds later, Chloe returns. 'Did you keep your promise, Ani?'

I can't control myself. 'Why didn't you tell me Mrs Kostas was planning to run away?!' This betrayal from both Chloe and Mrs Kostas/Dimas doesn't change my investigation – I'm still going to catch the murderer.

But it does change my feelings.

She was *packing*. She was going to leave me!

'Ani, you promised you'd be good!' Chloe sighs. 'I'm trying to solve this. I don't owe you anything. And I didn't want to upset you. But, for the umpteenth time, it isn't procedure to tell civilians – especially minors – investigational intelligence information. We don't know the full details about – well, anything.'

'Fine, sorry. But don't I deserve to know something?' My voice cracks. 'She was like a mother to me.'

Chloe turns to look at me. Her lips press together. Looks like she feels sorry for me.

But she doesn't need to feel sorry for me.

'And the autopsy –' I start.

'Is inconclusive,' Chloe finishes. 'We don't know the cause of death so we've requested for it to be redone.'

I'm going to break into Mrs Kostas/Dimas's flat myself and get answers – the truth – myself.

29

ANI

'Supersleuth's log –' I whisper into my phone – 'I've been kidnapped.'

'No, you haven't,' Mum snaps.

'The time is 7.17 a.m. Location: Anarkali's Paratha House. It's a Desi breakfast and brunch place. The food is tempting. Maybe laced with something addictive. My company is my female parent. I am here against my will.'

Mum sighs and sets down her mug of pink tea. 'Ani.'

I ignore her plea. 'Me and the SIT should be following a hunch. Plan's postponed. I know I promised not to investigate any more but this is urgent. Instead of following a hunch with Riri, I'm being *forced* to eat nice food. *Forced* to be here. Kidnapped, more like.'

'Hand over your phone.'

I don't argue. Because I do actually want to like her. And I want her to like me. I stop my recording. Lock my phone. Then hand it over.

'Thank you. Now, we've been here twenty minutes and haven't properly spoken.'

'You took a work call,' I remind her.

'And you did your supersleuth's log.' She sighs. 'I want us to start afresh. Your dad and Riri are getting on.' Riri the traitor has been sending nice notes under Dad's door all this time. I guess that helped with him coming out of his room – they'll be having brunch at 11 a.m. – so that makes me happy. 'Shall we start by discussing your feelings about me?'

I look around. Babies cry. People speaking in Dad's native language, Pōṭhawārī. A qawwali plays on the radio. Mum sways along – her native language is Hindko, which shares some similarities with Pōṭhawārī. 'You didn't come back to me and Dad for three years.'

Already, Mum's eyes water. 'It was a difficult decision. I didn't want to leave you, Ani. I love you so much.' She dabs her eyes. 'But adults must sometimes make difficult decisions. I'm happy we've reconnected now. The three years I didn't see you weren't easy.'

'You could've visited more,' I utter.

She sniffs. 'It's difficult.'

'So is growing up without a mum.'

'I know. I grew up without a mum. It's not easy. But it makes you grow up so strong. I see that strength in you, Ani. Riri has it too. Your dad's done a great job with you.'

I lick my lips. Taste seasoned ghee. 'You'll visit more? After summer, I mean.'

'Of course.' She tries to smile. 'Maybe you and Dad could come out to California.'

241

I don't expect to smile, but I do. Bonding with an estranged parent is a strange rollercoaster to ride. But I'm on it. So, I'll make the most of it. 'That sounds nice.'

She beams at me like she's taking a picture with her heart. 'Want to know a secret?'

'Yes.'

'I think you and me look more like twins than you and Riri.'

I carefully take her in. She's not wrong – we both have curly hair. Brown eyes. Full lips. Similar face shapes. 'Hmm.'

TUSC PROFILE

Name:	Ms Natasha Tariq (née Uddin)
Gender:	Female
Pronouns:	She/her/hers
Age:	33 years old
Occupation:	Head of Medical Affairs at Novastarr Labs

Physical characteristics:

1. Curly black hair
2. Plump lips
3. Big brown eyes

Observation: She works hard (at her job and at making me like her)

'I've told you a secret –' she sips her tea – 'now you tell me one.'

'I think your accent is funny.' Not funny bad. Funny different.

She grins. 'Do you want to know another secret? Yours is also funny. Oh, but I love it. I'd never change it. Could you teach me some Yorkshire slang? I've forgotten everything I knew.'

'"Cake 'ole" means "mouth". So, "shut your cake 'ole" means "shut up".' Mum laughs at that. I smile. '"Wazzock" means "idiot". "Wi'" is another way of saying "with".'

'Oh, so you don't pronounce the "–th?" OK then.'

My smile is getting bigger at her. 'How about facts now?'

'Yes! You go first.'

'I'm a great bowler. *Never* fail to get a strike.'

'Me too!' she declares.

'Dad is terrible,' we both say, then laugh.

'I think I know the answer, but I'll still ask –' Mum takes a bite of her aloo paratha – 'What do you want to be when you grow up?'

'A supersleuth.'

'That's so cool. I wanted to be Nancy Drew when I was little, actually. But when my dad was alive he used to always tell me that he wanted me to get a science degree.'

If Dad said something like that to me, I'd be unhappy. Even so, I grin at the fact that she would've tried to solve mysteries too. 'But do you like your job now?'

'Oh yes. I'll support you in whatever you want to be when you grow up,' she vows. 'I chose to get a science degree to honour your granddad's wish. Plus, I don't think I would've grown up to be a good detective or sleuth.'

'I could teach you.' Suddenly I feel shy. 'Help you find your lost skills. If you want.'

'I'd love that.' She glances at my half-eaten kebab paratha. 'Eat up.'

I do. The kebabs here might be better than the ones Dad makes. Between bites, I ask, 'How did you and Dad meet? You grew up in different countries.'

'I spent time in London during my gap year. But after six months, I needed a change and I'd heard a lot about West Yorkshire. That's when I met your dad.' She smiles, obviously remembering it fondly. 'Then I moved back to California. We kept in touch. He visited me. I visited him. When we finished our degrees, we got married and I moved here.'

'So, what changed?' Adults are confusing. She sounds fond of Dad at the very least. Isn't that love?

She's quiet for a beat. 'Adult stuff. You'll learn everything when you're ready.'

We don't talk while we finish off our parathas. Halfway through dessert, bhaṅgrā music comes on and dancers come out. I keep eating my mango halwa. Mum has nearly finished her seviya. The bhaṅgrā dancers do a great performance and I clap loudly for them.

Now, we're both drinking doodh phatti tea. I look through the window as the tea warms me up inside. Relaxed.

Rodolfo is staring at me.

He looks as grumpy at usual, but he creeps me out. Looks right at me. My heartbeat trips over itself. When I blink, he's gone. No matter how many times I try to shake off the weirdness of it, I can't. Is he the murderer? Is he watching me? Mum hasn't noticed.

I should've run out and questioned him. After all, we learned from Operation Cou-cou that he had the most time to kill Mrs Kostas/Dimas. And his motive is strong.

Our brunch date is now over and I've made progress with my maternal problems.

But not with my murder-mystery problems.

Oh well. As Mrs Kostas used to tell me, 'Well begun is half done.' Aristotle.

I'll keep going until I get the other half done. However long it takes.

30

RIRI

Now that brunch with Dad is over, I've just had an afternoon shower to scrub off the germs that are on me. It was nice to bond with him but it was difficult to ignore the funny looks we were getting from people. That's what made me be extra nice, talkative and funny to him – to make him smile. He seems to be doing better. Or rather, making the best of being the principal suspect in a murder investigation.

I go inside our bedroom. Ani's sitting on her bed, scrolling on her phone. I start refolding my clothes. The disorder of my possessions has been bugging me – I blamed Ani before brunching with Dad and she half-heartedly accepted responsibility.

I smooth out a T-shirt and work on refolding it. Ani smiles at me and then at the clothes I'm holding when I glance at her. It feels so much better that my OCD and autism are out in the open with her, like a weight has been lifted. There's nothing to hide now. I think this kind of openness is even making us closer!

Ani sings to herself while I move onto my bookshelf. I'm happy to see my books on a makeshift shelf me and Mom put up – with Ani's approval and supervision of course. I inspect the spines while straightening them. Anything that resembles the Leaning Tower of Pisa makes me feel funny. I see my old copy of *The Secret Garden* still in my bag and experience nostalgia as I hold it and flick through the pages. I then make a gap on my bookshelf, placing it beside *A Little Princess*, my current summer reread. My books are arranged by authors. 'Did you have a good time with Mom?'

Before Ani can answer, her phone buzzes with a notification. She scans the notification, her lips moving as she reads. 'It's from LaShawn.'

> Yo, Derek being Mrs Kostas's silent partner is spreading through socials like wildfire.

Ani is goggle-eyed. 'What?!' She dials him on speakerphone. 'LaShawn, explain.'

'Yo, Derek is listed as the *sole beneficiary* in Mrs Kostas's will.'

'How do you know this?' Ani asks.

'Me and Helin –' Helin greets us in the background – 'were walking and heard a group of coppers speaking. They should be more careful about what they gossip about in public. But it's all alleged so you would need to confirm that with the guy himself.'

I say, 'So . . .'

'Derek is in the Deed of Variation,' Helin says. 'Apparently he's the only one who can change Mrs Kostas's will.'

'If –' LaShawn adds – 'he wanted to make himself the *sole* owner of Cafe Vivlio.'

Ani nods. 'Yep. Dead partner means dead partnership. Unless something in the will states otherwise.'

Helin explains, 'If Derek doesn't change the will to make himself have full ownership of Cafe Vivlio, Mrs K's money goes to the Crown.'

'Yo, the coppers we overheard said that there might even be a chance of the cafe being up for sale. All speculation though.'

I exchange a look with Ani. Her brows are furrowed as she says, 'Derek isn't looking too good in this. We need to interrogate him about this.' I nod.

'Brace yourselves for the next bit,' Helin says.

LaShawn gives a drumroll. 'Cafe Vivlio is rumoured to be making *one million* in revenue. For a two-year-old business, that's magic.'

'So, the chances are even higher of Derek changing the will to make him the sole owner,' I say. Ani nods. 'Motive: greed. They had a fight the day before her murder and knew he was in the Deed of Variation so he would benefit upon her death.'

'Maybe he pushed her and ran,' Ani says. 'In a panic.'

I wince. 'But Operation Cou-cou –'

Ani's eyes glaze over as she realises something. 'Oh! If he was at the snack bar instead of at his table, then he had *more* time to slip into The Secret Garden and kill Mrs Kostas/

Dimas!' Now, her eyes widen as it sinks in.

'True,' Helin says. 'And Derek's a strong guy, gym regular. He could've even had time to kill.' She winces. 'Excuse the pun.'

I shake my head. 'This is only theory and unanswered questions.'

Ani cracks her knuckles. 'Then let's get our questions answered and our theories proven straight from the horse's mouth.'

Ani and I are now at Derek's house. It's a no-brainer that I'm sweating bullets on my way to confronting him. Although Ani will do most of the talking, I'll still be *standing in the same room as a murderer*. It's not the smartest thing to do – we should stay at our safe apartment and wait for Chloe to deal with it. But Ani believes herself to be the hero. And because, deep down, I think she wants to give Derek the benefit of the doubt.

'Derek, open up!' Ani's neck stretches to look up at his bedroom window. It's the same window that she threw pebbles at prior to Derek's initial TUSC interrogation.

He doesn't answer. Maybe he's out?

'Riri, give me a pebble.'

Looking for passersby is useless – sadly I'm an accomplice to my sister's shenanigans. From the pebble-less ground, I peep a look at Ani. Her head looks like it's about to roll down then slide off her neck with how much she's stretching it.

'Derek, Derek, open up, yarr! You've got nothing to hide.'

'I thought you weren't gonna be biased,' I remind her.

'We aren't. I'm trying to get him to open up. Literally. We need the door open.' Ani rolls up her sleeves. 'Riri, we're going in.'

'We can't! That'll be breaking-and-entering. Do you want me to get deported?' Despite myself, I look around, squinting against the sunlight but no one is paying us any mind – they're too busy eating ice-cream, riding bicycles and fanning themselves.

'Calm down.' Ani walks over to Derek's porch step and *she opens the door*. She definitely has a death wish and will go to great lengths to solve a case, which makes me feel queasy. Where will she draw the line?

Ani continues, 'It isn't breaking and entering if the door's unlocked.' She squints at me, likely playing one of her masterful mind tricks on me. Only I don't know what it is.

But I do know that this is where *I* draw the line.

'What do you mean, Ani? You can't force me –'

Then she pushes me! I'm in Derek's foyer, by force.

I let out a nervous sound. It's more of a suppressed cry that goes unheard against the loud music that's playing from upstairs 'Ani! This is where us helping the police turns into us giving them reason to arrest us.'

Ani, without a care, strolls in and walks past me. She even does a little dance to the song that's playing.

'Ani, I mean it.' I take a few steps back toward the front door.

'I've slid down the handrail of that spiral staircase before. Better than a rollercoaster.'

'If you're incapable of being serious for one second then I'm not joining you. And I'll call Chloe Li to put you in . . . i-is there a children's detention centre in police stations?'

'Would you get some guts, Riri? We need his answers which could lead to a *confession*. We're going to make the world a better place!'

'Fine.' I walk into the foyer, and stand beside Ani.

'Derek might be napping. Always talking about his beauty sleep, remember?'

'Maybe he is out.'

'Or . . .' Ani looks up and around. 'He never left. Everything appears normal. The blinds are up, sunrays shining through. But were they ever closed last night?'

I gasp at that, prompting Ani to give me a warning look.

'Keep to the right side of the staircase. The left is incredibly creaky.'

'Ani, I don't think I can do this. Look! My hands are shaking.'

'In America, when you can't sleep, do you guys count sheep too?'

'I don't know if this is a trick question, but yes.'

'Good. Then do that. One sheep with each stair. Just don't fall asleep. Now shut up and follow me.'

We creep up the stairs. Another song is now playing and even though it's loud and upbeat, it seems haunting. It's so distracting that I'm losing count of all the sheep in my head. I let Ani storm into each room as I keep lookout. However, if someone does come I don't think any sound will leave my mouth – or any limb movements that would be expected of an accomplished boxer in a compromising situation.

I make a mental note of the places Ani has confirmed the emptiness of:

Location: Derek Chase's house
- Both guest bathrooms
- Shower room
- Steam room
- Guest bedroom
- Other guest bedroom
- Both walk-in wardrobes
- The gardens

'Derek's bedroom, the master bedroom, remains unsearched.' Ani clears her throat and rocks on her heels. 'Uh . . . this is a major privacy invasion but what choice do we have?'

I can't answer because I'm too nervous. I'll never need to go to a theme park ever again. A summer in Castlewick gives me all the terror and thrills I would get on a rollercoaster.

I watch with bated breath as Ani slowly opens the door. She's silent. I can see Derek in a sleeping position. Ani's watching him, expressionlessly.

'Oh thank goodness. Look, he's just asleep.'

'He's dead,' she squeaks out. She looks at me and I can see the heaviness in her heart. I walk around the bed to be beside my sister. Then, I see it.

On this side, the white covers are red, and there's a bloody knife in his torso.

I try to swallow my nerves but my mouth is dry. My stomach is churning and –

I puke.

My English brunch – vegan sausages, hash browns, baked beans (a new food for me – they aren't a thing in America), mushrooms and fried tomatoes – has become vomit. Vomit *near* Derek. Thank goodness none of it hit him.

'Really, Riri?!' Ani pinches her nose, sounding nasally. 'Puke! What? Why?'

'It's . . . a d-dead body, Ani.'

'Hate to break it to you, sister, but this is the second body you've seen. You didn't puke when you saw Mrs Kostas!'

'Because she looked so peaceful!'

'Check for his pulse and a note. I'll look around for clues. Unlikely to be self-inflicted. I'll call an ambulance . . .'

I face Derek and let out a series of breaths, hoping to calm myself.

But then he moves. In fact, he's jerking and shaking. His eyes are still closed but that confirms he's alive . . . right? I think he's having a seizure.

Me and Ani start screaming and crying. Luckily the emergency operator can hear us.

'Just get here *now*!' Ani shouts then hangs up. 'Derek?' she gently asks.

No response.

The next thing that happens is a soundless blur. And I think I'll be haunted by it for the rest of my life – it's the sight of Derek lifelessly pulled onto the stretcher and taken away.

<u>Director Tariq's official statement</u>

Director Ani Tariq of the Tariq Ultrasecret Supersleuth Centre (TUSC) is requesting leave. Her official statement:

This case is wearing me thin. Back when Mrs Kostas/ Dimas got murdered, I didn't know where the line was. And then Dad got arrested. I thought the line was there. But now, Derek might be dead. Dead.

I think the line is here, the one I can't cross.

So, for now, this is it.

One day, when I'm strong enough, I'll be back.

I'll be back to solve this wretched case. To avenge Mrs Kostas and Derek. And to free my dad, once and for all. He is not under suspicion for what happened to Derek but he needs to be cleared for Mrs Kostas/ Dimas's murder. Chloe said the attack on Derek changes the focus from Dad, so that's a positive. But I'll make it all better, fully.

First, though, I need to get better.

Please respect my privacy at this time. Thank you.

31

RIRI

The investigation has been stalled. Not because we're out of leads but because Mom's taken all technology from us so that we can 'heal'. Our healing accelerated when we learned that Derek survived! He's in the hospital. Ani and I wanted to pay him a visit to ask questions but Mom said a non-negotiable no. We got applauded by every adult who saw us – for saving Derek's life. 'They finally accept and respect the TUSC!' Ani proclaimed later that day.

But lately there's been lots of sad silence. Before, we were soaring through our investigation and then Mom made us fall via forced disconnection. It's safe to say that parents fail to see the good intentions of their kids.

We've been in Leeds for the past three days and nights. After we discovered Derek, Mom decided that we needed to get away from Castlewick. Ani screamed and cried because she didn't want to leave Dad but Mom assured us it would be temporary.

I watched the scream-fest that was Ani vs. Mom as it reached a crescendo. As usual, I saw points in both of their arguments so I didn't say a word. Mom rang the hotel in Leeds to make arrangements. Within the hour, we had packed and left Castlewick.

Ani stretches with a groan then cracks her knuckles and twists her neck. 'Hotel beds look comfortable. That's a lie.'

'Have you ever been in a hotel before?'

'Nope. Never even been on an aeroplane either.'

I wish I'd known that before last night when I'd been happily reminiscing about me and Mom going to Disneyland Paris and Florida in one week for my birthday. I stupidly didn't stop there – I went on about us going to Germany, Tunisia, Peru and Singapore for Mom's work. In hindsight, that explains why Ani was silent. Since we've been banned from all technology, we've been exploring the city with Mom and playing loads of Cluedo (we call it "Clue" in America). Like *loads*. Instead of packing clean underwear, Ani packed Cluedo: Passport to Murder, Cluedo Party, Cluedo: Secrets & Spies, Scooby Doo Cluedo and Cluedo

Junior: The Case of the Missing Cake. Neither me nor Mom expected anything less, which is why I packed extra of everything. So did Mom.

Ani yawns, which prompts me to ask her when she slept because I fell asleep before her.

She rubs her eyes. 'Umm . . . I was getting some warm milk and – kinda – caught Mum crying.' My eyes widen and she continues in a quiet voice, 'So I had to hug her, obviously, and tell her it will all be all right. She admitted that it's been hard for her to stay afloat or something. Said she hasn't had enough time to process a lot of things. But she's trying to be strong for us. And for Dad.'

I give Ani a small smile. 'I think we're all trying to be strong.'

'Yep. "Fake it till you make it." Mrs Kostas/Dimas used to tell me that. It works.'

Now, day four, and we're heading back to Castlewick.

The air in The Skyscape greets us with its chilliness, like it's sad we left. Other than that, it looks the same as it did when we left.

Well, apart from a weird burning smell.

'Huh?' Ani sniffs deeply. 'Yeah, that's only barbecues. It's summer, Riri.'

'Maybe but something feels weird, different.'

'Nothing here has changed. As usual.' Her words are moot because we've only gone from the car to The Skyscape; we haven't explored all of Castlewick to see if anything has changed. Feeling something different in my bones today, I tell Ani that.

'Look, you wouldn't know about barbecues because you're vegan.'

'Ani, you said it yourself that I would develop feelings about certain things when I become a proper supersleuth and even though I'm a SIT – I can't explain it but something is wrong. And that smell is getting stronger.' She shakes her head at me.

I let my confusion nag me while we go into the apartment.

Dad greets us all and it's nice to see him. The elephant is still in the room – everyone's trying hard to not talk about Dad's arrest. We're all warily eyeing the tracking anklet that he still has to wear. It looks uncomfortable. 'I missed you a lot,' he says. 'I'm glad you're back.'

After settling in, Mom looks at Ani and then at me. Addressing both of us, she says, 'I'll give you your things back if you go and unpack. OK?'

She means my reading books and Ani's phone and laptop. We both nod and speed-walk over to our room and set down our bags.

'I'm only unpacking so I can get my phone and laptop back,' Ani tells me. She makes absolutely no effort to tidy up. 'Mum said nothing about tidying up.'

'They're one and the same.' We dash out of The Skyscape, the sun shining down on us. 'We're gonna continue with our investigation as we left it, right?'

'Uh-huh.'

That doesn't convince me. 'Are you sure? I mean, you put out that statement and I – well, no one, really – would blame you for not being able to return so soon.'

Ani steps closer, her face serious. 'Thanks for the concern but I'm totally fine. Taking a break in Leeds was good for me. Honest. I have to solve this.'

Slowly I nod. 'OK. I think I remember these streets . . . Mimi's house is closest so let's check in.'

'Why?'

'Her and Derek were friendly; she must be hurting about what happened to him,' I say.

'Fine.'

'Good. Someone she cared about is critically ill, remember.'

Ani chews on her lips and squints at me. 'Surprised you don't wanna wander around Castlewick to find Frankie Chase.' She smirks. 'For condolences and kisses.'

I ignore her. When she's being silly like this she doesn't deserve my words.

She deserves a brief but feeble shove. So, I do just that.

Her retaliation is to chuckle. That's all. I don't know which one of us has won this round. But we soon laugh, in sync, and that's that. We have an odd relationship but I can sense that we're closer than ever before. I like her and she likes me. 'Hey, are you happy I'm here?' I blurt out, hopeful.

'Yep,' Ani admits then skips round the block that'll lead us to Mimi's house, always eager to get in front of me.

'Me too!' I squeak out after her.

I squint against sunlight as Ani circles back to me.

'So, this might be the most serious bad news I've ever delivered. Before this, the worst news I've delivered is telling this tourist in The Case of the Runaway Squirrel that the runaway squirrel who'd shimmied into his bag had a rare case of leptospirosis.'

'What? What are you talking about?'

Ani looks serious. It's a scary kind of serious. 'Mimi's house is on fire.'

32

RIRI

Mimi's house is on fire?

'Huh?'

'Just hurry!' Ani grabs my hand and leads me round the block.

'Oh my gosh!' I shriek.

Ani scrutinises the crowd watching the house burn as firefighters battle the blaze. Most of it already looks burnt down. Included in the crowds are photographers and journalists, their phones and cameras aimed at the house like the hoses. Ani mentioned on the drive from Leeds that she imagined the press sensationalising how crimeless Castlewick is quickly becoming West Yorkshire's crime centre.

'Police Constable Margaret Ribar, is that you?' Ani says in a sinisterly pleasant manner, prompting someone in police uniform to turn. 'Oh, it is! How are you? I still think about our little conversation in the interrogation room almost a month ago.'

'Ani,' PC Ribar curtly replies. 'I thought you were staying out of the way.'

'Good joke. Care to tell me what we have here?'

PC Ribar sets her thin lips in an even thinner line. 'I will, if it means you won't stick your nose in official police business.'

Ani nods her head. I know her mentality – if she doesn't say it verbally, then the lie doesn't count. Not that lying keeps Ani up at night. Unlike me.

'Someone set the house on fire two days ago.' I do a quick calculation in my head – two days ago was twenty-eight days since the murder, twenty days since the TUSC investigation launched and thirteen days since Dad got arrested. 'Terrible sight. And now it's reignited. Apparently that can happen with the hot weather, oxygen or chemical reactions.'

I gasp and cover my mouth. 'Oh no.'

'That's horrible,' Ani adds. 'How's Mimi doing? PC Ribar, that's her *nickname*, by the way. She prefers to be called Mimi.'

PC Ribar shakes her head. 'We don't have any information about Miss Bloodworth's whereabouts at the time of the first fire or since. But we haven't finished searching for remains. She's officially a missing person. Now run along. Go on and play like kids do.'

Ani groans and walks off, past whatever's left of Mimi's house. It seems like we're both in a state of shock and disbelief that Mimi could be dead but just have different ways of showing it. A small group of people's overlapping conversations are audible and Ani heads off in their direction.

She's gonna get us in trouble *yet again*. I huff and try to stay where I am but let's face it, I have to follow her.

Me and Ani go unnoticed by this group as we linger on the outskirts. About twelve people are talking about Mimi's house burning down. Ani looks at me and puts a finger on her lips, telling me to be quiet.

And that's when we overhear it. Someone says, 'Firefighters stumbled on a necklace that they expect will match the description of the one the homeowner always wore. That's all that's left of her.' I tiptoe to see who he's speaking to, but I can't see over the others. Is it someone genuine? 'She's legally dead.'

My heart shatters louder than a vase that slips out of someone's grip. A numb glance at the bodyless ambulance, police cars and fire engine imply that they're trying to salvage something, anything. Someone.

Mimi is dead.

I look at Ani, lost for words. She asks me in a low tone, 'How much do you wanna bet the necklace they found is Mimi's? The amethyst one she never takes off.' Ani has a point, and I see her try to withhold her emotions; her nostrils flare as she stares at me.

We hear someone say, 'At least Abderrazzak, bless him, isn't being blamed for the housefire. He's lucky his anklet showed him being at the flat when it started.' My heartbeat quickens, but with relief. Maybe Dad forgot to tell us about that when we reunited.

Ani's face is a steeled mask of emotions and she's off in a flash. My feet start moving, steps in sync with her before I know it. I glance around and, away from the crowd, there's Rodolfo. He's staring at me, like a haunting shadow.

I catch up to Ani. Rodolfo's disappeared but I still feel watched. And I know that death happens everywhere all the time – even in California – but it's never been so personal.

'Derek's injured, Mimi dead. We need to find the murderer. Now or never, SIT.'

'Girls, you're going to have to say something,' Dr Chandra says. 'It's been half an hour. We're at halftime in this session.'

Dr Chandra's joke doesn't get a laugh or even a smile out of either of us.

'OK, let's be serious for a second. I can use all my experience to fill the silence like I have for the past half-hour but that's pointless if I don't know what's on the tip of your tongues. You're both strong girls who've had a tragic summer that keeps on getting worse. Just as you've come to terms with your first bout of grief, you're hit with more. I'm sorry about that. Riri, obviously you didn't know Mimi well, but it still hurts. How does hurting make you feel?'

'Sad. It's upsetting that we're losing so many people.'

'Very good. Anything else?'

'I-I don't feel safe in Castlewick with a murderer on the loose.'

'You're not the only one. That's why the Castlewick Police has issued these leaflets to all educators, healthcare professionals and businesses.'

I take the leaflet and flick through it. I learn about some

basic ways to deal with grief and see steps to take if there's anyone suspicious around. Rodolfo comes to mind.

'Wonderful honesty there, Riri. Ani, is there anything you'd like to say?'

Ani sighs and for at least three minutes that's the only sound that comes out of her. I'm uncomfortable in this kind of silence because it reminds me of a standoff. There are no winners or losers in therapy but Ani clearly disagrees.

'Would you like Riri to wait outside?' Dr Chandra gently asks Ani.

Ani does a funny shaking-her-head-and-shrugging motion. 'I'm done with words.' As if to express that actions speak louder than words, Ani pretends to cry and pulls out a tissue from her sleeve. Her eyes are watering. She's faking, I know it. If Dr Chandra can see through Ani's act she doesn't say or do anything other than console her.

'Your mum told me you're trying to free your dad,' Dr Chandra tells Ani. 'That's brave. Care to share anything? What's said in my office stays in my office.'

'Our investigation's classified,' Ani utters but the real answer is that we don't know. We don't know if Fred is still around. We don't know if Dad will be officially cleared.

'OK. You've had a lot of changes this summer. Let's discuss that. What do I always say? Even if you think you don't need to talk about it, you do. So, let it all out.'

'I'm fine.'

'Ani, come on. Let it out. Only then can you let it go.'

'What if I don't want to let it go?'

'Then it'll eat you alive. Remember what I told you about

the Dolichogenidea Xenomorph wasps? They inject you and eat you from the inside out. Grief is like that. Unless you cover yourself with your words as a shield.'

Ani's unfazed but the thought of wasps is making me feeling tingly and itchy.

'Ani, stop biting the insides of your cheeks,' Dr Chandra scolds. 'It means you're anxious about something.' Ani doesn't rush to confirm or deny what she's hearing. 'Your tablets – are you still taking them every day?'

Ani nods.

'Excellent. Any problems or side-effects?'

Ani shakes her head.

'No words? OK, I know what'll make you talk. Let's circle back to the TUSC. You said it was confidential. Is that supersleuth code for you being at a standstill?'

Ani works her jaw. To me, that confirms it.

'Well, with The Case of the Ripped Trousers, do you remember what I told you?'

'No, I don't. That was one of my first cases, years ago.'

'More times than not, you'll find what you seek by taking a deep breath and looking around with fresh eyes. What you truly seek was right under your nose the whole time.'

'We'll remember that.' Ani smiles, sweetly.

Dr Chandra wraps up the session. A knock on the door shows us that Mum is here, on the dot, to collect us.

'Everything all right? Any concerns I should have?' Mom looks nervous.

'All I can say is that we had a productive session.'

As we get ready to leave, Mom starts chatting to Dr

Chandra about NovaStarr Labs's medicines and trials.

Dr Chandra asks, 'Will I be seeing you at the vigil?' At our confused expressions, she explains that there'll be a vigil for Mrs Kostas and Mimi.

We'll definitely be there.

Director Tariq's
official statement

Life thought it had broken me down. But now I'm out of my faraway safehouse, back on the clean but crime-ridden streets of Castlewick. My time away allowed the dust to settle.

But then, Mimi died. In the worst way as well — her house was on fire, her body burnt to a crisp. No — *she got murdered*.

Police Sergeant Chloe Li of the Castlewick Police, a TUSC ally, has confirmed in a press conference that her team are treating the tragic death of Mimi as a murder.

Everyone thought I'd be done for, hopelessly demotivated. I don't blame them.

But actually I'm hopefully motivated.

You see, with my experience, it would be stupid for me to allow the possibility of the murders and attempted murder being linked to not be considered. The TUSC is doing what we can to either prove or disprove this.

Think about it: a crimeless town suddenly has two murders and an attempted one? All three victims are linked. We know that Mrs

Kostas/Dimas wasn't who she said she was —

And well, we still don't know a lot about her.

For this investigation to move forward, I must learn more about the Mrs Kostas/Dimas's backstory.

I need to go into Mrs K's flat and see if I can find something that'll link the murders and reveal the murderer.

Director Ani Tariq of the TUSC is BACK and here to stay.

TO-DO LIST

- Sneak into Mrs Kostas/Dimas's flat to see if there are any clues about the murderer.

The best time to sneak into the flat is when most of Castlewick is in one place to not catch me. AKA the night of the vigil.

UNANSWERABLES

- Was she really planning to run away?

- Or was the murderer setting it up that way?

- Maybe the police missed something?

- Who killed Mrs Kostas/Dimas???

33

RIRI

TUSC timestamp
32 days since murder
24 days since TUSC investigation
   had launched
17 days since Dad got arrested
6 days since Derek was attacked
2 days since Mimi's house was
   initially on fire and she died

When you're not actively pursuing an investigation, time goes by slowly – hours felt like days, as day turns into night. Me and Ani were killing time by watching TV. We couldn't agree on something to watch. I wanted to watch a NASA documentary and Ani wanted to watch *Murder, She Wrote*.

We're now on the umpteenth episode of *Murder, She Wrote*.

'This is so old and boring,' I complain.

'Hush, this is one of my favourite episodes.' Ani doesn't move as she watches it. I'm pretty sure she hasn't blinked in so long.

Bored, I grab the remote and click "info". The episode is called *Twice Dead*.

'So, let me get this straight –' I say, as I watch on – 'the scientist faked his death –'

'And then actually gets murdered, yep,' Ani finishes. 'Now, stop talking.'

For the next half an hour, I watch it. But I can't focus – the words *twice dead* ring in my head. 'Hey, Ani?' She looks over at me. 'You said not to leave any stone unturned so – Mimi's body wasn't found. Could she have run away before being burnt to death?'

Ani quirks her lips. 'Well done, SIT – that's a good mindset to have. It is plausible. Maybe she thinks she's being threatened and has left to save herself.'

'True. Or maybe she escaped injured, but is too scared to come out of hiding.'

'Very good, Riri! Anything else?'

I bite my lip. 'Maybe . . . maybe she faked her death?' I cringe.

Ani pauses. 'What's your evidence?'

I shrug. 'Well . . . I-I can't explain it. So, m-maybe we should just let the dead rest.'

'Girls, it's nearly 7 p.m.,' Mom comes in, grabbing the

remote. 'Get ready for the candlelight vigil. I bought candles from the organisers. Don't lose them.'

I follow Ani into her room and we quickly change clothes. Ani wears a black tracksuit and I wear a black summer dress. I can't shake my earlier thought. 'Ani, do you think any of the dying or dead in this investigation have faked their death?'

Ani laughs, loudly and never-endingly. I feel foolish for even suggesting it. 'No, silly sister. Why? You're wondering . . . Well, let me break it down for you. We saw Mrs Kostas/Dimas's body. Declared her dead ourselves. Saw Derek unconscious. He was bleeding but he's recovering. And Mimi? All that's left of her is her necklace. Maybe they'll find some teeth.' After saying that, Ani rubs the back of her neck and stares off into the distance. It looks like she's reflecting on the fact that's finally hitting her. 'We might be at a crossroads but I'm not giving up. I have a lead.' She puts her hand under her pillow and pulls out a scrunched-up piece of paper. It's stuck together with bubblegum. Ew. She straightens the paper and shows it to me:

TO-DO LIST

- ~~Question Derek Chase~~ †

- Look in the victim's flat for clues

'You're surprisingly thorough, Ani – you even included the dagger symbol next to Derek's name to show that we thought he might be dead,' I say then pause. 'Wait, you want us to go into Mrs Dimas/Kostas's apartment?'

'Yeah. I can feel it, Riri. *Something* is there. Are you scared?'

'N-no.' I swallow, trying to be OK with that lie. How can she ask that? Of course I'm scared of breaking into a murdered person's apartment! 'Is this logical and necessary?'

'Riri! There could be something there! Maybe something about her past that'll lead us straight to the murderer. I refuse to leave any stone unturned.'

The vigil is held in the park. It's 7 p.m. and there are loads of people. Their candles are already lit and with the lilac summer sky, it looks like a park of stars. A huge sign says: DEREK CHASE IS <u>NOT</u> DEAD! DON'T BELIEVE EVERYTHING YOU READ ON SOCIAL MEDIA!

There are huge, smiling pictures of Mrs Dimas/Kostas and Mimi. They look so happy. Derek's picture says, 'Pray for my recovery.'

'The fact that Mrs Kostas/Dimas and Mimi are gone forever is feeling a lot more real now,' Ani quietly admits. Her eyes don't leave the pictures; she doesn't look at me.

I reach for her hand. Mine is warm – hers is cold. They fit and it feels nice, like finding my long-lost puzzle piece and feeling complete. 'I'm sorry you lost these great people,' I tell her. 'Just remember the good times. Not the endings.'

She smiles and nods her head, still holding my hand.

The mayor is here now, standing beside a priest, who starts off by speaking into a microphone that's been set up at a podium. 'We're gathered here this summer evening to remember the lives of two bright souls, who are now angels in Heaven. Mrs Polina Anastasia Kostas and Miss Tammy Jacqueline Bloodworth. Derek Chase is recovering, so let's fill his recovery with some prayers and good thoughts.' A low murmuring dances through the crowds. It sounds like little cries and sniffles. 'Mrs Kostas, a revolutionary figure in our community . . .'

As the priest continues his speech, I look around. The park is even more crowded now.

Ani sighs, all shaky. 'This whole thing – injury, death and more death – sucks.'

'Big time,' I agree.

Soon, the priest's speech is done. I swear, I hear a sigh of relief in the crowd. In their defence, the speech did go on for over forty-five minutes. The priest gets down and people take it in turns to say nice things about Mrs Kostas and Mimi.

While the speeches happen, about a dozen people in total come and give condolences to Ani. I get introduced to some and politely respond, but I'm not too focused.

Instead, I'm having doubts.

Sure, I want Dad's name to be cleared, but I'm just not sure that it's right for TUSC to pursue it.

There are three taps on my shoulder. Nervous, I turn.

It's Frankie.

'I'm so, so sorry about Derek,' I say to him.

'Thanks. I owe you and Ani for finding him just in time. You two saved his life, so thanks a lot.'

I give him a small smile. 'It – it was nothing. How is he? Have you seen him?'

Frankie sniffs. 'We visited him. He's drowsy but recovering. It's been a shock for all of us. I can't even believe it, like –' He shakes his head, too upset to talk.

Clearly he needs someone. In a crowd of thousands, he wants to talk to me. That means a lot.

More people come to hug Ani – and now, Frankie – including Helin and LaShawn and his mom. I watch Miss Monique lead him and Helin away, using the opportunity to glance around. Fred, the only living/uninjured suspect, isn't here. That's weird.

I go closer to Ani. In her ear, I say, 'Where's Fred?'

She swats me away. 'Forget Fred, yarr. Let's sneak into the flat and look for clues!'

She's so loud that Frankie does a double-take. Oh, great. I'm surprised that others haven't heard. Or maybe they're just used to Ani blurting out silly things.

'So –' I start, hoping to distract him.

'I mean it,' Ani presses. 'Let's go now. It's a great chance to slip away, undetected.'

Does she not see that Frankie is standing next to me? 'No, Ani, we should stay here.'

She frowns. 'But –' she sharply inhales – 'we need to get the last thing done on our to-do list. Everyone's out here so we won't get caught!'

'No, Ani. It's disrespectful. Let's stay here.'

Ani slits her eyes at me. 'I knew it. You are evil!' I remember her calling me her evil twin when I first came here. 'Do you even care?' Heads turn towards us as she gets louder.

'Of course I do,' I say quietly. 'I just think we need to rethink our approach.'

'What approach?' Ani's red in the face. 'Go on, say it! What approach?'

'You're always like this!' I sound awkwardly loud. 'You're too irrational, illogical.'

'So? At least I have guts. Unlike you.'

'Ani, I don't think now is the best time to fight –'

'Shut up! Stop caring what other people think! Say what you wanna say!' she dares.

I let out a breath. I'm not gonna stoop to her level.

'Come on! Cat got your tongue? Say something. Have the guts –'

'I don't like the way you are! I don't think you actually care about anything. You're too invested in your mysteries.'

She's shocked at my words. In all honesty, I'm shocked too. Deep down, I think they've been brewing for a while. That doesn't mean it was the right thing to say.

'I'm going alone!' she declares. 'I don't even need you. Go back to California!'

With that, she runs off.

My heart sinks. I'm sad, but I don't run after her. In fact, I think I feel relieved.

'What was all that about?' Frankie asks, uneasily. I can't

believe none of the crowd – including Mom – have come over to investigate. Maybe everyone is simply too wrapped up in their grief. I would be too, if I didn't have an annoying sister to deal with. But then, as Mrs Dimas used to quote, "Nothing exists except atoms and space, everything else is opinion." Democritus said that. I can still hear her voice telling me those words.

'Nothing.' I keep my glassy eyes on the candlelight. 'Nothing but the usual.'

34

ANI

'My stupid evil twin and her stupid crush and her stupid accent and her stupid awareness of other people,' I utter under my breath, as I stomp over to The Skyscape. I don't need her. I don't need anyone. I founded the TUSC *alone*. I can do anything myself.

In front of me, The Skyscape is empty.

I use the stairs to go to Mrs Kostas/Dimas's flat.

Not the lift. Why? Because lifts can malfunction or get hacked. With stairs, even in a fire, you'll be able to tell your way around.

It doesn't take me long, even though hers is the twelfth floor. Ours is the fourteenth. No thirteenth floor in this building.

Ripped police tape is outside Mrs Kostas/Dimas's door even though it's no longer police priority. I've wandered up and down the corridor and around the staircase. Nothing.

Moment of truth: I'm not ready to go inside.

'Yes, you are,' I tell myself through gritted teeth. 'Pull yourself together, Ani.'

I can do this.

I can do it. I can do it. I can do it.

I can just pretend that Mrs Kostas/Dimas is alive.

If that doesn't work, then I have one thing to remember – my mission. To avenge Mrs Kostas/Dimas and to free Dad. I have no choice here.

I remember telling my evil twin that Mrs Kostas/Dimas 'used to call me to help her find items that she'd misplaced and that made me love mysteries'. That means I know where Mrs Kostas/Dimas's hiding spots are.

I'll find the clues in no time.

Having Riri – I mean, my evil twin – around would only slow me down.

I creep beneath the police tape. I don't even need my spare key because the door is open. Did the police leave it open? There's no time to think about it.

Mrs Kostas/Dimas's signature karidopita scent hits me – cinnamon, walnuts and cloves with lemon zest. But I'm not ready for it. I bite my bottom lip. Focus on the police tape. Blue and white. Blue and white. Blue and white.

'Remember the mission,' I say to myself.

I see the suitcases.

Maybe Mrs Kostas really had wanted to leave.

No, I convince myself. She wouldn't have done that to you.

'Mrs Kostas –' I decide to speak to the flat's energy – 'it's me, Ani. I found out who you were. Sorry about that. But I'm sure you'll understand. I'm trying to solve your murder.'

I swallow. 'I love you and I don't want to let you go. Uh . . . I was working with my twin sister. She's kinda cool but we've fallen out now. You might've liked her as Mrs Kostas – she's obsessed with the bookshop inside Cafe Vivlio. Well, she was – the place has been closed since, uh . . .

'Anyway, my evil twin knew you as Mrs Dimas in California. I hope that was a happy coincidence and you didn't plan to cross paths with us. Seems shady, if not.' I release a shaky breath. 'I miss you so much. Thanks for looking after me and, I guess, putting up with me. Thanks for all the memories.' Great, now my eyes are tearing up. 'Gosh, your life was unique. Never would've expected it, sorry to say. I'm struggling to imagine you as a criminal, when you were the opposite of one in Castlewick. You were *on the run*. I mean, does one bad thing in your past make all the good things you've done since irrelevant? And you being an art thief led you to me, indirectly, so should I be grateful? What a thought to have! Would you have crossed paths with me if you weren't on the run? I feel like I don't know enough about you to answer anything.' I wipe my eyes. 'So . . . I'm sort of asking for you to throw me a bone,' I whisper, breath shaky, 'I think you were killed because of your past and that's so unfair.' I sniff. At my normal volume, I continue: 'Please tell me where to look. I need a clue, something that'll tell me who killed you. I've searched and searched but . . . It's painful, looking through your things. Being here, knowing you won't burst into the door.' My heart was feeling heavy. Now, it feels fluttery. Is fluttery the same as light? I don't know.

For a few seconds, because I'm trying to open my mind, I wait. Wait for a sign.

Nothing happens.

Until I trip over the air. I put my hands out to the small table in front of her bookshelf to catch myself before I fall. It's like someone gently pushed me.

But no one is here.

I stamp my foot, frustrated. I think I'm losing touch with my skill versus superstition. I stamp my foot again, commanding myself to focus and to *think*.

I hear it first. Like a creak and a swoosh. I turn my back to the bookshelf and look at the door. It's still closed. The windows too.

Then I feel something. Or my foot does – it's like a pedal is hidden under the carpet. And that's what I accidentally stamped my foot on, twice. I shake my head and look around.

Now, something catches my eye.

The bookshelf has opened.

It's a secret passage!

Unafraid, I go straight inside. In the gloom, I can see rolled-up canvases and artwork stuffed in the cracks and crevices. So, *this* is where Mrs Kostas had been keeping all the artwork she'd stolen.

I splutter on the dusty air. Then I hear someone opening the front door AKA the only entrance to the flat. A cold wave of panic shoots through me. What do I do? I look around. Hopelessly. Helplessly.

There's a big red button in the secret passageway. I press it. Hold my breath.

Silently the door closes.

I'm safe.

I'm also in complete darkness. Except for one sliver of light shining through a crack. I'm happy I turned my phone off – if it makes a sound then whoever's in the flat will find me. But who knows how long I'll be here?

Despite my views on the afterlife, I don't think this was a happy accident. I truly believe that this was Mrs Kostas/Dimas looking down on me and out for me. I whisper a thank you.

The bricks are engraved with writing. It says, 'The tongue has no bones but bones it crushes.' That's a Greek proverb that Mrs Kostas/Dimas told me *every single day*. She said it to me at the barbecue, and she said it to Derek when they were arguing. It's fitting that it's caught my eye now. I think I need to rethink how I spoke to Riri. I'm still angry at her, but I don't want her to be crushed by my words. I lean closer to the peephole and peer out.

It's Fred.

He's dressed all in black. A scowl is scrawled on his face. He's in a rush. If I didn't know any better, I'd say he was about to run away.

He's holding a huge black duffel bag. He's throwing Mrs Kostas' things inside it. I've never seen this expression – or this behaviour – from him.

But then, one of the rules of supersleuthing is to never underestimate someone.

Anyone can be capable of murder. That's, like, the golden rule of murder.

'Great,' he says, 'I need to take a leak.' He walks off.

I grimace. But then an idea strikes me like lightning. The bathroom is down the hall from here. On the other side of the flat. So, if I use the front door, he won't see me. If I'm super quiet and careful, he won't hear me.

It's disappointing, though, isn't it, that Fred is the murderer. How obvious, for him to murder Mrs Kostas/Dimas and then try to murder the other regulars/suspects. It has to be him because he knew Mrs Kostas/Dimas's real identity and wanted hush money. He didn't want anyone else to find out her identity when they could also want the hush money so he killed Mimi and tried to kill Derek before . . . what? Running away forever? That's my theory. Now I just need to prove it.

With Fred out of sight and earshot, I press the big red button.

The bookshelf opens.

But someone else has entered the flat. No!

It's Riri. I mean, *my evil twin*. She has to ruin everything – I sigh with a huge amount of disappointment. 'SIT!' I whisper. My evil twin looks over at me. 'What are you doing here? I said I didn't need you.'

'Oh, so you're talking to me now? Whispering, no less. Finally – I've still got your shouts ringing in my ears. Despite that, I still came over here because I could feel something was wrong!'

'Talk quietly,' I hiss. 'The murderer is in the bathroom! Do you want to get murdered?' Because Riri came to find me, feeling like something was wrong, then fine, I'll admit that

I also care about her well-being. I don't want the murderer to murder her.

Her eyes widen. 'Oh my gosh! Who is it? Wait.' She looks past me. 'The bookshelf is a secret passage! Awesome! Please, *please* let me come inside.' She steps closer.

'No,' I whisper. 'We need to get out of here before he comes back.'

'Fine. But don't you want to know why I'm here?'

'No, but why?'

'Because – well, is twin telepathy a thing? I shouldn't believe it – it's illogical. But I'm pretty sure I heard you panic in my mind.'

I roll my eyes. 'Shut up and get out. I mean it. I'm older than you so listen to me.'

Pouting, she turns toward the door. I stride out of the secret passage and quickly press the table, shutting the bookshelf behind me.

'But thank you,' I say to her with a small smile. 'For looking out for me.'

Riri smiles back. 'Thanks as well, for having my back.' We nod at each other before giving in and just hugging. It's nice. We fit together.

We're now walking, in sync, towards the door.

But before we get there, Fred says, 'Where do you think you two are going?'

35

RIRI

As a former bed-wetter, I can accurately predict when I'm next gonna pee my pants.

That would be now.

What's the point denying it? It's not like I'll have any dignity left when Fred, the serial killer – well, almost-serial killer – chooses to mutilate my body.

'Fred, we know what you did,' Ani says, calmly. How is she keeping her cool?!

'No, you've got it all wrong, Ani. You don't know what you're talking about.'

'When they were beginning to suspect you, you murdered Mimi and then left Derek for dead, thinking you'd killed him too.'

'I did not.'

'Because you knew who Mrs Kostas really was and wanted money to keep the secret. When she refused to pay you more, you pushed her to her death.'

'*I didn't!*' he snarls through gritted teeth. He's redder than before, evil-looking.

'Please, good sir!' I cry out. 'Please don't kill us. We're so young! We have so much to live for. Do you know that I aspire to be the first brown, female, hijab-wearing, Muslim person of South Asian descent to be President of the United States?' I'm actually in tears now, full-on waterworks. 'That's so many minority boxes to check off in one go. Please!'

Before I can politely mention that I'm a great boxer, like an off-switch he's no longer red, scowling and angry. Setting down the bag, he runs his hands over his face. If anything, he now looks exasperated. 'Girls, I'm so sorry for lashing out at you.'

'Shut up, murderer!' Ani yells.

I hold up my hand. 'Ani, be quiet for a minute.'

Fred is sobbing.

I glance at Ani. 'Do murderers normally sob this much? Whoa, he's about to make a puddle of tears on the floor,' I note. And here I was thinking I was about to make a puddle of pee on the floor. Life is funny like that.

'I don't think so,' Ani says. 'But then, this is my first human murder investigation. Plus, adults are "layered" and "complicated" so what do I know?'

'I'm not a murderer,' Fred wails, slumping to the floor.

Ani circles him. 'Fred, Fred, Fred,' she taunts. 'The one who was a student-turned-teacher at the "illustrious" Columbia University. You say you're not a murderer so I have to ask –' she pauses for dramatic effect – 'what exactly are you?'

Fred's hands move from his face. If he wasn't a murderer then I might feel sorry for him. 'I'm her son. Polly – Anastasia Ophelia Dimas's – real son.'

What?!

Me and Ani are silent. Both of our mouths fall open with shock, and my eyes are wide. Ani shakes her head in disbelief.

Fred's words keep echoing in my ears. In my peripheral vision I see Ani massaging her temples.

'OK, I think I'm ready now,' she says, more so to herself than to me and Fred. She narrows her eyes at Fred. '"I'm Polly's real son",' she poorly mocks his voice. 'Explain that.'

'I'm her real son.' He shrugs. 'I moved here about a year ago to find my birth mum. Did a DNA test and everything. My grandmother brought me up and she never told me anything about my mum. My grandmother died ten years ago. I could only bear to go through her things last year and I found all these postcards to her from my mum. I did some research about my birth parents and saw that they were a Greek version of Bonnie and Clyde. Mum was on the run forever.'

'Nice story,' Ani snaps. 'That might make a great movie one day. But if you truly are her son you need to give me the evidence. *Now!*'

Fred lets out a shaky breath. 'I'm her son, I swear it. I've been following the postcards but they're all old and there wasn't one for Castlewick. I don't know where she'd been before then – I saw a damaged postcard but I couldn't salvage it.'

I gulp, hating that I have to tell him this. 'Before Castlewick, she was in California.'

The shock on Fred is sad to see – there's a chance he's telling the truth. He covers his mouth. 'Sh-she was in the same country as me?'

'She did say she was moving to the UK to look for a long-lost relative.' I speak softly to make him feel better.

Fred is on the verge of happy tears. 'Maybe she was looking for me too! Her search probably led her to the UK because I was born here – my grandma wanted to put Greece behind her – but I studied and worked in the USA.'

Ani clears her throat. I don't think either of us are sure about what Fred's saying.

Fred stammers as he explains, 'That DNA test I mentioned – I took a piece of Mrs Kostas's hair without her knowing. It's a match but she didn't know.'

'So . . . why didn't you, I don't know, tell her this?' Ani shouts.

He sighs. 'It's complex. I was trying to play the long game. Let her get to know me.'

I cringe. 'I hate to ask but . . . are you who you say you are? We have to be sure.'

Fred is silent for a beat before dropping a truth bomb. 'I didn't show you anything on my laptop at first in case you saw the scanned documents of the postcards and figured out who I really was. And . . . Fred isn't my real name.'

'Ew!' Ani screams, disgusted. 'What kind of a – I thought you said you wanted to get to know her! How is that genuine?! Ah! You wanted to get to know her based on a lie? What on earth is wrong with you, Mr Not-Fred-Hunt?'

'Ani, it's still me. I'm just . . . a college dropout who never studied screenwriting. My real name is Kristoff. Here's my birth certificate.' He gets it out of his pocket, his thumb covering his surname. Despite that, Ani authenticates it but it has me wondering – what's his surname? 'And more proof – Mum's Cafe Vivlio email address was my name backwards.' I remember when we hacked into Mrs Dimas/Kostas's Apple Watch and her email was ffotsirk@cafevivlio.com.

'How did you come up with the name Fred Hunt then?' I wonder.

He blushes. 'Long story. Gran gave me one of my mum's aliases but by the time it came to searching, my mum had stopped using it. Gran said Mum changed her alias every two years, on the same day – my birthday. Mum had sent Gran a message – the first in many years, I'd been told – that she was looking for me, to reconnect. Gran said I'd moved and referenced something called "the lists". Gran died after that exchange but I found the lists. One was of cities Mum had lived in. Like the postcard, this list was also damaged except for the title, so I couldn't have known about California. The other list was of the cities she'd go to next. The top of that list was Castlewick, making that the next city. Gran always talked to me about us moving there one day – maybe that was the place where Mum and Gran would finally reunite. But Gran was dead so I went there instead. I figured Mum would be at Leeds-Bradford Airport and went there to ask anyone, everyone I could. Some people reported seeing her on a flight arriving from LAX Airport. Ended up in Sheffield. An hour away from Castlewick but that's what you get when you rely only on eyewitnesses. Anyway, I tried so hard to find her even after Google-searching came up blank.'

'Wow, you have a lot of free time,' Ani utters.

Fred or 'Kristoff' gives her a brief glare, but it isn't that threatening. 'I learned she was in Castlewick by stumbling upon one of Derek's sponsored Instagram posts where she was in the background. I don't think she knew she was being photographed but I instantly knew it was her –' a smile tickles his lips – 'and that she was my mum. She looked so similar to Gran. I knew where she was and what she did for a living so I went to someone to make me a fake ID, National Insurance number, CV, backstory. I didn't know which name to choose! I thought of how cool Derek Chase's name is and I thought maybe a similar name to his will give her a clue that I was her birth son.'

Ani and me frown at the same time. 'How is Fred similar to Derek?' we both ask.

'Put them together. Fred plus Derek is Frederick. Chase and Hunt mean the same thing, I don't know.'

'I would've named myself something legendary like –' I think for a second – 'Oh! Like Athos Aramis.'

Ani nudges my arm. 'What? Who's Thanos –'

'Athos,' I correct.

'Whatever his name is. Who's that?'

'It's two characters' aliases from *The Three Musketeers*.'

'Oh.' Ani is unbothered.

'Well, anyway –' Mrs Dimas/Kostas's birth son says – 'my

biggest regret is that I didn't tell her who I was before she passed away.'

'I would've thought your biggest regret was looting a dead woman's flat,' Ani retorts.

'N-no, no, I'm not looting. I'm trying to escape. But only because someone's framing me!'

'Prove it,' I challenge.

'Come on, isn't it obvious? The police are going to dig deeper than ever for Mimi and Derek and soon enough they'll find out that my alibi of a life as Fred Hunt doesn't add up. The real murderer used your poor dad as a scapegoat for the first murder. But I know the spotlight will be on me now. I was collecting some of her things as keepsakes.'

In a weird way, that's sweet.

'OK, Fred – can I call you Fred?' Ani asks. 'Or Kris? How do we go on after this?'

He shrugs. 'Fred, Kris, whatever. I don't even know who I am anymore.'

'Hey, you're the son of one of the greatest women ever,' Ani snaps. 'Know that.'

He nods, grateful.

'Are you aware of inheritance laws?' Ani takes the question out of my mouth.

He shrugs. 'Sure . . . from the movies, I suppose. Why?'

I decide to answer, 'Because, by the universal laws of inheritance, you – Kristoff Kostas/Dimas – are entitled to your mother's part-ownership of Cafe Vivlio.'

The look in his eyes at this news implies that it is bittersweet for him to hear. Understandably. 'Wow, I –'

'So, tell me the truth here,' Ani says. 'Did you attack Derek? He's confirmed to be Mrs Kostas's silent partner for Cafe Vivlio.'

'No. I was sorry to hear about what happened to him but I just want my mother. I don't want her cafe.'

Something inside of me believes him. I glance at Ani. Her expression shows that she does too. 'Fine. But dial the police right now and come clean. You have to.'

He nods, and starts dialling.

Even though we've solved another mystery, we still don't know who the murderer is. I'm about to lose hope in mine and Ani's investigation skills.

But then, someone else barges into Mrs Dimas/Kostas's apartment.

It's Rodolfo.

Me, Ani and Fred all turn and stare. He stares back at us – from me to Ani then again.

Then he runs, faster than the wind.

So . . . maybe we *do* know who the murderer is.

36

ANI

'RODOLFO! Come back! You have to listen to me! I'm the Director of the TUSC and you're a murderer!' I shout while in pursuit of him. 'Stop in the name of justice!'

'Ani, he might be dangerous!' Riri warns from behind me. She's so slow and she better be keeping an eye on Fred.

'RODOLFO, STOP RUNNING!' I keep running. I'm sweating all over, winded and panting like a dog, but I don't care. 'Slow down and tell me why you did it!'

I can see now that it totally makes sense that he's the murderer. Here's the evidence:

```
- He's always been mean
- He had public arguments with Mrs Kostas/Dimas
  about his disapproval of the new chef vacancy
- He lied about taking a smoke break at 4.30 p.m.
- He was staring at me and Riri in the street
- He didn't want Mrs Kostas/Dimas to hire
```

```
another chef. At EEE, he said, 'We were coming
to an arrangement.' As in, he killed her and
that sorted it out
```

True, right now he's unemployed but *someone* will buy Cafe Vivlio, if not Derek. I doubt that anyone would apply for the chef vacancy, so Rodolfo might have the upper hand if the new owner needs an experienced chef who's also a familiar face to customers. I don't know if being a chef is worth killing for, but murderers be weird like that.

```
—  He ran out of Mrs Kostas/Dimas's flat, the
   same flat that the murderer might've set up
   to look like she was running away
```

I'm going to get a confession now. I stop and inhale deeply. Then I charge for him.

'Ow, get off me!' Rodolfo shouts. All I did was bump into him at high speed. At least he's stopped now. 'And I'm not the murderer!'

Once they hear that, Riri and Fred run over to me and Rodolfo. Chickens. But Riri and Fred are foolish – Rodolfo's word means nothing. We need proof.

And at the most inconvenient time, my supersleuth senses are telling me to think about the article where Mrs Kostas/Dimas/Anastasia saw Detective Larsson die outside her childhood home. I ignore it . . . for now.

'Prove it,' I tell Rodolfo. 'Otherwise, the police will be here so quickly – they're probably on their way over already.'

Rodolfo shakes his head. He looks pained. There are creases on his face and his Adam's apple bobs. 'I shouldn't have run –'

'And you shouldn't have stared at us like a-a creepy murderer!' Riri squeaks.

'I only did that because I wanted you to pass on a message to the police from me!'

'You couldn't do that yourself?' I stare at him like I don't believe him. 'You could've gone to the police to confess.' I dial Chloe's number.

'To confess? No, I'm not confessing to anything. Look, the murderer is after *me*.'

'How?' While I don't believe him, my interest is piqued. There's an anguished look on his face.

'Because –' he pinches the bridge of his nose – 'I-I saw something. I saw Polly and Mimi having a disagreement that day.' I raise my eyebrows. No one mentioned anything negative between Mrs Kostas/Dimas and Mimi. That's suspicious. And I'm angry that not only Rodolfo lied about this, but Mimi did too during the interrogation stage. 'And now Mimi is dead. I don't think her house-fire was accidental. I just *know* it was the murderer who started it. And he must've seen me see them so he's coming after me too.'

'How do you know that? Did you see the murderer?'

'No. But we know the murderer wasn't them two – they're both dead! And I'm next!'

'Rodolfo –' I say – 'you are the murderer and you killed Mimi as well, in case she said something. Maybe she saw you and Mrs Kostas arguing.'

'No!' he yells. 'I would *never* kill Polly. Her and me, we go way back. Back to when her name was Anastasia Dimas.'

I freeze. 'How do you know about that?' I whisper because I'm afraid my voice will break.

'Me and Mrs Kostas were the same age. When she was younger, she was an art thief. Me? I was the security guard at a Spanish museum. I was the guard in charge of *Infante and Dog* by Diego Velázquez. It was a lost painting that my boss had managed to buy back. But when the curtain lifted, the painting was gone. Her partner, Nikolaos, he sent the newspapers a letter confirming it was him and Anastasia who'd stolen it. I was disgraced – I lost everything. Eventually my name faded from the news but whenever I tried to apply for a job, it all came back up again. I lost everything because of Polly.'

Suddenly I remember all the clues that were right under my nose all along.

a) The day before the murder, Rodolfo said to Mrs Kostas/ Dimas, 'Remember everything you've thanked me for, Polly.'
b) Also on that day, he said, 'If it [covering the counter] gets too much, then I can always go outside and play guard. Right?'
c) Regarding the *Poppy Flowers* situation, Rodolfo said something about the painting days later, in the kitchens. Maybe she'd told him because he already knew everything?

d) When we interrogated him at EEE, Rodolfo said, 'I might head back to Spain, relax a bit. I could go back to being a security guard, I guess. Not sure.'

He was getting revenge on Anastasia, coming back to haunt her! He *so* did it. 'Well, that's motive enough for you to kill her, Rodolfo.' I look at my phone. 'Did you get that, Chloe?'

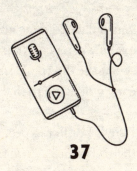

37

ANI

'Ani, you're good,' Chloe admits through the phone. I smirk because where's the lie? 'Who's there with you, your mum?'

'Nope. It's me, Riri, the murderer and Fred.'

'OK. Fred and Rodolfo, both of you need to stay exactly where you are. Try running and I'll hunt you down. Ani, go back to your flat with Riri. I mean it, don't lurk around. My officers will be there in two minutes.'

'No, no!' Rodolfo cries out. 'Please, someone listen to me! That wasn't the whole story! True, I lost everything but she helped me get everything back.'

'Huh?' Riri says.

'My mum was British so I have dual-citizenship. My Spanish family don't talk to me because of the museum incident so I saved up to come here. My only plan was to stay with a cousin in Leeds but that didn't last long. I was unemployable and homeless. Then, I don't know if it was magic or a miracle, Polly – Anastasia – found me. She turned my life around – helped me buy a flat. Told me about this cafe she wanted to open. Helped me get a cooking diploma, saying she felt so bad about what she did to me years ago. She was a *good* person. I have my whole life to thank her for. So no, I didn't *kill* her.'

I gape at Rodolfo. Well, I didn't expect that.

'Why did you run then?' Riri asks. 'You tried to creep into her apartment, saw us, then ran. That's guilty behaviour, mister.'

Rodolfo runs a hand over his now-sweating face. 'I . . . have to go back home. There's nothing for me here and I just . . . She said if something ever happened, there was a cheque for me. And Ani, she wrote you a letter. She told me.'

'That still doesn't explain why you ran.' Riri isn't speechless like me. 'That only explains why you came here in the first place.'

'I was more scared because the door was unlocked – Polly gave me a key. Then I saw Fred . . . I thought he was the murderer.'

That prompts Fred to admit that he was Mrs Kostas/Dimas's long-lost relative – her son – and the two of them have a moment.

'Hello?' Chloe says. 'So, there's no killer there with you?'

I groan. 'Nope. Come on, Riri.'

38

ANI

TUSC timestamp
35 days since murder
27 days since TUSC investigation
   had launched
20 days since Dad got arrested
9 days since Derek was attacked
5 days since Mimi's house was
   initially on fire and she died

Three days have passed since we saw Fred Hunt/Kristoff get taken away in handcuffs. They arrested him for having a fake ID and he's officially under investigation over the murder of Mrs Kostas/Dimas and Mimi and the attempted murder of Derek. Dad is still under investigation too and that sucks. But now that so much new information has come to light, we're optimistic that Dad's name will be cleared. Rodolfo has been told to stay in the country for the time being and asked for police protection at his home, adamant that the murderer would come after him next.

Again, my supersleuth senses are telling me to think about the article where Mrs Kostas/Dimas/Anastasia saw Detective Larsson die outside her childhood home.

And I think I finally know why.

I've been reading the letter Mrs Kostas/Dimas addressed to me for two days now. The first time, I drenched it with tears. It was like Mrs Kostas/Dimas was speaking to me from the dead. Like she was in her flat with me.

My dearest, darling Ani,

I'd hoped to be around to see you flourish into a seasoned supersleuth. But my life has been a rocky road-trip of teenage mistakes that bled into adulthood regrets.

It's only fair to get to the point – I must leave Castlewick. I'm so sorry. I'm being threatened and it's getting worse. When you asked me about Poppy Flowers, years ago . . . I'd stolen it. Then it was stolen from me. Whoever did it started taunting me.

And they didn't stop with that painting.

But how could I report that to the police without coming clean about who I was? I think it's someone who lives in Castlewick but I see so many people enter Cafe Vivlio so it has been hard to find out. It's now too dangerous for me to stay here – and for you too. Shocking, I know, but it's true. I was an art thief on the run for decades.

Long ago, something happened involving a car. And the emotional scars I got meant I could never drive again. Not when I envision Kristoff, my love, everywhere.

I've finally figured this bit out. Mrs Kostas wasn't in love with Nikolaos in the end. Somewhere down the line, she fell in love with Detective Kristoff Larsson AKA the copper hunting her! *His* first name was Kristoff too. And what's Kristoff backwards? Ffotsirk, as in Mrs Kostas/Dimas's Cafe Vivlio email address. Now, undeniably, this is super strange – the detective trying to catch her fell in love with her at some point. She was pregnant with *his* baby. Fred is Detective Kristoff Larsson's son. I'd assumed Fred was Nikolaos's son.

Plus, I was pregnant. I had to give my son up to my mother and be on the run forever. I sent her postcards of wherever I'd settled. She knew the dangers of visiting me so never did. She promised to never tell my son about the foolish mistakes I made.

Nikolaos taunted Kristoff by telling him me and my baby were dead. Then, from prison, Nikolaos arranged Kristoff's murder in the car when he was outside my childhood home. Because he knew about us. I couldn't do anything. He had killed Kristoff, so what would stop him from coming for me and my baby next?

The statute of limitations ended ages ago but I can never live a normal life. What a shame that is – I would love to live as Mrs Kostas in Castlewick near you forever and ever.

Why an art thief, you wonder. Well, Hippocrates once said, 'Life is short, the art long.' Maybe that's why. I can't be sure, myself. I regret the lives I messed up because of my naive thrills – like Rodolfo's, and the millions of pounds' worth of losses and damage because of me. If I could relive my life, I would come straight to Castlewick, simply as Mrs Kostas.

Ani, I'm sorry if you take this news badly. If it's any consolation, hiding all this from you was one of my biggest regrets. But then, a life on the run would've never led me to you. And you to me. Ani, be unique. Be you. Forever. To quote Thales, 'The most difficult thing in life is to know yourself.' But you already do. Hold onto that.

Another confession: I befriended your amazing mum and she told me all about Castlewick, your dad and you. She told me about how her and your dad always wanted to move there. Me and my mum also wanted to move to it for the quietness and the community – it was like fate! If I came here, I knew I would be around good people, and I didn't think I'd ever run into your mum in Castlewick because of her life anchoring her in California with your twin sister, Riri. Your family is remarkable.

To Riri, I'll give you the same advice: Be unique. Be you.

I hope you take care of The Secret Garden. Remember to water the plants!

Lots of love,

Anastasia Ophelia Dimas (AKA Polina Anastasia Kostas and Ophelia Polina Dimas)

Update about Derek: he is recovering fast. The investigation into who actually stabbed him – he can't remember – is still underway. But by the police, not by the TUSC.

We're still determined to solve the murder case eventually but we've decided to take a short break from sleuthing. For our mental health and because our parents want us to have a healthy distance from sleuthing and murder.

I'm at Helin's house now.

She's practising a TikTok dance. Begging me to join her. I refuse, time and time again. I don't dance. Never have, never will. Instead, I'm watching TV.

I glance over at LaShawn. He's playing Fortnite with Riri. I'm excited to continue being a supersleuth soon. But it's kinda nice being a kid for a bit.

'Aww, look,' Helin says. She comes with her phone over to me. 'Look, it's Mimi's old TikTok page.' We glance through the videos. Mimi's infectious smile bursts through the screen. I miss her.

'Crazy that she's just gone,' I say.

'I know, right?' Helin then says she's going to check the Castlewick Moors' Stables's website. Her parents have finally gifted her with horse-riding lessons.

I continue watching TV, glad Helin's stopped dancing. But one minute of silence soon triples. I look over at Helin. She's frozen. Wide-eyed at her phone screen.

'What's wrong with you?' I ask. Peer over her shoulder.

'Ani, Mimi is on the updated staff photo on the stables' websites,' Helin whispers. Sounds like she's seen a ghost. I go still. 'It's her face, just with a different hair colour and style.' She zooms in and there's Mimi. Dark red curly hair and she's dressed in all black. That's not the Mimi I knew.

'No. That can't be true.'

Can it?

Hours later. It's still eating me alive.

Me, Helin, LaShawn and Riri are watching some movie. Well, I'm not – I'm thinking. Thinking about Mimi.

About the possibility that she still may be alive.

Exactly like in that *Murder, She Wrote* episode, people *can* fake their deaths. I shouldn't have brushed it off when Riri suggested it. This is all wrong. But –

'Ani, yarr, you're creating a draught.' LaShawn mimes shivering.

'Yeah, stop pacing,' Riri says.

I can't. 'Guys, my gut is telling me something.'

'Ugh, mine too.' LaShawn holds his stomach. 'My gut is telling me that I should *not* have dipped my Doritos into that cheese sauce!' LaShawn, who actively ignores the fact that he's lactose intolerant, runs to the toilet. 'I'm The Gingerbread Man!'

I laugh at LaShawn, now out of sight. 'Let's check out Mimi's house.'

Helin cheers. 'Let's go, Team TUSC!'

'Well, without LaShawn – looks like he's otherwise engaged. OK, let's go.' I motion to Riri and Helin.

Riri frowns. 'But . . . it's burnt to a crisp. What else could there be?'

'I don't know but I have a feeling I can't explain. Let's just go.'

I'm a walking plate of jelly. The trek from Helin's house to Mimi's burnt house is not pleasant. What am I nervous about seeing?

'This will be my first TUSC mission ever successfully

completed!' Helin exclaims. I don't think she understands the danger we could be in. Maybe it's the adrenaline. 'Riri, are you excited?'

'Kinda,' my sister says. 'Maybe more nervous.'

'As long as you can box us out of problems, you'll be fine.' I think about the *Murder, She Wrote* episode about faking a death as we keep going.

We're at the house. Head inside whatever's left of it.

There's a lump in my throat, just looking at it. Nothing left but rubble, debris and parts of metal structures. Inside, it still smells of smoke and ash. Only that three-foot glass vase is still standing. Wait a sec –

'Shouldn't the vase be burnt as well? Little shards of glass maybe?' I say.

'Glass isn't flammable,' Riri and Helin say at the same time, then giggle at each other.

Helin totally has the wrong energy for this crime scene – she skips over to the vase. 'Ooh, I love the designs.' She reaches over to trace them. The vase wobbles. It's the same one we saw at Mimi's house during her interrogation. Nice designs carved on the glassy exterior. A stand supports it. The roses have been burnt to nothing.

It wobbles harder and faster.

'No!' My heart is beating fast. 'Helin, catch it!'

'Argh!' Helin squeaks. In her defence, she tries reaching for it. But she's too slow. It topples and shatters instantly, the sound deafening.

'Who do you report a broken vase inside a burnt-down house to?' Riri asks.

'I'm sure we could tell Chloe . . . *after* we've made a breakthrough,' I say.

All that's left is the foot of the vase. It's drilled into the floor, like Mimi told us. 'Guys –' Riri falls over the foot of the vase. Two of my SITs are clumsy. Great.

The foot wobbles. And reveals a square, metal manhole cover.

I look at where the vase once stood. 'That's weird.'

'What's weird about it?' Riri asks.

Riri and Helin haven't already figured it out. 'The house was on top of a manhole.'

Helin frowns beneath her sunglasses. 'Umm, how is that possible exactly?'

'That's what I'm saying. It isn't possible unless –'

'The manhole was a hideout!' I say at the same time as Riri.

I go on, 'Made secretly *after* the house was built. Oh my gosh – the hole in her living room! It was really a manhole and the vase had been moved to cover it!'

'Back up,' Helin says. 'Why would it even need to be built inside a house?! Manholes are for outside use for maintenance and inspection.'

I shrug. 'Let's look around. Dr Chandra always says that the clues that seem the hardest tend to be right under our nose.'

And so, we look around.

We find a lot of dirt.

Riri sighs. 'Ani, this is hopeless.' I ignore her.

'I think I agree,' Helin adds. I ignore her too.

The foot of the vase keeps catching the corner of my eye. I crouch on the soot-coloured ground to get a closer look. Something small, almost unmissable, is tucked inside.

A picture.

Of a man in a police uniform. 'Uncle Kristoff' is written on the back. And a date of thirty-four years ago.

Uncle Kristoff, Uncle Kristoff. Uncle Kristoff . . .

I've got it – *Uncle Kristoff is Detective Kristoff Larsson*. This feels overwhelming. I don't know if it's drop-tower-at-the-funfair overwhelming or Barbecue-of-Bad-News overwhelming. Wait a second –

The vase! It looks exactly like the one that Larsson is standing beside in his profile piece for Nikolaos's trial. He looked younger in the article but it's undeniably him.

I think we've done it! And I didn't even have to use my little pot of black powder, white paper, sewing measuring tape and magnifying glass!

TUSC findings:
- Detective Kristoff Larsson investigated Mrs Kostas/ Dimas/Anastasia and Nikolaos, her partner-in-crime
- Kristoff vowed to find her even if it killed him
- Kristoff and Mrs Kostas/Dimas/Anastasia fell in love at some point
- Outside her house, his car blew up and he died
- Further research showed he had no extended family
- But this photo could prove that he lied — and he did indeed have extended family

I update Riri and Helin. A chill slithers through me. Nothing feels right.

'Maybe the internet was wrong,' Riri guesses.

Helin nods. 'Maybe he did have family but it was unreported.'

'Both of you, prove it then,' I say, simply.

'Hmm. Could we ring – ?' Riri starts but I cut her off.

'I know! Let's call Chloe.' I start pacing. No answer. My heart rate quickens and this time, I know that's a bad sign. 'Ugh, it's on voicemail. Hi, Chloe. It's Ani. Um . . . I need a *huge* favour that could solve this case! Please, *please*, call me back. 'Kay, bye.' With the picture in my hand, I leave the burnt house.

'I know what you're thinking,' Riri says. 'And if you're right, then that was why Mimi had a hole in the floor – for her getaway.'

'No way,' Helin loudly whispers. 'LaShawn would be freaking out if he were here.'

I agree with Helin but I don't focus on that. My swallow sounds like a gulp. 'The fire could've been started by Mimi. And the necklace planted while she snuck through the manhole.'

Riri looks worried. Helin gasps. I ignore it. My only priority is waiting for Chloe to return my call.

```
Suspect List 3.0
 — Mimi Bloodworth(+?)
```

308

TUSC call transcript

Caller = Detective Sergeant Chloe Li
Receiver = Director Ani Tariq
Call placed five hours after photo discovery

Ani: Hi, Chloe. Thanks for ringing me back.

Chloe: I'll always call you back. But this sounded urgent.

Ani: If we weren't in competition, I'd say you were great.

Chloe: (chuckles) Well, I'm not ashamed to say that you are. What can I do for you?

Ani: Chloe, we found a picture of Detective Kristoff Larsson inside a vase in Mimi's burnt-down house. He's the detective in charge of catching Anastasia/ Mrs Kostas/Dimas and they fell in love – it's a long story. So, I was wondering if you could run a name through the system.

Chloe: Oh. Uh . . .

Ani: That's a real thing, isn't it?

Chloe: It is, but there's a process for it. And the higher-ups will know who I've been looking into and that raises questions . . . Oh well, I'll say it was a lead. Tell me who I'm looking into.

Ani: See if Detective Kristoff Larsson had any relatives.

Chloe: (types loud and fast) . . . Hmm . . . It doesn't look like – oh, hang on. Yes. His half-sister had three children. All were born and bred in the UK. I'm seeing criminal records for each family member, all except one. What happened to Larsson negatively impacted them forever. They made some bad choices.

Ani: That's grudge-worthy, wouldn't you say?

Chloe: I would. Now, who's this squeaky-clean family member? Oh - there we have it. Although something tells me you already knew this, Ani. Detective Kristoff Larsson's niece is one Tammy Jacqueline Bloodworth. AKA the Mimi we know - uh *knew* - rather.

Ani: Yes! OK, Chloe, so you need to take a team back to whatever's left of her house -

Chloe: Wait, wait, wait. Mimi's dead so there's not much I can do here. Sure, it links her to the case with a motive, but I need more. Much more for your dad to be cleared.

Ani: We were looking into the wrong kind of long-lost relative all along! I should've delved deeper into everyone's past for sad childhoods and family issues - especially Mimi's! Plus, Chloe, there's an actual manhole in her living room.

Chloe: *What?!* How did my team miss this?!

Ani: It was hidden beneath a vase foot that was drilled into the floor.

Chloe: I'll be having words with my team . . .

Ani: You're welcome for the lead! Got to go!

Chloe: Ani, you're a real one. Well done and thank you.

39

RIRI

'Supersleuth's log,' Ani says into her phone in the living room as we all wait. 'Even after a major breakthrough yesterday, much of life can end up being a boring waiting game.'

'Agreed,' I utter, on the sofa, drumming my fingers on the armrest.

'Silly girls –' Mom tuts – 'thinking you can confront a murderess at the stables by yourselves. We're to wait here for Police Sergeant Chloe Li to update us on the investigation. You've both done your part. Hopefully it's a success so your dad can put all this behind him.' She motions to his room where he's making calls.

Ani continues, 'Chloe's destination is the Castlewick Moors' Stables. Basically, SIT Tariq deduced that the potentially un-dead suspect was a horse lover.'

Evidence: a few horseshoes hanging on the wall, and some pictures of a younger mimi posing with a horse.

Ani keeps talking. 'We have reason to believe she is hiding there, evading murder and attempted murder charges while faking her own death. The police went down the manhole when the TUSC showed it to them. It was to an underground sewer tunnel that led to houses near the stables so Mimi used that to escape. There were disguises in the tunnel.'

Ani goes on and on with her log, 'The TUSC took another look at Mimi's motive. Turns out, it wasn't over fame but *revenge*. It all made sense but we weren't looking at it properly – she mentioned an uncle whose death ruined her family.'

I continue reading a book. That doesn't last long because Mom's phone rings. She, after telling us to stay put, leaves the room to answer it.

'Chloe's just confirmed that Mimi's at the stables,' Mom says.

'Yes!' Ani hollers. 'I knew it.'

'I knew it too,' I say.

'Can I continue?' Mom shakily holds her phone. Me and Ani exchange a confused look. What's going on? Whatever it could be has me worried. But then, I'm a constant worrier so it's probably nothing. Mom's dramatic by nature anyway.

Mom continues, 'Chloe's got Mimi but she's refusing to confess unless . . . well . . . Chloe, do you want to explain? You're on speaker now.'

'Thanks, Natasha. Ani, Riri, confirm if you can hear me clearly,' Chloe commands.

I say, 'Yes', while Ani says, 'Roger that, Police Sergeant. The TUSC to the rescue!'

Chloe chuckles but it's brief. 'Girls, this is serious. She's willing to confess but wants to talk to you two first. Now, she isn't saying what about but we can all wager a guess, right? I'm asking for you both to come out to the stables – your mum will drive you. You'll be constantly supervised by me and my officers so nothing can happen to you. We need this confession to free your dad. If you can't do this, tell me now. My team are telling me you're just kids but I know you're both special. And you'll still be special if you don't feel you can do this.'

'Chloe, of course we can do this!' Ani cheers. She's clearly happy to have a deeper role in this investigation.

Me, on the other hand? I'm the complete opposite, from my shaking hands to the sinking pit in my stomach.

The car ride is weird up to the point where we're received by Police Constable Margaret Ribar at the Moors. She leads us through the grasslands to the stables. Here, even though we're hunting down a potential murderer who faked her death to frame a non-murderer, I feel different. I don't know if it's fear-and-pee-your-pants different or brave-then-jump-and-drown different. The air is fresh, leaves blowing in the summer breeze, and the grass is so green. On the horizon, there are some cottages. Could one of them be Mimi's new place? It must be where the sewage tunnel led to.

Soon enough we see the stables, swarmed by loads of officers and police cars.

Ani, either unaware of the danger or just unbothered, runs over.

'Hey!' PC Ribar dashes to catch up to Ani.

Mom sighs. 'She is uncontrollable but amazingly brave. Come on, let's go.' Hand-in-hand, we run over to the scene. By the time we get there, my legs are throbbing and Mom's curls are frizzy. Yards away, I can see horses eating grass, whickering, unfazed.

I can't *not* look away from Mimi when I see her. She smirks at me. Her hair, like in the staff photo, is now red and curly and her eyes are scary – like they're reflectors of what she's done. Deep into her blue eyes, I can now see the darkness that she's been projecting into the world all along. Handcuffed, she wears a polo shirt with the stables' logo on it. So, she *has* been working there.

It's not a surprise to hear Ani chuckle. Three officers circle her, stopping her from going closer to Mimi, who is held by Chloe. 'Mimi! Welcome back from the dead! Everyone, give her a round of applause.' Obviously none of us do. 'Tough crowd. Never mind. Mimi, so, you're a murderer and a downright evil person. Tell me more. Including why you want to speak to me and Riri. I'm here for your apology for framing my dad and your confession.'

'You don't want to hear *why* I did it? I want you to tell me.'

Ani shrugs, bored. 'We already know. But I'd much rather hear Riri's voice instead of yours.' She looks at me. 'It's your time to shine, sister.'

I take a deep breath, ignoring all the eyes on me. Before, I didn't realise that some officers were surrounding me like protective trees. 'You killed Anastasia because your uncle, Detective Kristoff Larsson, was investigating her childhood home when he got blown up in his car. His death broke your family, maybe even more because he told everyone he didn't have one. You lied about being estranged from your family –' this is an assumption but we've used it to bridge the gap between her motive and what she told us before – 'you're actually close to them. But it's easier to blame others. This was an act of revenge. You wanted to avenge your uncle and get revenge for the way his death ruined your family. But how did you figure out she was really Anastasia Dimas?'

'Mmhmm,' Ani says.

I continue, 'You were threatening her. Rodolfo heard you having a disagreement the day of the murder. Ani remembers Mrs – Anastasia – commenting on getting "silly prank" messages. She downplayed it for Ani's sake. That was you threatening Anastasia, wasn't it?'

Mimi smirks like a supervillain but a flicker of panic is in her eyes. She actually thought she could get away with this. 'Secrets cost money. I found out the real identity of sweet Mrs Kostas almost immediately. I helped her carry boxes into her flat when she first moved to Castlewick, two years ago. I was new to this town as well.'

I remember back to me and Ani interrogating Mimi, during the quick-fire round. 'Oh yeah, you were born in London.'

Mimi nods once. 'There was a scrunched-up newspaper clipping underneath a jewellery box. It was a random good deed. But also, a sign from the universe – the woman who ruined my family was right in front of me! If not, then I would've hunted her down – my family knew people.' Her features darken. 'The resemblance was there. I kept the secret for two years. She was so oblivious that I had to shake her up – I found her Californian address, handwritten overleaf on the newspaper clipping, and contacted her landlady. She said *Mrs Dimas* had sent off a huge parcel before leaving, addressed to an art museum. But for whatever reason, it was returned. I told the landlady to send it to me. She wanted to get rid of it so didn't ask much. It was the original *Poppy Flowers*.'

'Whoa,' I utter.

'My family all agreed on one thing – the blame for my uncle's death fell on Anastasia Dimas. Uncle Kristoff was supposed to come back home in time for my tenth birthday. He was my favourite person in the whole world – he sent me postcards and told me fun stories about catching bad guys. He was like a father to me. And that *witch* Anastasia, she gave him a lead just before my birthday that he followed like a cat to a mouse. All the way to Greece.'

'Her childhood home,' I say. 'And that's when he died. If you were ten when he died, thirty years ago, then you lied to us about your age.'

Mimi clicks her tongue. 'Yes. Me and my family agree that she killed him – he was so close to finding her and putting her in prison . . . where she deserved to be.'

'So you pushed her to her death –' Ani says – 'to get revenge.'

A shadow crosses over Mimi's face. 'It took me years to plan this. *Years*. I had to change my hair and my personality.

Everything was calculated, even the murder – it was supposed to look like an accident!' She glances at Chloe. 'What does the autopsy say?'

Chloe swallows. 'We're still waiting for it to be redone after returning inconclusive.'

'No need – I'll reveal my secrets. First, I put laxatives in the Cafe Vivlio baristas' drinks so they wouldn't be well enough to work. Then I blocked the cafe's facilities.'

'But they ended up working,' Ani says. 'Fred used them, so you did a lousy job.'

Mimi smiles, indifferent. 'On her last day, we were on the hillock. She was drinking tea. She laughed when I told her I was Kristoff Larsson's niece. *Laughed!* Like *she* was hiding something. She was wearing a silk scarf and I strangled her. Then I pushed her down the hillock's stairs and left her, unmoving. She wasn't dead yet but was slowly dying. I needed an alibi, so I went back inside, back on the SparxPix app. I knew there were no cameras inside the cafe. I wasn't with her when she took her last breaths and that's how I avoided suspicion.'

I shake my head, unable to fathom her evilness. 'Without a second thought, y-you left an old woman who had arthritis alone, knowing she wouldn't be able to get up easily. She managed to answer Rodolfo's call and then what? Why did she call out Dad's name?'

Mimi clicked her tongue, looking smug. 'All of that is correct. She called out for Abderrazzak whilst I was strangling her because she thought she saw him in the street. It wasn't him but she thought he would save her.'

317

A chill creeps through my body and I avert my eyes from her evil ones.

'How about your visit to the cafe at 6 p.m.-ish?' Ani asks. 'After the murder.'

'That was to plant the note. I printed it weeks ago. The note was made to look like your dad was taunting the police. It would've been too risky, in my opinion, to come back so soon to plant it so I had to wait. I knew no one would start a search party for her in just a couple of hours. It's summer, after all! People are too busy to look past themselves. At least, at first.'

'But why our dad?'

'Wrong place, wrong time. But it was always my plan to use someone as a scapegoat. As soon as I met your dad, I knew he'd be the one.'

I shudder and Ani does too. Then, she holds her phone up. It's Derek in the hospital bed, on a video call. Mimi gasps. She truly was expecting him to be dead. Derek looks better, and I can't ignore the half of Frankie that's in the frame.

'I should've been sure,' Mimi utters. 'I should've gone to the hospital.'

Ani scoffs. 'Are you saying you planned to kill Derek as well?'

Mimi shakes her head. 'I hadn't planned to kill him but he was getting suspicious. I just got the knife to threaten him – it was stupid but then we fought and I fell. And I didn't know what to do – I couldn't turn myself in because I had to get my family back together. That's the whole reason I did this.'

'You could've called for help and even used a payphone if you were scared,' I say.

Mimi chuckles, wickedly. 'I thought about it but my own goal overtook me. As it should've – I'd been planning this for years.' Rolling her eyes, she curses. 'But he survived, because of you two.' She glares at me and Ani.

'You don't feel any remorse?' Ani asks.

'Of course. I loved him once and he was never part of my plan. But getting him out of the picture did help things. I thought about it. I did. Ultimately the end justifies the means.'

I shake my head at the woman I once admired. 'Derek, care to explain why you were near the snacks and "on the phone" at the time of death?' Fred confirmed he was on the toilet.

He clicks his tongue. 'Yo, I was rustling the snack wrappers to make it seem like I had a bad line. I was . . . trying to break up with my boyfriend, Toby, once and for all.'

Ani tuts at him then looks at Mimi. 'If you killed Mrs Kostas to avenge Kristoff, and you cared about him so much, then why did he deny having any immediate family? You read that article, right?'

Mimi's chuckle sounds dark. 'I did. He lied to protect us of course. The article tells you that Nikolaos had ties with assassins and abductors even when in prison. Uncle Kristoff wanted to protect his family. He knew that this case would haunt his nights and weekends and didn't want to put anyone else in danger because of it.'

'And the vase?' Ani asks Mimi. 'Did he give it to you?'

'No. It got shipped to my family after he died. My parents

kept it in the attic for so many years – they said it was too painful to look at his things – until I asked them for it.'

I look at Mimi, moving on. 'So, you got our dad's boot and fingerprints –'

Mimi looks at me tauntingly. 'From his flat. I took my laptop and phone over to him to repair loads of times.'

Poor Dad.

'But how did you know Dad wouldn't have a solid alibi?' I ask.

Mimi smirks. 'Before I killed Anastasia, I left a device with a recording of Ani shouting on the staircase of the fourteenth floor. And another on the fifteenth and sixteenth. I broke the CCTV cameras of The Skyscape's staircases and remotely activated the recordings.'

Ani gasps. 'So you sent Dad on a wild goose chase. And he must've thought he was imagining it and would be silly to say that was his alibi if I was safe. But what if another resident heard and came outside to enquire?'

Mimi smirks again, this time deeper. 'I put leaflets under each of their doors for a fake antique sale raffle on the other side of Castlewick. They all RSVP'd and if they didn't, then I would've found another sure-fire way to get them out of the building.'

I let out a shaky breath but recover when I realise that me and Ani will be the last ones laughing. 'Well, you should know –' I say – 'that Kristoff didn't hate Anastasia. In fact, she was pregnant with his baby when he died. They were *in love*. He was watching the house in order to look out for her. That's why he said he would find her even if it killed him – to reunite them.'

Mimi looks like she might explode. Her eyes are wide and she's frowning. Chloe nods when Mimi looks at her for confirmation.

'Hard cheese, Mimi. Keep going, Riri,' Ani says.

But I don't.

Instead, Mimi has an outburst. 'I never cared about fame but it could work out after all. If you weren't here, I could've made a podcast about how your dad is guilty. Podcasts are so in now. But, look at me! I'm exactly the kind of person that will get a short sentence because of good behaviour. I'll publish my autobiography and get a Netflix movie deal. Either way, I'll be immortalised.'

Chloe guffaws. 'You can try but that is not happening on my watch, I assure you.'

Then, Chloe takes Mimi into the police car and away forever. And that's that. TUSC Case: Closed.

TUSC closing report

Director Ani Tariq and SIT Riri Tariq attended the funeral of Anastasia Ophelia Dimas yesterday. Here is the director's closing report:

It took us 35 days since the murder happened. 27 days since the TUSC investigation officially launched. 20 days since Dad got wrongfully arrested. Derek had a near-death experience and Mimi faked her death. But we've finally solved the case!

Fred/Kristoff Jr (actually Kristoff's son) was temporarily released from prison to attend the funeral. We could all feel Mrs Kostas/Dimas/Anastasia and it was weirdly beautiful. It's sad that after all those years on the run, a misunderstanding about her past got Anastasia killed.

Derek and Frankie are getting on with their lives just fine. Derek is the rightful owner of Cafe Vivlio but it's still closed while he figures things out. Novastarr Labs offered Mom to relocate to the UK to manage the Leeds office. She accepted, although it could be temporary. Still, SIT Rtyuiop could be starting secondary school with me and fellow SITs Hgfdsa and Lkjhgf in September. Wild, I know.

The TUSC is now thriving. We're getting a lot of cases coming in — missing pets, missing money, missing clothes. Thankfully they're not as grisly as this case.

Because of our demand, SIT Rtyuiop said it's time for a change. She's typing up all my notes. We haven't fought in three days. She's slowly becoming my best friend (putting Helin and LaShawn tied in second place, which is still good).

Dad's name has been cleared! He's doing fine and even got promoted at work.

All the art I found in Mrs Kostas's flat was given back to the museums that she stole them from. The story has been sensationalised the world over.

Everything seems perfect. For now, at least. Murder lurks, you see, just like sharks.

Now that the funeral is over and the case has been closed, there's one last thing I need to do. I walk through the flat and find Riri with Mum and Dad. It's great to see Dad happy again. I give him a tight hug then turn to Riri. Hand her a plaque and some jeera biscuits.

'My official promotion from SIT to Sleuth?' She hugs me. I hug her back.

'Yes, but don't get too big for your boots. You still have to work your way up to being a *super*sleuth. That takes hard work and dedication.'

She has crumbs all over her face. 'I know I'll be fine, Ani, because I have you.' She hands me a bottle of mango juice.

I mean it when I say, 'I'm happy you're sticking around, sis.' I take a few gulps but then scrunch my face up. 'Kinda sad I didn't get to use my little pot of black powder, white paper, a sewing measuring tape, magnifying glass and wristwatch.'

'There's always next time. This is only the beginning.'

Riri's right – this is only the beginning.

Acknowledgements

Dear reader, thank you so much for reaching the end of *Murder for Two*! I hope you didn't guess the murderer before the big reveal!

Writing this book required a lot of time and effort – and I couldn't have done it without many wonderful people.

Family first – I'd like to send my love and endless thanks to my mum, sister and brother. I pitched this book to you three first and you were all so excited. Look at how far we've come! I love you all. Thank you for being patient and understanding as I dedicated most of my time on this, and for believing in and supporting me when I told you I wanted to write books. To Mum for never letting me quit my dream, even when the rejections felt insurmountable. For always being there for me, for your joy and advice, for introducing me to Agatha Christie and *Murder, She Wrote*, and for all the bookshop and library trips in my childhood. 🐾

And Noor, you're a cat and I'm certain you can't read but I hope through all the cuddles and treats, you know that I think you're pawsome (sorry).

To my grandma and granddad – thank you for all that you sacrificed for us. Thank you both endlessly for filling my childhood with stories and for never allowing us to forget our culture (shout out to all those in the diaspora). Grandma, I think – I hope – you would've loved this book. I'm sad you never got to see me become a published author but I'm happy for the time we had together.

Grief truly is the price of love – and I'm proud to grieve you forever. Granddad, you're the strongest, funniest and outright best person ever. Thanks for all the biscuits and jokes. I love you both forever.

To my uncle, a father figure who taught me a lot, I treasure you and our introspective, enlightening chats. And to my entire extended family, you've all shaped me. Lots of love.

Next, I'd like to thank my literary agent, the amazing Gemma Cooper. Without you, none of this would be possible. Thank you for seeing something in my query and sample. My infinite gratitude for your patience, personality and editorial skills – as well as for always being in my corner. I'm lucky to be in this business with you. Here's to many more books! And thanks to your brother for helping us iron out the police/crime scene specifics!

To Ruth Bennett, my countless thanks. Your feedback and edit letters are amazing – your guidance has transformed this story from a Word document to a book. Thank you for *getting* the characters and the story. The book wouldn't be what it is without you, and our emails delight me. ☺

I'm so pleased to have the honour of working with the talented, brilliant team at Piccadilly Press, namely: Talya Baker and Ruth from the editorial team, Aimee White for proofreading, Dominica Clements from design, Samara Iqbal from marketing, Pippa Poole from publicity and Charlotte Brown from audio. Katie Foreman, thank you for bringing the town of Castlewick and Cafe Vivlio to life with your beautiful maps! Many thanks to Lil Chase for your phenomenal copyediting, Krish Jeyakumar for kindly sensitivity reading, and Nikki Patel for spectacularly narrating the audiobook!

The cover blew me away the first time I saw it – Caroline Garcia, I'm so thankful your vision aligned with mine and the team's, and that you said yes on such short notice! Thank you for bringing it to life through your amazing art.

Murder for Two has been kindly endorsed/blurbed by some amazing authors – including the amazing Sophie Anderson – so thank you all so very much!

Special shout out to some of my author friends: Tanvi Berwah, Zeena Gosrani, Rachel Greenlaw, Nadine Aisha Jassat, Khushboo Patel, Courtney Smyth and Amanda Woody. If I've missed anyone out, I'm sorry but know that I do value you so much!

My thanks will never run out for the booksellers – including the phenomenal team at Read Holmfirth – librarians and schools who have supported me and *Murder for Two*. You're so important to the industry – and my love of books came from the school library and the local bookshop, so thank you. I'm so grateful to Parrot Street Book Club for your support as well!

To anyone who's read *Murder for Two* and/or passed it onto a friend and/or recommended it to a friend/family member/neighbour and/or posted about it, then from the bottom of my heart, I thank you.

I'd be remiss to not acknowledge, with a heavy heart, the parents, children and *people* who are refugees, asylum seekers and living in conflict. To the ones who never got to return home before their final breaths, and to those who didn't see the conflict's end. Here's to the imploration that children living in conflict or asylum get access to books and safe skies as well as the human right that is education.

Last but absolutely not least – thank you to you, the person reading this, for reading all the way to the very end. I hope you enjoyed *Murder for Two* – and will join Ani and Riri for the sequel!

Niyla Farook is a writer from West Yorkshire, where she still lives. When she's not writing, she's either working in a pharmacy (just like Agatha Christie!) or winning every murder mystery game she can (which isn't a lot!). As a woman of colour, Niyla is passionate about portraying authentic diversity in her books.